PAGING THE DEAD

Selected as *Library Journal*'s Mystery Debut of the Month

"Bonner successfully combines an intriguing cast with the promise of an unfolding romance and a spritz of the paranormal in her winning cozy debut."

—*Library Journal* (starred review)

"Bonner adds a nice mix of genealogical scrapbooking info and . . . romantic entanglements."

—*Publishers Weekly*

"The past and present intriguingly collide. . . . There are plenty of suspects plus loads of clues . . . and some clever humor adds to the entertainment."

—*Single Titles*

"Engaging and touching. . . . Goes beneath the surface of family trees, and gets to the roots of relationships."

—*Mystery Scene*

also by brynn bonner

Paging the Dead
Death in Reel Time
Picture Them Dead

Dead in a Flash

Brynn Bonner

Pocket Books

New York London Toronto Sydney New Delhi

Pocket Books
An Imprint of Simon & Schuster, Inc.
1230 Avenue of the Americas
New York, NY 10020

This book is a work of fiction. Any references to historical events, real people, or real places are used fictitiously. Other names, characters, places, and events are products of the author's imagination, and any resemblance to actual events or places or persons, living or dead, is entirely coincidental.

First Pocket Books paperback edition September 2016

POCKET and colophon are registered trademarks of Simon & Schuster, Inc.

For information about special discounts for bulk purchases, please contact Simon & Schuster Special Sales at 1-866-506-1949 or business@simonandschuster.com.

The Simon & Schuster Speakers Bureau can bring authors to your live event. For more information or to book an event, contact the Simon & Schuster Speakers Bureau at 1-866-248-3049 or visit our website at www.simonspeakers.com.

Manufactured in the United States of America

10 9 8 7 6 5 4 3 2 1

ISBN 978-1-4767-7682-8
ISBN 978-1-4767-7684-2 (ebook)

For Katian, Stephanie, May, Bobby, and Kevin.
You amaze me; each of you and all of you.

acknowledgments

I am thankful for insights, suggestions, and encouragement from the Weymouth Seven: Sarah Shaber, Margaret Maron, Alexandra Sokoloff, Kathy Trocheck (Mary Kay Andrews), Diane Chamberlain, and Katy Munger. And, as always, for help and support from my family.

one

"NOW YOU'VE GONE AND DONE IT!" MY BUSINESS partner, Esme Sabatier, said, lifting a cucumber slice off one eye to glare at me. "You know better than to say such a thing."

"All I said was I can't believe how smoothly this job has gone," I said. I'd meant to put more punch into the protest but my voice came out dreamlike and warbly. The spa attendant was wrapping me in warm, wet sheets and I was bonelessly content.

"And now you've jinxed us," Esme said with an exaggerated sigh. "Never say a thing like that until the job is done and the check's cleared. We're a long way from that—we still have the scrapbooks to finish and that last interview this afternoon."

Any other time, Esme's warning would've set off my alarm bells. When Esme gets one of her vibes, it pays to listen. But at this particular moment, I wasn't sure I could remember how to worry.

I've never seen myself as a spa kinda gal. Before today, I'd thought of spa denizens as wealthy, pampered women in need of rejuvenation after a particularly arduous shopping spree. I, Sophreena McClure, a self-employed thirty-something, am not pampered, nor am I wealthy, though I make a decent living from my genealogical services company. Plus, I have a little locker room phobia left over from encounters with mean girls in high school gym class. But when a client rewards you for a job well done by giving you a free pass for the full treatment at the town's new luxury spa, you say, *Thank you, ma'am,* even if you suspect you'd be too self-conscious to redeem the offer.

Esme, a fifty-something who'd been impervious to mean girls, had no such qualms. She'd dragged me out of bed before daylight, startling me out of a deep sleep by throwing back the covers and tossing a pair of jeans at my head. She'd prodded me to get dressed and thrust a go-cup of coffee into my hand as she herded me out the door. She'd piloted her SUV through the streets of our little town of Morningside, North Carolina, in the rosy glow of dawn so we'd be first in line when Mystic Lake Spa opened for business.

Our first treatment had been a mud bath, and I was ready to throw in the towel, literally, right then and there. Esme and I are a comical-looking duo—even fully clothed. Esme is over six feet of latte-toned woman. She carries herself as if she's royalty and doesn't worry over a little extra cushioning here and there. I'm a very short, very white woman with ungovernable auburn hair and have both the looks and the well-earned reputation of a nerd. We stood side by side and dropped our towels to step into a huge tub of goopy mud. I caught a glimpse of the attendant trying to suppress a grin and I wanted to pack it in. If Esme hadn't threatened me with all manner of dire consequences, I'd have bolted.

After the mud bath, we got full-body massages, which left me so loose-limbed I felt drunk. I found I cared much less about the attendant's tittering after that. Then came a mani-pedi, then a facial, and now we were stretched out on adjacent tables wrapped like mummies in steaming hot sheets with more stuff slathered on our faces and cucumber slices on our eyes. Zen-like music played on the speakers and I felt as if my spirit might actually be disengaging from my body. I couldn't remember when I'd ever felt this serene. But now Esme, with her work talk, was disturbing my aura or misaligning my chakras or something. It was making my muscles kink up into their usual pretzel shapes again.

"We've got to stay on our toes," she said, though she didn't sound like she could have gotten to a sitting position, much less to her toes. "If we deliver on this one, it could mean a lot of business coming our way."

"Yes," I said, "well, we're working for a senator. We've already got feathers in our caps just by landing this job."

"Mm-hmm," Esme said. "Big old peacock feathers. All the more reason we've got to come through with the goods without any glitches."

"You're right. And granted, today's interview may be a little touchy," I allowed, "but it's not as if we'll be asking about anything that isn't already public record. It'll be fine."

Snagging this job really had been a coup. It had been a different twist from the normal family history searches that are our bread and butter. In this instance we'd been not only tracing family history, but documenting a long public service career as well. Along with the heritage scrapbooks we'd designed, we did separate books that highlighted Senator Stanton Sawyer's decades-long career as a senator from the great state of North Carolina. These were going to be displayed at a birthday shindig held in his honor here at the new hotel and spa on Saturday. The elegant luncheon, carefully planned down to the last painstaking detail by the senator's family, would draw not only a who's who of North Carolina bigwigs, but dignitaries from all over the country.

It had all gone surprisingly well considering we were dealing with a politician—a species not known for harmonious collaboration. Senator Sawyer, or Senator

Stan as he was known to his admirers, was now in the ease of retirement. As he approached his eightieth birthday, he was in a retrospective mood and had been forthcoming, even about things he regarded as missteps in his career and foibles in his personal life. But today we were slated to talk about a family tragedy and both the senator and his sister, Lenora Morgan—the one who'd actually hired us—found it a difficult and sensitive subject and had put it off until the very end. Still, I didn't expect any real problems. I'm a professional genealogist and I've had plenty of experience with delicate family matters.

"You know, Esme, I feel like sort of a slacker on this one," I said.

"What do you mean?" Esme said, and I didn't need to lift my own cucumber slice to know she was glaring at me again. "I've worked my tail off. My back forms the letter C from being hunkered over the worktable sorting photos and putting together those scrapbooks. I feel like one of the Village People." She started flailing her arms and singing "Y.M.C.A." while the attendant was trying to wrap her up. The patient attendant reminded her, in a voice ever so soothing, that she was supposed to be searching for serenity, not getting her '80s groove on.

"I'm not saying we didn't work hard," I said. "But the senator's family has been in Quinn County since roughly around the time the earth cooled. So much has been written about them over the generations, it seems there isn't anything left to discover. We didn't have to do much digging."

"Uh-huh," Esme said. "But you know there is such a thing as too much information. There was a ton of stuff to plow through and narrowing it down to the highlights was no easy task."

I thought of the many boxes of Sawyer family archives stacked around our workroom. "You're right," I agreed. "The senator has lived a long and well-documented life, a charmed life, really. Look how many times he was re-elected."

"That's true," Esme said, "but he's had his share of challenges. Losing his baby brother in that house fire was a major childhood trauma for him and Lenora, and you know they hate to talk about it. And then there's Lily Rose's illness. That's a heartache for him, too. Can you imagine being married for fifty-six years? And they've seldom been apart in all that time. There's no doubt he wants her by his side when he blows out his birthday candles. Is she going to be able to come?"

"It's wait-and-see," I said. "Her disease is degenerative, some sort of ataxia. You've seen how it is. She has good and bad days and never knows which it'll be until it gets here. But I tell you, her mind is still sharp and she has a phenomenal memory. She was able to answer all our questions with precision and clarity and she seemed to enjoy it, though she tired easily. It must be awful to be trapped in a body that won't obey your commands," I said, then realized I might experience that myself when I tried to get up off this table at the end of our session.

"Mm," Esme said. "Senator Stan got a good genetic draw, I guess. He's spry for a newly minted octogenarian. He's a hoot, isn't he? Lord have mercy, how that man loves to tell stories."

"Yes," I said, "he's a mesmerizing yarn spinner. I'm going to miss him and the entire family when this job is done. It's such a pleasure to spend time with them, it hardly seems like work."

"I told you not to say stuff like that," Esme scolded. "Take it back."

I laughed as the attendant layered on another warm wrap.

I should've listened to Esme.

The senator's retinue had taken over the entire top floor of the hotel. The structure was only seven stories—not exactly a skyscraper—but it was the tallest building in Morningside, and from its perch high on Crescent Hill it commanded a breathtaking view of Mystic Lake and the town below.

Some of Morningside's citizens had been enraged by the prospect of the hotel and spa locating here, chief among them the residents of Crescent Hill, the most affluent section of town. To them the words *commercial development* were the most vile in the English language. But after a long wrangle, the Village Council turned a deaf ear to their complaints and opted for the tourism dollars. Now that it was a fait accompli, I suspected a considerable portion of the spa's business came from the people who'd worked hardest to keep it out.

As Esme and I stepped off the elevator later that afternoon feeling totally rejuvenated, we were drawn to the top-floor viewing window directly across the hallway from the bank of elevators. Four gigantic full-length windows overlooked the tennis courts, the pool, the boat launch, and the exercise trail, all located on the lake side of the hotel. The exercise trail featured a series of workout stations located along a meandering path. It ran through a copse of pine and deciduous trees and wound back around to the lake's edge, which sloped gradually down at the boating and kayak center, then rose sharply to a bluff overlooking the lake. All this had been carved out of land previously deemed unsuitable for residential building. Looking at it now made me realize what millions of dollars can accomplish—even Mother Earth had been bought off and forced into compliance.

Lenora opened the door to her suite and gave us an uncharacteristically tense smile as she ushered us in.

The senator was pacing, waving his lanky hands in the air. "Jackals, hyenas," he thundered, paying no attention to our arrival. "Mr. Jefferson remarked on the subject of a fourth estate that our liberty depends on freedom of the press and that cannot be limited without being lost. Well, I can only but wonder how far from his lofty ideals the profession has fallen. These so-called reporters aim for cheap and momentary titillation. They skew the facts or make up things from whole cloth."

"Told you you'd jinx us," Esme said out of the side of her mouth.

"Would you care to explain to me how this came about?" Senator Stan said, stopping in front of a wan-faced Lincoln Cooper, the young ghostwriter who was helping the senator with the long-awaited autobiography he'd finally agreed to write. We'd worked closely with Lincoln over the past few months and I felt for him at that moment. He looked miserable.

"Oh, Stanton, for heaven's sake, leave the boy alone," Lenora scolded.

"Well, someone's responsible for this. If not him, who? You two?" Senator Stan narrowed his eyes at Esme and me.

Esme, for once in her life, was tongue-tied. But I drew myself up to my full five foot nothing and answered in the strongest voice I could muster. "Senator, I can assure you that whatever has happened and whatever the press is on about, Esme and I are not the source. We hold the confidentiality of our clients as a trust."

"Of course you do," Lenora said, leading the senator to the sofa. "Now, let's all sit down like ladies and gentlemen and see if we can't sort this out and decide what, if anything, can be done."

"Yes, yes," Senator Stan said with another wave of his hand, "you must forgive me. I endure this calumny for myself, I signed up for this sort of scrutiny when I went into public life, but for my parents' memories to be so maligned yet again is beyond the pale. Will they never be allowed to rest in peace?" He sat down and put his head in his hands, and Lenora rubbed his shoulder.

Esme and I sat on the sofa opposite and Lincoln Cooper took a side chair, perching on the edge as if he might need to make a quick escape. Esme and I stole a glance at each other as we waited for someone to clue us in, but the senator just continued to shake his head.

"I take it you two haven't seen the news today," Lenora said. "There was a story in a local magazine yesterday about Stanton's birthday celebration, or at least we were led to believe that's what it would be about. It ended up being the worst kind of tabloid trash about our house burning all those years ago and all that tragic event wrought."

I nodded, but I still hadn't figured out why the senator was in such an uproar. The fire and their brother's death was a matter of public record and had been written about many times.

"It's a well-known family tragedy," the senator said as if reading my mind. "And it is true that baby John's death haunted our mother and father as this reporter, Chad Deese is his name—damn his eyes—has written. But he slanted the story so they come off looking like lunatics. It's disrespectful to folks who deserve reverence. I want him sanctioned. I want a retraction."

"That won't happen, Senator," Lincoln said. "And other news sources have already picked up the story." He closed the cover on his iPad and peered over his glasses at the senator like a rabbit might eye a fox.

"All in the same tenor?" Lenora asked.

"'Fraid so," Lincoln answered.

"This cannot stand!" the senator roared, getting to his feet again. "I'll make a statement. I'll file suit."

"You'll do nothing of the sort," Lenora said. "You know full well that will only make matters worse. Let's try to get on with life and let this fizzle out on its own. It always does, you know. Something juicier will come along tomorrow. Sophreena and Esme are here to do our interview and I'm sure Lincoln has work to do." She looked in Lincoln's direction and he nodded vigorously and scurried from the room.

The senator fumed and paced for a few more moments, and Lenora gave us a patient smile.

Finally, anger spent, he sat and drew his hand through his silver hair, a stray lock falling back over his forehead. "I am reticent to talk of this incident in our lives," he said, patting Lenora's knee. "Though it's distant in time, it is forever engraved on our hearts and on our psyches. Truth be told, I was planning to give you two the essential facts this afternoon and let it go at that, but now I feel we should have a thorough recounting so you can fully understand why this is so upsetting and help us put it in the proper context in our family history."

Esme and I both took out notepads but the senator held up a hand. "I'd like to tell this my own way, without the question-and-answer format, if you please. It's difficult."

"Of course," I said, though I hoped he wasn't saying he was unwilling to answer questions after he'd made his recitation. This sounded like just the kind of story that would demand some follow-up.

"The year was nineteen forty-seven," he began. "It was a different world in those simpler days. We grew up in a little farming community in Quinn County where everyone knew everyone and neighbors helped one another in a pinch even if there was personal enmity. You might denounce a fellow as a sorry excuse for a man one day, and help him get his mule out of the ditch the next. It was a code of conduct in our culture. That's important to keep in mind.

"One hot summer day my father and I went into our little town of Coventry to buy farm supplies. My father was an attorney, but he fancied himself a gentleman farmer and we kept considerable acreage under cultivation. We had a farm manager, Luther Hamilton, who ran the farm in all the practical ways, but our father liked to keep a hand in. It was an idyllic life. I loved following Luther around and learning how the place operated, and he was tolerant of my tagging along. And in the small-world way of things, it's Luther's son, Cyrus Hamilton, who owns this very beautiful hotel in which we sit. The American dream in two generations.

"But I digress. On that August day my father and I, as was our habit, went to a greasy-spoon burger joint we liked and had a hamburger and a Coca-Cola while the men loaded our supplies into the truck. I remember feeling perfectly happy. I loved spending time with my father. He was a learned man and very witty. I was a boy of twelve and felt honored and validated that my father treated me like a man and talked to me as he might have spoken to a peer. That is my last precious memory of life before. You see, for Lenora and me life will forever be cleaved into before and after that day.

"As we drove home that afternoon, we had the windows down to get some relief from the sweltering heat. We were badly in need of rain, and one could smell baked earth in the still air. I leaned my elbow on the window ledge in imitation of my father and squinted out across the stand of tobacco growing in our nearest neighbor's fields. In the distance I saw a plume of smoke and asked my father what he thought that might be.

"A look of panic came over his face and he started muttering 'Oh, dear God,' over and over. My father was not one to blaspheme and his doing so made my blood run cold. We approached a bend in the road and as I got myself acclimated, I realized the smoke was coming from our house. He turned down our gravel road and pushed the truck to its limit. The road was in a sorry state and we jostled along with me bouncing until my head hit the cab's roof—this in the days before seat belts. I wanted to tell my father to slow down, but instead urged him to hurry. I tried to convince myself it was just our mother burning trash or that Suzette, the woman who came sometimes to help Mother with the household chores, had taken it into her head to make homemade soap at the wash pot as she sometimes did. But I knew that was far too much smoke for either of those possibilities.

"When, at last, the house came into sight, it was an abomination to behold. It was in full flame and the structure was starting to break apart. We flew into the yard and my father was out of the truck before it had completely stopped moving. I caught sight of Mother and Lenora at the edge of the yard with two of the neighbor men and saw some field hands wrestling with a hose, trying to get it to reach the house from the outdoor spigot, though it was useless. Mother was in hysterics and pulling against the men, who were holding her back, and Lenora was on the ground crying and coughing, holding desperately to Mother's dress tail." He turned to Lenora and gestured to her to continue the story.

"Mother had already run back into the house twice, trying to get to Johnny," she said, blinking back tears. "It was too late to hold any hope he'd survived, yet she was straining to go back again even as the house began to fall. When she caught sight of Daddy, she screamed that Johnny was still inside, and he ran toward the conflagration. But at that moment it collapsed."

"It was sheer horror," the senator said. "For all of us."

"Was there no fire department?" I asked.

Lenora sniffed. "It was a volunteer department. We had a fire chief and one ancient pumper truck. But the notification was by phone tree and some of the volunteers didn't even have phones, so someone had to actually go out and find the men."

"Needless to say, the response time was not what one would call swift," Senator Stan said. "They finally arrived over an hour later and put out the last glowing embers. All the damage had already been done by then, but alas, there was more, less tangible, damage to come."

Lenora heaved a sigh. "You see, despite all the evidence to the contrary, neither of our parents could accept that Johnny died in that fire. They simply *couldn't* accept it. Mother latched onto the idea that he'd been kidnapped and the fire was set to cover the crime. And in some sort of folie à deux Father came to believe it, too. Each was haunted by the conviction that Johnny was still alive out there somewhere. They searched for him until the end of their days. It was a shadow over their lives and over ours."

"Indeed." The senator nodded. "But it didn't turn them into different people. This article makes them look like obsessive nuts, which they weren't. They were simply parents who'd lost a beloved child and their heartbreak was so immense, it would've surely killed them if they'd let in the grief, so they built a different reality for themselves. I've mentioned that our code of conduct was to help those in need, and our parents were surely in need. There were folks back then, most well-intentioned who encouraged them in their denial, like alchemists trying to spin sorrow into hope. And sadly there were others who spurred them who might not have had such pure motives." He spat the words, his face hardening into a stony glare.

"We learned to live with this," Lenora said, her voice

quiet. "In the early years, from time to time, a person would show up with a toddler or a young boy claiming he was Johnny, and our parents would be filled with hope, despite their efforts to remain skeptical. Then we'd all live in limbo until the claimants were investigated and found to be charlatans. It was taxing. And it didn't help matters that the case was horribly bungled, leaving the door open for these people to take advantage."

Just then Lincoln opened the door and stuck his head inside as if afraid to enter. "Sorry to interrupt," he said, "but Mrs. Dodd has arrived and wonders if you and Lenora are free for dinner."

"Yes, yes, of course," the senator said, "please tell her we'll be right along—a half hour at most. And Lincoln, I'm sorry for having shouted at you earlier. This whole thing has put me in ill temper. Are you sure there's nothing we can do?"

"I'm sure, Senator," Lincoln said. "Nothing's been said that was patently untrue. You know better than me about libel laws."

"I do know," the senator said with a sigh. Then he turned back to Esme and me, and something about the look on his face made me tense.

"When all this brouhaha over my birthday is done with, I'd like to engage you two to prepare a report for me to sort out all the facts surrounding that fire and lay the rumors to rest once and for all."

Lincoln took a step into the room. "Uh, Senator, I could do that for you," he said. "I'm not sure—"

"No, no," the senator said. "You're needed elsewhere. We have to get this confounded book finished. It's been three years now and two extensions. The publisher is losing patience. And besides, these two have a reputation for digging into the past and getting answers. Sophreena and Esme, will you take on this investigation for me and Lenora?"

"Senator, this is a little out of our wheelhouse," I said. "We're not private investigators or public relations people. We don't have press contacts. Even if we researched this for you, we'd have no way of getting the story out."

"I have people for that," Senator Stan said. "You just look at the evidence and document the findings. We're not asking you to solve a mystery. There is no mystery. Let me be clear, neither Lenora nor I have a shred of doubt that Johnny died in that fire. We were both there, after all. It's just that we don't want our parents remembered only for how they reacted to this tragedy."

"And there's a more practical reason we'd like your help at this particular time," Lenora said, turning back to the senator.

"Yes, our parents had a proviso in their will," he said. "They set aside a sum of money in a trust that was to go to Johnny in the event he was ever found. It's not a jaw-dropping amount, but it's enough to bring false claimants out of the woodwork, and since Chad Deese mentioned this fact in his despicable scribblings, the timing could not be worse."

"But surely those claims could be dealt with easily enough with a DNA test," I said.

"Yes, our entire family got tested as soon as it was accepted in the courts. Lenora and I and our parents are all on file. But while DNA testing would eliminate claimants in short order and the onus of proof is on the claimant, it is a terrible intrusion into our family life, and every new claim will likely attract more bad press. The money reverts to Lenora and me on baby Johnny's birthday this year, which is one month hence. We plan to use the funds to establish a foundation in his name to provide educational opportunities for low-income families. Our good friend Dinah Leigh Dodd has offered to match our seed funds, and my grandson Damon will direct the foundation. I want no hint of scandal or legal entanglements to become attached to this endeavor. This is to be a credit to our parents and our dear baby brother, not more fodder for the rumor mill."

"But, Senator," I protested, "that's even more reason why a lawyer or an investigator would be a much better choice."

"Trust," Lenora said softly. "That's the key. We *trust*

you two to handle this. Would you be willing to take it on, as a personal favor to us?"

Esme and I looked at each other and while she didn't say it aloud, I got the message clear enough. *I told you you'd jinxed us.*

two

"I FEEL LIKE I'M CARRYING A HUNDRED-POUND sack of expectations on my back," Esme said as we passed through the cathedral-like lobby of the Mystic Lake Hotel. "I'm happy those two have confidence in us, but I don't know if we can deliver on this one, Sophreena. We should have told them so."

I sighed. "I tried, but you're right, I should have been more emphatic. You saw how distressed they were. And anyway, as you said this morning, Lenora hired us for this gig and we owe her."

"Yeah, but the flip side is it could hurt us—and them—if we fail," Esme said. "I can't imagine we'll be able to find out anything now, all these years later, that a whole passel of law enforcement folks and fire investigators overlooked more than a half century ago."

"Probably not, but it won't hurt to put fresh eyes on it. And anyhow, they're not asking us to disprove findings, only that we certify them, right? Who knows, maybe we'll get lucky and you'll get some back-channel information we can use."

"Sophreena, you know better than anybody that's not how it works," Esme said. "It's a one-way call from Beulah land."

The "it" was Esme's gift, or her curse, as she often pegged it, of being able to receive communications from the dead. Most often these were maddeningly enigmatic messages composed of images, cryptic words, vague feelings, or occasional musical passages. There had been times when this helped us spectacularly in our family history searches, but more often it was just a pain. It created confusion and only made sense once we turned up solid facts with more conventional research methods and could see it in context.

"I was kidding, sort of," I said, looking up to admire the sparkle of the massive chandeliers suspended from the two-story atrium of the lobby. "We'll just have to give it our best, and anyway, we've got to finish up this job first. We'll worry about it later."

"Okay, Scarlett, we'll think about it tomorrow," Esme said.

"Ms. McClure," someone called, and I turned to see a young man in a bright blue blazer sporting the hotel logo on the pocket. He was trotting in our direction.

"Yes?" I said. "I'm Sophreena McClure."

"Glad I caught you," he said, nodding to Esme. "Senator Sawyer sent me to find you and ask you both to come to the restaurant if you would."

"Okay," I said, drawing out the word, "though I'm not sure I'm dressed for that."

He gave my black polyester pants and only slightly stretched-out cotton top the once-over and assured me, very unconvincingly, that I looked fine. Esme, as always, was totally dolled up, so I tried to trail along in her wake as we followed the young man, Esme mumbling every step of the way. "What do they want now? Are we to find Amelia Earhart's plane? Or maybe track down a yeti?"

As it turned out, they wanted to treat us to dinner in the swanky hotel restaurant for which reservations were next to impossible to get. As a waiter passed carrying a shrimp dish to a nearby table, the aroma made my stomach growl, and my attire suddenly seemed inconsequential, at least to me.

"We've already ordered, I'm afraid," Lenora said. "We weren't sure we'd be able to catch you." She asked the waiter to bring more chairs and everyone scooted to make room for us.

Introductions were made as we settled at the table. The attractive older woman sitting on Lenora's left was Dinah Leigh Dodd. She offered her hand with a warm smile and introduced the younger woman as her assistant, Chelsea Bremer.

The name Dodd sounded familiar but I couldn't piece together who she was.

"Dinah Leigh is a dear friend and one of my most stalwart supporters. Has been for years," the senator said as if reading my mind again. "She's supported me financially, psychologically, and spiritually since I ran for my first public office in nineteen fifty-six. I won that election and became county soil conservation director, for which I was paid the munificent sum of seventeen dollars a week."

"Times have certainly changed, haven't they, Stanton? What did you spend on your last campaign?" Dinah Leigh asked, her tidewater accent rolling off her tongue in an indolent flow.

"I don't like to think about it," he said, grimacing. "Were I a younger man, I would've stayed and entered the fray on campaign finance reform. But I'm too old and weary."

"It's absurd," Lenora said. "So much money spent, even with Stanton running practically unopposed." She turned to Esme and me. "The political arena aside, Dinah Leigh and I were childhood friends. Well, she and Stanton were childhood friends, too, but you know how big brothers can be."

"We were dismissed as tagalongs and pests, which I'm sure we were," Dinah Leigh said with a laugh. She had a nice laugh and an easy manner. I supposed she and Lenora were around the same age. But while Lenora was a handsome woman and very classy, Dinah Leigh looked much younger, perhaps due to her stylish, intentionally messy haircut, the artful makeup job, and the sparkle of mischief in her eye.

The waiter brought us menus, and it took only a few seconds to put in our order, as we'd already heard talk around town about the signature dish called Cioppino à la Aaron. It was the chef's take on a classic seafood stew with shrimp and mussels and was rumored to be heaven in a bowl.

"So you grew up together in Quinn County?" I asked Dinah Leigh.

"Yes and no," Dinah Leigh said. "I lived there until I was seven and then, in the most heart-wrenching episode of my young life, my parents moved us to Norfolk, where my aunt lived. My father had lost his job when the graphite plant closed, and he'd gotten on at the shipyards up there. I thought I would absolutely roll up and die from missing Lenora. But we were dedicated pen pals for years, and then the cosmos made up for separating us by granting both of us acceptance at Chapel Hill. We roomed together all four years of college and we've stayed close ever since."

"We're like sisters," Lenora agreed, "and we like to do things for each other. Which brings me to a question. I hope you won't think we've invited you here under false pretenses. We really did only have in mind for you to meet Dinah Leigh and Chelsea and share a meal with us. But we were singing your praises about the job you've done for Stanton's celebration while the fellow was trying to find you, and well, one thing led to another. We'd like to ask a favor of you. Our second request in one day, we realize."

"And if it's not workable, just say so," Dinah Leigh put in. "You see, my little brother is getting married in two weeks and he's lately become a family history buff." She leaned across the table and wrinkled her nose. "I don't think he's very good at it. I'd like to hire you to do a family tree for him as a wedding gift. Lenora showed me the one you did for Stanton, and it's stunning."

"Thank you," I said, tilting my head in a way I hoped would indicate modesty. Though I had nothing to be modest about. The illustrated family tree *was* beautiful. I'd worked very hard to make it that way.

"The thing is," Dinah Leigh went on, "I'd like it done before the wedding and I know that's short notice."

"Let me just check our calendar," I said, bending down to get it out of my bag. I used those moments to rack my brain for an excuse and mumbled vaguely. "We've still got a few things to finish up for the senator and then we'll be working on that other assignment for you," I said, giving Lenora a pointed look.

"No need for veiled language, Sophreena," the senator said. "You may speak freely in front of Dinah Leigh and Chelsea. In fact, talk to anyone you please about it. You have our blanket permission. It's not as if it hasn't all been laid bare over the years. Especially by callow writers and ignominious so-called documentarians!"

"Don't start in on that again, Stanton," Lenora said. "You'll just upset yourself and ruin this lovely dinner. "

The senator nodded, but huffed one last time.

To my surprise, Esme put her hand down near my bag and gestured an emphatic thumbs-up as she pretended to help me find my calendar. I glanced at her face, and she gave me wide eyes and whispered, "Say yes," through her clenched teeth.

Fine. She'd been the one complaining earlier. I supposed we could work a few late nights to do a favor for a friend of the senator. I told Dinah Leigh we'd be happy to do what we could in the time allowed. "This isn't the time or place to talk about our price list. Would you like me to call you tomorrow?" I asked.

"It'll be fine," Dinah Leigh said. "If Lenora and Stanton trust you not to gouge me, that's all the assurance I need. Just send the information to Chelsea and if you need an advance or deposit, she'll take care of it. Otherwise, just send the bill."

Chelsea took the card I offered, slipping it into the

case of her iPad. She passed one back and I stuck it in my calendar. There was something about her smile that made me think she considered these bits of paper quaint in this electronic age, but for some things I still prefer something I can hold in my hand.

Later on I'd come to see that exchange as the pivot point, the moment we took on the second of what should have been two easy jobs that turned out to be anything but.

Our meals arrived and we gave the food the attention it deserved. I'd heard rumors the chef was a superstar they'd lured with an exorbitant salary and plenty of perks. And I'd also heard some people sniff about the arrogance of his naming this dish after himself. But whatever they were paying him, he was worth every cent.

"How long have you been with Mrs. Dodd?" I asked Chelsea, who'd remained quiet but somehow still engaged during dinner.

"Thirteen years," Chelsea said, which took me by surprise. She looked to be about my age. She was pretty in a girl-next-door way and seemed sure of herself and perfectly comfortable in her role.

"Can you believe it?" Dinah Leigh said. "And by the way, Mrs. Dodd was my late mother-in-law, may she rest in peace. I'm Dinah Leigh. Chelsea came to me as an intern. She was still in college then and she proved indispensable from day one. She's never left me, thank all the gods in the pantheon. I don't know what I'd do without her."

The talk turned to the senator's birthday celebration, and Dinah Leigh, Lenora, and the senator chatted about who would be in attendance and the activities that were planned. I felt a little forlorn that we wouldn't get to see the fruits of our labor, but we hadn't been invited. Then I tuned in to what Lenora was saying.

". . . and, of course, we've reserved a table for you two and your plus ones if you're bringing someone," Lenora said.

The surprise must have registered on our faces.

"You got your invitations, didn't you?" Lenora asked. "You should have received them weeks ago."

I thought of the mail still piled on the console in our foyer. We'd been out of town on a job earlier in the month and still hadn't plowed through the stack.

"We'll be there with bells on," Esme said, sidestepping the question. She leaned toward me. "I could get used to this," she whispered.

I'd been thinking the same thing. First a spa day, then a fancy dinner, and now an invite to the affair instead of being asked to deliver the scrapbooks at the back door with the rest of the hired help.

"We're honored to be included," I said. I was itching to pull out my phone and call my plus one to invite him to this grown-up version of prom. But that would have to wait.

The food was wonderful and the table talk stimulating, but there was a part of my brain that was setting up a worry-buzz about the deadline for Dinah Leigh's "little job." Finally I could resist no longer.

"Would it be terribly gauche of me to ask a few questions about your family now, Dinah Leigh, so we can get off to a fast start? Senator? Lenora? Would you mind?"

The senator gave a hearty laugh. "Young lady, you are speaking to an old pol who has spent half his adult life at rubber chicken fund-raising dinners and pig pickin's. Or standing around being bitten by mosquitoes as I've wolfed down potato salad at the family reunions of numerous clans not my own. It surely will not offend my sensibilities. For me, every meal is a working meal."

"And I've generally been right there beside him, except I don't wolf down my food," Lenora said. "Though I might make an exception for that Chocolate-Mocha Volcano dessert they have here. Who's in?"

All hands went up except the senator's. "I'm afraid I must watch my girlish figure," he said, rubbing his hands over his midsection, which was flat enough to make a gym rat envious.

"That means he'll be eating half of mine," Lenora said with an eye roll.

"Not to worry, this will be short business," Dinah

Leigh said as I dug my trusty notebook from my bag. "I know our parents' names, of course, and our grandparents' on our mother's side and my paternal grandmother's name I think was Edna. She died long before I was born." She paused and puckered her lips. "And I'm afraid that's about it."

I tried to smile but it took effort. This wasn't enough for a shrub, much less a family tree.

"Conrad will know more," she said. "Like I said, he's developed an interest of late. He'll be here tomorrow and you can talk with him then. I'll be meeting his fiancée for the very first time. I really hope we like each other. I dote on my baby brother, always have. It'd be dreadful for him if the two women in his life didn't get along."

I did some math in my head and puzzled over her description. "Could you give me your brother's full name and date of birth?" I asked.

She smiled and recited his full name and the date. "I remember the day he was born like it was yesterday. It felt like Christmas, my birthday, and the Fourth of July all rolled into one. And yes, he's now sixty-four years old, so it's silly to keep calling him my baby brother, but that won't stop me from always thinking of him that way. This is his first marriage. And his bride-to-be is forty and it'll be the first trip to the altar for her as well. Can you imagine? I think this could go two ways. One, they're both so set in their ways they can't bend and the marriage will dissolve before the ink is dry on the marriage license. Or two, they've waited so long for the right person they'll cherish each other and be happy together to the end of their days. Course, I'm hoping for the second scenario. That's what Conrad says, that Phoebe is the woman he's waited for all his life. Isn't that sweet?"

"It is," Esme agreed, and I could have sworn her eyes were misting. Esme's not overly sentimental, so I had to wonder if she was thinking of her own situation with her beau, Detective Denton Carlson of the Morningside Police Department. They'd been seeing each other for a long while, but Esme hadn't allowed things to progress because she'd been afraid to tell him about her unusual gift, for fear he'd be repelled by the whole notion. I'd threatened to tell him myself, but she let me know straightaway that wouldn't play. Finally, a couple of months ago, she'd gotten tired of holding back and told him. He'd accepted it without question, which is more than I can say for myself when she first told me.

I asked Dinah Leigh a few more questions but saw it wasn't going anywhere and gave up.

"My aunt Yvonne can tell you more, too," Dinah Leigh said, actually shivering as she spooned up a mound of chocolate lava. "She's coming to the birthday celebration and I'll ask her to bring along anything that might help. And I'll call down to my house in Charlotte and have my housekeeper send up the one box of family memorabilia that survived my mother's constant household purgings."

"That'd be great," I said. "But I want to caution you—with this tight schedule we may not be able to trace your lineage back many generations. As a rule, the further back you go, the more time-consuming it gets."

"Oh, I understand," Dinah Leigh said. "Just do whatever you can. I'm hoping you find enough branches to fluff out a pretty tree. That'll be enough to please me, and Conrad will be happy with whatever you turn up."

We enjoyed our chocolate with unladylike groans of pleasure. Lenora swatted away the senator's spoon as he tried to steal a bite, then laughed and relented. He stopped with one bite. I admired his discipline, but found this behavior incomprehensible. What kind of person could resist this chocolate concoction once they'd tasted it?

When the meal was over we thanked our hosts profusely and said good night. On the way through the lobby, I turned on Esme.

"Were you not the one bemoaning all the work we have to do when we were walking through this very lobby earlier? What changed your mind? Why were you so hot to take on this job for Dinah Leigh?"

"Do you even know who she is?" she asked, unperturbed by my chittering. At my blank look she plowed on. "Her husband, Preston Dodd, was the founder and sole owner of Dodd Enterprises, one of the biggest privately held companies in the southeast. I can't tell you what they manufacture, doohickeys and thingamabobs, but I know they're big. When her husband died back in the early nineties, Dinah Leigh took the helm. Everybody thought she'd sink the company within five years, but instead she built it to nearly twice its size in less than a decade and kept it in family hands."

"That's impressive," I said. "And how do you know all this?"

"A friend from my church used to work for Dodd Enterprises. She can't say enough good things about the Dodds and how they looked out for their employees."

"Good to know," I said, realizing why Esme had been so eager. It's not that we market ourselves exclusively to rich people, but only the financially comfortable are likely to hire us, especially for our deluxe services, which involve archiving materials and producing heritage scrapbooks in addition to our genealogical research.

"So, worth the midnight oil," I mused. "Plus, I like her. She seems like a fun lady."

"And even better than that, she's a chatty lady. If we please her, she'll spread the word. She and Lenora share a lot in common, don't they? They're both widows, both have daughters approaching middle age and younger sons with wanderlust. Course, Dinah Leigh's filthy rich and Lenora's not, but Lenora's got grandbabies and I'm betting she feels herself the richer of the two."

"No doubt, Lenora dotes on her grandkids. Too bad they both came down with the stomach flu. She was already upset that her son couldn't come for the celebration. Now her son-in-law and grandkids will miss it, too. But as far as finances go, Lenora's no pauper," I said.

"No, she gets by fine enough," Esme said. "But she's not cost-is-no-object rich. You remember how she questioned us about every little line item when she hired us? Dinah Leigh just said 'Send the bill.'"

"Must be nice," I said.

"Oh, I imagine it is in some ways, but sometimes money makes more problems than it solves, or so I've heard."

"Yeah, well, I'd like to find out firsthand if that's true, just for a little while. But for now we've still got to hustle for a living. I'm worried we've overcommitted. We can't call in the cavalry right now, remember?"

The members of our Tuesday night genealogy club, otherwise known as our closest friends, are normally available to help when we get into a bind on a job, but not this time. Marydale and Winston Lovett, the newly wedded senior members of our group, had gone off to visit Marydale's daughter in Chicago. Coco Newsome, our resident hippie and most talented scrapbook designer, was at a sustainability workshop with a former client of ours, River Jeffers. And Jack Ford, the youngest, and I might add the handsomest, member of the group, needed to concentrate on his new role as my boyfriend. Jack and I, after being pals for years, had finally fessed up about our feelings for each other. And, as my grandmother McClure used to say, *thanks be to God and all the saints*, it turned out the feelings were mutual.

"We're pretty much on our own," I said.

Esme sighed. "But still, it's worth some sleep deprivation."

"But, Esme, you're going to be moving in the middle of all this, too."

"That's flexible," she said, "and anyhow, as you keep telling me, I'm not moving cross-country. And as long as you're not planning to rent my room out from under me, there's no big hurry."

Esme and I had been roomies in the house my parents left me for more than five years, ever since she came from Louisiana to join my genealogy business. I'd invited her to stay in the mother-in-law suite over my garage until she found a place, but the arrangement had suited us both so well she'd never quite gotten around to finding a place of her own. But now that we were both involved romantically, privacy had become more of an issue.

Esme had decided it was time to go and bought a house less than a block away. She'd had to replace the faulty furnace and have some structural work done before she could move in, but the house was almost ready, and both of us were getting more apprehensive about what the change would mean to our lives. I was going to miss her desperately but we both knew it was time. Jack and I had agreed to take things slow, fearing that if we rushed it and things went badly, we'd lose our friendship. But Esme and Denton were an established couple, and everyone except Esme seemed to recognize they were ready for the big step. Denny would have to overcome Esme's prejudice against the institution of marriage and her distrust of any arrangement that infringed on her independence. But my money was on Denny.

"I'm not planning to rent the room out," I said. "I didn't intend to rent it to you in the first place, but you insisted on paying."

"Well, I wasn't going to mooch off you," Esme said. "I like to pay my own way."

"You like to *have* your own way," I said. "Anyhow, every penny you've paid in rent I've socked away in a contingency fund for house repairs. I'm in good shape and not at all interested in taking in boarders."

"Don't blame you," Esme said as we pushed open the doors and got a blast of warm, outside air in our faces. "Not everybody's as easy to live with as I am."

I gave that the raspberry it deserved as we side-stepped the valet and headed for the visitors' parking lot.

As we made our way down the hill in the gathering twilight, we met Lincoln, who was so preoccupied, he would've walked right past us if Esme hadn't spoken.

"Lincoln, are you okay?"

He seemed surprised to see us, then produced a tight smile. "As okay as a man who's been royally shafted can be, I guess," he said.

"Shafted?" I asked.

"That article," Lincoln said, "it was all my fault."

Lincoln was a handsome guy if you liked the elbow-patched scholar type. Normally his dress was tidy and his grooming precise. But now he had his shirttail hanging out and his dark hair was tousled.

"I vetted that reporter, Chad Deese," he went on. "I'm the one who convinced the senator to do the interview. The guy totally snowed me. He all but promised me—no, he *blatantly* promised me—a puff piece, a local-son-does-us-proud homage."

"But that's not what you got, I take it," I said. "We haven't actually read the article yet."

Lincoln shook his head. "It's bad. Trashy tabloid stuff. Total hatchet job. The senator's parents come off looking like dolts, and that is one thing he cannot abide."

"So we've seen," Esme said. "Did you know this reporter?"

"I'd met him before," Lincoln said, taking off his horn-rimmed glasses and polishing them with his shirt-tail. "He gave me this spiel about his attachments to Quinn County, and you know how the senator is all about the home folks. So Deese tells me he's got family back there and how his folks knew the senator's folks and all like that. Like it was all old home week. So I set it up."

"Reporter's tricks," Esme said. "You shouldn't beat yourself up. You couldn't have known."

"Yeah, that's the thing," Lincoln said. "I should've looked into him further. The damage is done, but I can't let this stand. I've been out looking for the guy. I just wanted a few select words with him. Didn't find him, but I found a guy who worked with him. He says Deese has a well-known sore spot when it comes to the sena-tor. He's been writing attack pieces and shopping them around to newspapers, magazines, blogs, everyplace, but he never got a take until he landed the interview. If I'd asked around I'd have known that. So, yeah, it *is* my fault."

"Any idea why he's gunning for the senator?" I asked.

"No, his coworker didn't know; he thought maybe it was some kind of family feud thing. But the senator didn't recognize the name and I haven't been able to turn up any family connection. I can promise you this, though, I *will* find out what Deese's issue is."

"Normally I'd advise you to let it go," Esme said, "but I'm not inclined to waste my breath and I can see you've got your teeth into it. Just don't do anything foolish. I'll see you in the morning, right?"

"Yep, I'll see you then," he said, giving a two-fingered salute before heading up the hill.

"You'll see him in the morning?" I asked.

"I promised he could have a sneak peek at the scrapbooks. He wants to make sure there's nothing that might catch him flat-footed if anyone asks about it. I gather writing this book with the senator has been like herding cats. Lincoln can't get him to concentrate, and as entertaining as his storytelling tangents are, it's hindering their progress."

"I can understand that," I said. "The senator's a great storyteller, but like all the great ones, he tends to stretch the truth and sprinkle fairy dust on it. Lincoln will have to force him more into the *Dragnet* mode—*Just the facts, ma'am*. And I think he's just the man for the job. Gentle, but determined. Do you know how Lincoln got picked to work with him on the book?"

"I think there's a Quinn County connection there. And Lincoln's a friend of Dinah Leigh's son, whose name escapes me. Anyhow, he recommended him.

Lincoln's double-dipping, you know. He's writing his doctoral dissertation on some bill the senator championed back in the sixties, so he needs facts, not stories."

"Well, Lincoln's right about one thing: the senator seems to enjoy gathering his home territory folks into his inner circle and weaving in all those connections. And I think there may be another one being formed. Did you catch Lincoln peeking in the doorway as we were having dinner?" I smiled as I recalled the look on his face.

"No. You think he was feeling left out?" Esme asked as she slammed the SUV's door and adjusted the mirror.

"I don't know about that, but he was definitely making eyes at Chelsea Bremer. And she was makin' 'em right back. I think they may have a thing going."

"No doubt that's a union everybody would bless," Esme said.

"Or maybe not," I said. "Dinah Leigh's son—his name is Ken, by the way—might object. I overheard Lenora telling her daughter that she thinks Ken's hot for Chelsea. Only, Lenora is a lady, so she said *smitten*. They were speculating about whether Ken would show up for the event. I think he's in Uzbekistan or Kazakhstan or one of the -stans. Anyhow, their conversation didn't mean anything to me at the time because I hadn't met any of these people, but I took note because Lenora is usually so circumspect and I was surprised she was gossiping. She said she thought Ken's desire to see Chelsea would bring him, even if the obligation to honor the senator wouldn't."

"You sure picked up a lot," Esme said. "I guess it's true about little pitchers having big ears."

"I prefer to say I'm observant and a good listener. Anyhow, I'd never repeat any of that to anybody but you—and maybe Jack."

"Let's hope you never turn to the dark side," Esme said with a smile. "With all the family secrets trapped in your little head, you're a walking Pandora."

"True," I said, "but I'll always walk in the light and I know to keep my lid shut. Now, let's talk about the schedule; it's gonna be tight." I sighed, feeling blue at the realization I'd have little time to spend with Jack over the next couple of weeks. "But it's doable. Unless something weird pops up to bite us."

"And there, you're doing it again," Esme said, giving me an exasperated look. "What did I tell you about saying things like that!"

I smiled, but I felt a twinge of apprehension that wasn't helped by the yellowish tint in the sky and the clouds roiling into a thunderhead in the east.

As soon as we got home, Esme and I headed for the workroom. The first thing I did was track down that troublesome article online. Lincoln was right. It was *bad*.

"I thought maybe Lincoln was overstating things," Esme said. "But this sounds to me like this Chad Deese set out to paint the senator's family in a bad light."

"Sure looks that way," I mused. "Or maybe we're not objective. Anyhow, we can't get sidetracked. While you finish up that last scrapbook, I'll see what I can find out about the fire investigation."

We worked companionably for an hour or so, the silence broken only by the clacking of my computer keys as I ferreted out what I could about the house fire that killed little Johnny Sawyer back in 1947. The actual incident and subsequent investigation seemed pretty cut-and-dried, though there was reference in one newspaper article to a "proper" death certificate being issued. As opposed to what? An improper death certificate?

In the early days there had been numerous stories, some quite sensational, about the parents and their quest to find the child they believed had survived the inferno. Gradually the interest in the case had petered out, and as far as I could tell, there hadn't been any stories in print about the parents' obsession since the mid-sixties—not until today.

Esme's phone trilled. "That'd be fine," she said to

the caller, "long as you don't linger. We've got work to finish up tonight."

I didn't need to ask who it was. Esme has an iron-clad rule for Denny—no unannounced visits. He has to call before he comes over, and she gets to set the limits on how long he stays.

Denny is a patient man. He obeys the letter of Esme's law, but he must've been sitting in his car at the curb when he called, because he came into the work-room about a minute and a half after she clicked off.

My house has normal, to-code doorways, and Denny didn't need to duck when he came in the room, but I suspect he's cracked his head enough times that it's a built-in reflex by now. "How are the night toilers?" he asked as he straightened to full height.

"Busy," Esme said. "You just getting off? I could fix you something to eat, but it'd have to be scrambled eggs or something else quick."

"I'm good," he said, plopping into a chair with a whoosh of breath. "I had a supper break. You about fin-ished with Senator Stan's project?"

"Last scrapbook," Esme said, "so we're set for Sat-urday, but I've got a hunch we won't be done with the senator for a good while yet."

In response to his quizzical look I told him about being hired to look into the fire.

"Nineteen forty-seven," he repeated. "You'll be after

sheriff's department records. I wouldn't expect much; written reports from back then tend to be a bit sparse."

"I hope they wrote their pencils down to stubs in this case," Esme said. "We need every fact we can scare up." She told him about the article that had caused today's uproar.

Denny nodded. "Oh, yeah. I remember. And no disrespect to the senator, but from what I recall, his parents *were* pretty obsessed."

"What could you know about it, Denny?" I asked. "You weren't even born when that fire happened."

"Nope," Denny said, "but when I was a kid there was a billboard, sort of a homemade thing, set up on a state road that runs through Quinn County. It was on the route we took to my grandmother's house. It was huge and hand-lettered, so it got your attention. It offered a reward for information about a missing baby, John David Sawyer. The senator's father put it up."

"Okay, still," I said, "if they believed their child had been abducted in those early stages, that doesn't seem too unorthodox a thing to do."

"Billboard's still there," Denny said. "Least it was the last time I was out that way. It's grown over with weeds and untended now that the senator's father has passed. But he maintained it faithfully till he died, upping the reward every now and again. It used to be a curiosity to me and my sister to see what the reward amount was each time we went out to see Grandma."

"Was there any good reason to believe that baby *did* survive the fire?" Esme asked.

Denny shrugged. "I don't know much about the case. I just remember seeing that billboard growing up and thinking that was a long time for a person to hold on to hope in spite of evidence to the contrary, which there surely must've been. Either there was something really wrong there with the way the case was handled, or the child's death drove the parents over the edge. I don't know which. I know some people over in Quinn County—want me to ask around?"

"Yes, please," I said, feeling my skin start to prickle.

"And we've got another job stacked up in front of that," Esme said and told him about being hired by Dinah Leigh.

Denny whistled, long and low. "First the senator, now Dodd Enterprises? You two are in high cotton," he said.

"You, too," Esme said with a smile. "We've been invited to the big shindig on Saturday as actual guests. You'll be my plus one."

"I'll go dust off my glad rags," Denny said, rising to go. "And I think I'll need to do some manscaping." He patted his close-cropped hair as he bent to give Esme a good-bye kiss.

We quickly got reabsorbed in the work at hand, both of us lost in our own thoughts.

After a long while, Esme's words whispered into the silence. "Yes, it is," she said. "That's a *very* long time to hold out hope."

three

DINAH LEIGH'S BROTHER WAS NOTHING LIKE I'D pictured. While Dinah Leigh was fair and petite, Conrad Nelson was tall and rangy, with a golden tan and a prodigious shock of brown hair shot through with gray. But like Dinah Leigh, he was fit and energetic and had the same laugh and amiable nature.

When she introduced us he gushed so effusively, I felt like a rock star. I don't get that much—people who aren't into family history generally find the whole subject a big snooze. I like to think that's because they don't appreciate how important it is to know about the people you come from and how their stories shape your own. But Conrad had latched onto his family history quest with all the rabidity of a European soccer fan.

He started rattling off what he'd learned before we even sat down, and I had to stop him. "Let me get set up," I said. "I don't want to miss anything."

"Sorry," he said with a laugh. "I get carried away."

"And so shall I," a woman's voice rang out. I turned to see her sweep into the room. She was snugged in a terry beach wrap and wearing flip-flops. "Get carried away, that is," she said, walking over and putting out a hand. "I'm Con's fiancée, Phoebe Morris, and I'm so glad you're here, Sophreena. Dinah Leigh has told us all about you, and you are my rescuer. I love this man madly, but I can't listen to one more telling of the begats or my head will spin off."

Phoebe Morris was one of those women who could make time stop when she entered a room, and I realized I'd frozen with my notebook and cell phone halfway to the coffee table. It wasn't just that she was gorgeous, though she was that. She had a full mane of golden-brown hair with a streak of pure silver framing her face and the largest, greenest eyes I'd ever seen. But she also had that quality of being simply a presence. I sincerely hoped she and Dinah Leigh *did* take to each other. It would be a battle royal if they ever locked horns.

"I'm off to the pool," she said. "But I wanted to remind you, Con, we're supposed to take your aunt Yvonne to lunch."

"Oh, joy," Conrad said with a grimace. "I'll need a workout before I face that. I'll be down to join you shortly."

"No hurry," she said, bending to give him a peck

on the top of his head. "I'll do my laps while you talk." She turned to go, then looked back over her shoulder and mouthed a silent but heartfelt *thank you* in my direction.

"She's lovely," I said as I flipped open my notebook.

"That she is," Conrad said, gazing after her. "I'm a lucky man." Then the smile disappeared as he looked down at the table. "I hope you won't find me insufferable for saying this, but it's a particular pet peeve of mine; must we have the cell phone out?"

I smiled. "I promise I won't answer if it rings, but I use the camera a lot, and I see you've brought some notes. If you have no objection, I'd like to snap a photo of those. I'll take my own notes as we talk, but sometimes it helps to have something to cross-check."

"I'd never thought of that," Conrad said with a laugh. "I'm hopelessly old school. I still go to the library carrying a bag of quarters for the copy machine."

Over the next half hour, Conrad shared everything he'd discovered about his family lineage and I took copious notes. He'd actually uncovered more than I'd dared hope for and I felt less pressure about the job. Conrad was a proud man, but not arrogant. He'd spent his entire working life as a city planner in various cities across the nation. He'd been retired for two years, which had allowed him free time for family research. "I always wanted to do it," he said, "and at my age I'm getting philosophical. The whole idea of what it means to be family is of keen interest to me now."

"Me, too," I said. "I have blood kin out there somewhere that I've never met, yet most of the people who form my family aren't related. It's complicated."

Conrad leaned forward and clasped his hands together. "Just so you understand a little of where I'm coming from, let me share how Dinah Leigh and I grew up. If you ask Dinah Leigh, she'll whitewash it and tell you we had a lovely childhood with loving parents and only sunshine and warm puppies all of our days. Dinah Leigh's good at seeing the picture she wants to see. But sadly, that wasn't our reality. Our parents loved us, but conditionally, *very* conditionally. Our father doted on Dinah Leigh, but hardly seemed to remember he had a son. He was injured in an accident at the graphite plant and it left him scarred in more ways than one. There were times when alcohol was a problem for him—and therefore for us. And our mother, as if to make up for his deficiencies, coddled me to the point of suffocation. She was, on her best days, a little capricious. On her bad days, plain scary. Also, the folks fought a *lot*. And they weren't quiet arguments hoarsely whispered in the night. They were loud, disturbing altercations. I'm surprised they stayed together and honestly I think it was only out of inertia that they did. They weren't self-aware people and they were dreadful at communication. I know that sounds disrespectful"—he nodded as if deep in thought—"but it's honest. They had their good points. They kept us clothed and fed and tried to make sure we each got a good education, but they didn't leave us a good model for family life. I think that's why I've been alone, by choice, all these years. Dinah Leigh was luckier. She fell in love with a patient, persistent man and had a happy family, the marriage part anyhow. The parenting part? Jury's still out on that one. She was devastated by Preston's death—that's why she threw all her energy into the company. People underestimate Dinah Leigh at their own peril. She may come off like a flibbertigibbet sometimes, but she's a strong woman and smart, uncommonly smart. But I digress. I wanted you to know I have my own reasons for looking into our family history now that I'm making this big commitment," he said, glancing toward the door Phoebe had exited. "I'd like to understand what made my parents' relationship what it was and avoid that if I can. Maybe find something in our tree that's a bit more admirable." He smiled, but it was a sad smile.

"I understand," I said with a nod. "And, of course, I think that's a wise pursuit."

I glanced at the clock and realized I needed to wrap this up. "I can tell you this," I said, "your sister is very devoted to you."

He chuckled. "Dinah Leigh decided long ago she needed to look after me. It's the Hansel and Gretel syndrome, I suspect, where the siblings form an especially close bond because there's something lacking in their parents' care."

"Happens in lots of families," I said.

"I was a sickly baby, or so I'm told," he said as he walked me to the door. "Dinah Leigh helped look after me back then and she's never gotten out of the habit of worrying about my welfare. It's sweet and I love her for it, but sometimes it can get a little restrictive, if you know what I mean." He tugged theatrically at the collar of his shirt.

I thought of my relationship with Esme. She looked after me with all the tender love and care of a mother. And, like *some* mothers, she interfered in my life with unsolicited advice and unwelcome admonitions.

"Yes," I said as he opened the door. "I know precisely what you mean."

As I stepped out of Conrad's room, Esme and Lincoln were coming down the hallway. The elevator dinged and as the doors opened, we saw Chelsea craning her neck to see around the cardboard box she was carrying. Lincoln broke into a trot and took the box from her as the elevator doors started to close.

Chelsea laughed as she thanked him and in the moment of silence that followed, both of them looked like kids caught with their hands in the cookie jar. "I was hoping I'd see you," Chelsea said to me once she'd gotten her grin under control. "This is the family stuff from Dinah Leigh's house. She's asked me to organize it and make copies of everything. I can bring it to you later if you're headed out."

"I'll be here awhile longer," I said, glancing at the box. It was bigger than Dinah Leigh had indicated, but smaller than I'd hoped. "I'm to interview Dinah Leigh's aunt Yvonne when she gets here. I'll text you before I go to see where you are with it."

"Okay," Chelsea said. "Dinah Leigh's down in the café if you want to check in with her."

"We'll do that," I said, looking at Esme, "if you're all done, that is."

"All done, I think," Esme said, looking a question at Lincoln, who seemed distracted by Chelsea's proximity.

"Yes, great," he said. "You did a phenomenal job. Really great." He turned to Chelsea. "I can carry this for you."

Chelsea directed him down the hall and they disappeared into her room.

"Hm," Esme said. "Not sure how much work she'll get done in the next little bit."

"Wonder why it's such a big secret," I said. "They're both single and free to see whoever they'd like, right?"

"Yes, but it might not be that simple," Esme said as

she pushed the call button for the elevator. "Chelsea's devotion to Dinah Leigh runs pretty deep, from what Lenora told me. I suspect she'd be hesitant to leave Dinah Leigh just now. She grew up poor and without much family support and not many prospects. One of the first things Dinah Leigh did when she took over the company was award five full-ride scholarships to promising students, and Chelsea was one of the chosen that first year. Dinah Leigh took a personal interest in her scholarship kids and that's when they first met. Chelsea was seventeen. She's almost like a daughter to Dinah Leigh. And as you picked up, I think there might be some sort of history between her and Ken Dodd. Maybe Chelsea doesn't want to disappoint him and by extension Dinah Leigh."

"Maybe," I allowed, "but Dinah Leigh would have to be blind not to notice the vibe between Lincoln and Chelsea."

Esme shrugged. "Sometimes people won't see what they don't wanna see."

As we stepped into the elevator, I realized Conrad had just told me that very thing about Dinah Leigh.

When we got to the ground floor Esme went off to locate the event planner to find out where the scrapbooks were to be set up, and I went to the café. I spotted Dinah Leigh with a younger woman I hadn't met at a window seat overlooking the pool. As I approached,

I spotted Phoebe Morris still swimming determined laps.

". . . flake and gold digger," I overheard as I moved toward the table, the comment coming from the younger woman.

"Well, I think you're wrong," Dinah Leigh said. "I like her."

Both women looked up as I drew closer, and the younger woman gave me a bright smile. But when Dinah Leigh introduced me to her daughter, Patricia, the smile dimmed. "Yes, nice to meet you," she said with all the sincerity of a door-to-door vacuum salesman.

"Patricia, would you go tell Aunt Yvonne that Sophreena will be up in about fifteen minutes," Dinah Leigh asked, giving me an apologetic look. "She'll need a little time to get herself together. Poor old love is slowing down these days. The trip was hard on her and she's exhausted. She'll just be getting up from her morning nap."

Patricia looked to be in her early forties, with Dinah Leigh's good looks but without her affable manner. She gave an eye roll worthy of a teenager and rose. "Wouldn't we all love a nap," she groused, jerking her head in my direction. "She'd best come up before Auntie gets into her cups." She gave me the smile again, more genuine this time, though on the malicious side, and continued. "Auntie operates under the rule she can't drink while it's light out, but as she's fond of saying, it's always dark under the porch."

As she walked away, Dinah Leigh shook her head. "That's my daughter. Patricia has decided to run for public office in this fall's elections. She has most everything she needs to be successful—she's well funded, she has good connections, she's smart, she's attractive, and she's determined. Now she just needs to work on that personality thing," she said dryly, motioning for me to take the vacated chair.

"Ah, but she's right about Aunt Yvonne," Dinah Leigh said with a *tsk*. "She loves Jesus, her family, Virginia Slims, *American Idol*, and Wild Turkey bourbon—not necessarily in that order. But she should be in good shape right about now." She gave me the room number and glanced at her bejeweled watch. "Just give Patricia a few minutes to get her situated. I only hope they don't peck each other to death before you get up there."

I declined coffee and looked out the window to where Phoebe was still churning the water. "I met Phoebe briefly upstairs; she seems very nice," I said.

"Yes." Dinah Leigh beamed. "I think she's the real deal. And Conrad's giddy as a schoolboy. The only problem is she's making me feel like the world's biggest slug. I think I'll go see if there's a yoga session I can get into."

I took that as my cue and started up to interview Aunt Yvonne, feeling confident, despite the warnings.

When would I learn?

"I don't understand why we're dredging up all this old stuff. Who cares?" Yvonne demanded. She was a dry husk of a woman. Her skin had the sallowness of the dedicated chain-smoker, and deep wrinkles were carved from each side of her mouth down to her chin, giving her the look of a marionette that had been stuffed in a trunk too long.

"It's for Conrad," I said encouragingly. "It's a wedding gift from Dinah Leigh."

"Worst gift I ever heard tell of," Aunt Yvonne muttered. "What's wrong with a compote bowl, or some nice percale sheets, or in Dinah Leigh's case, why doesn't she just buy him a house? She bought me one, you know."

"That's very generous," I said. "Maybe this is something you can do for her in return. It means a lot to her."

Aunt Yvonne gave a resigned sigh. "Fine, ask your questions and I'll tell you what I want you to know."

What she wanted me to know wasn't a whole lot. She had a few names from her branch of the family, Dinah Leigh and Conrad's maternal line. She knew a little about family occupations and some family lore about a migration pattern, but it was like pulling crabgrass to get a factoid out of her. "Me and my sister didn't give a rip about all that old stuff," she said. "Marie was like me; she lived for today and for Dinah Leigh and Conrad's future. Those people who came before are all dead, they can't do us any good."

After getting nowhere and enduring her fourth tirade about how unjust it was she couldn't smoke in the room that Dinah Leigh had "paid out the ying-yang for," I decided to pack it in. The whole time we talked, Yvonne was continually toying with an old cigarette lighter or flipping a pack of cigarettes on the tabletop. She definitely needed a nicotine fix. I put away my notes and quickly texted Esme to tell her I'd be stopping by Dinah Leigh's room to check on the status of the box of family artifacts, then I'd be set to leave.

"Conrad needs to come to it that all that stuff from the past doesn't mean anything," Yvonne harrumphed as I headed for the door. "He's his own man and well into his years. Much as Dinah Leigh likes to make over him, he's no boy."

I couldn't think of what to say to that, and anyway, a reply wasn't needed. Aunt Yvonne pushed past me and headed for the elevator, intent on getting outside for a smoke.

*   *   *

"Dare I ask how it went?" Dinah Leigh inquired, grimacing as if she already suspected.

"I got a little new info," I said. "She's not really into the whole family history thing, is she?"

"No," Dinah Leigh said, making her mouth form a perfect circle as she drew out the word. "Not the sentimental sort, our aunt Yvonne. She can be a bit tart."

"No problem, I've dealt with lots of reluctant people. She's not the worst," I said, but I was thinking Aunt Yvonne might still be in the running for that title.

"Good, then. I think Chelsea is almost done. Would you like to wait or should I have the things sent over to your office?"

"I'll wait, if that's okay."

"Oh, surely," Dinah Leigh said, gesturing to a chair beside her. Her suite had a sitting area as big as my living room, with a little kitchenette in the corner and a gorgeous view of Mystic Lake.

"If you have the time, would you mind if I asked you a couple of questions about what happened to the senator's family all those years ago? He says I can speak freely to you about the fire."

"Of course, but I doubt I'll be much help. I was a child when the fire happened and we were getting ready to move. In fact my mother had already gone ahead of us. She was pregnant and Aunt Yvonne came down to pack up the house for her. I was left behind to help. I was miserably unhappy about the move. I hardly saw Lenora after the fire because her family was in mourning. Then we moved to Norfolk and I didn't see her or Stanton again for a long while."

"Did your parents ever talk about it?" I asked.

"Not a whole lot—not around me anyway. I did overhear them a couple of times over the years discussing how foolish it was for Alton and Margaret to continue believing Johnny had survived."

"I understand they weren't the only ones to suggest the parents were delusional," I said.

"No," Dinah Leigh said with a sigh. "I know it pains Stan and Lenora, but their parents did go a little off the deep end when they lost baby Johnny. They were mad with grief and grasping at straws, which I'm sure would be exactly the way I'd react myself. What a horrible, horrible thing to lose a child, and in that awful way."

"Do you have any idea what, specifically, made them believe the baby had been kidnapped?"

"I'm sorry, Sophreena, I don't know any particulars. We had a sheriff back then named James Ogdon. Big Jim, people called him. He was a very sweet man, but I came to realize as I got older that he probably wasn't the brightest bulb on the Christmas tree. Maybe they simply didn't trust his conclusions."

The door opened without a knock and Patricia came into the room followed by a man a full head taller than her and strikingly handsome. She flopped down on the sofa and started filing at a nail with such industry I expected her to quickly strike knuckle. She looked over at me with a wicked grin. "How'd it go with Auntie? She's a sweetheart, isn't she?"

"Patricia," the man said, stretching her name into a caution. "Watch the cynicism."

It fell to Dinah Leigh to introduce Marc Benton, Patricia's husband. He extended a hand and I feared my arm might suffer tendon damage if he didn't stop shaking it with such vigor.

"Marc is trying to teach Patricia to be more prudent about sharing every opinion that comes into her head, which is a good skill to possess, especially in politics. He's her campaign manager," Dinah Leigh said.

"And he's right, I'm a terrible crank," Patricia said. "I need to learn to be winsome." She vamped a moment and fluttered her eyelashes.

"Maybe your brother can give you some clues," Dinah Leigh suggested brightly. "He called about a half hour ago. He's on his way from the airport. I told you he'd come."

"And of course he never disappoints you," Patricia said.

Dinah Leigh ignored her and addressed her comments to me. "We weren't sure he'd be able to make it. Ken's a doctor; he works with a group called Physicians for Peace in areas of the world where there's substandard medical care. I haven't seen him in three months, so I'm very pleased he could come home. I only wish Lenora's son, J.D., could've made the trip. I know she's disappointed he can't be here, but he's off in some jungle somewhere like Dr. Livingstone. Only he's a PhD doctor, not the medical kind. I know she's proud of the work he does, but honestly, it seems like he could have taken a few days to come for this. Anyway, be sure you come by our table tomorrow so I can introduce you to Ken."

"You can curtsy and kiss his ring," Patricia said.

There was a light knock on the adjoining door, and Chelsea pushed it open with her foot and came in with the box of family archives. She was wearing a strange expression. Her face was flushed and she seemed distracted. I wondered if she and Lincoln had spent a bit of quality time between document scans.

"Marc can help you get that to your car," Dinah Leigh said.

I tested the box and demurred. It wasn't that heavy, just awkward. I took out an elastic-band-and-webbing contraption I keep in my bag for just such occasions and slipped it onto the box, forming a handle.

"Chelsea, would you fix me a cup of tea? Earl Grey, please," Patricia said, again filing away at the problem nail.

"Chelsea is not your maid," Dinah Leigh said calmly, but with a razor's edge.

Patricia looked up, her eyes drilling into Chelsea. "Of course not, whatever was I thinking? She's the daughter you wish you'd had, right?"

Chelsea blanched and turned to go back into her own room. I couldn't help but notice her hand was shaking as she reached for the knob.

"Patricia! Really!" Dinah Leigh scolded. "Sometimes you go too far."

By the time I headed home the clouds that had been gathering all day were sending heavy raindrops spattering onto my windshield. I hadn't brought an umbrella and I'd had to run for my car. I was wet, tired, and grumpy and in no mood to work tonight and intended to tell Esme so, even if she pushed.

But when I arrived I found Esme had lit a fire in the family room fireplace. There was tomato-basil soup simmering on the stove and grilled cheese on my favorite Italian bread on the griddle. We took trays into the family room to eat in front of the fire and shared our day. These were the times I was going to miss when she moved out.

I told her about my interviews with the Nelsons, the pleasant one with Conrad and the flinty one with Aunt Yvonne.

"So sorry I missed that," she said.

"Sarcasm doesn't become you," I told her, which is a line she uses on me frequently. She gave me an overly sweet smile and took a bite of her sandwich.

I told her about Dinah Leigh's seemingly brittle relationship with her daughter.

"Yes, I met her. She's quite a contrast to the other daughters," Esme said. "Lenora's daughter, Judith, is quiet and kind, and so is the senator and Lily Rose's daughter, Sarah. I think of them as dutiful daughters and I don't mean that in a dismissive way. They're always the ones to recognize when people need a chair or something to drink or when their parents are overtaxed, and they see to it without any fuss or bother. I don't think I'd want to come up against either of them if they decided their children or their parents needed defending, but otherwise they tend to blend into the background."

"I seriously doubt Patricia would ever blend," I said.

"Not her nature," Esme said. "But we don't know her story, so I won't judge. Not unless she gets snippy with me personally."

"I think she's smarter than that," I said with a laugh. "But she does seem to take after her great-aunt Yvonne a bit."

The rain had let up, but I knew it wasn't done for the night. There were still low rumbles of thunder off in the distance and the weather forecasters had predicted bands of rain coming throughout the night.

"I hope this doesn't last into tomorrow," I said. "I was hoping we'd have a beautiful North Carolina spring day for the senator's big event."

"It's supposed to stop by morning," Esme said, reaching for my tray. "Now, I don't know about you, but I've got things to prepare for tomorrow's gala. I always wanted to say that, tomorrow I'm going to a *gala*."

"So we're not working tonight?" I asked, relieved I wouldn't have to mutiny.

"You can do as you please, but I've got things to attend to. I'm going up now to hang my dress in the bathroom to steam it. And while that's happening I'll pick out my accessories and decide which shoes to wear. Then I'm going to take a nice long, hot bath using that bath bomb Marydale gave me for Christmas. You need to get your things ready, too."

"Oh, I will," I assured her. She left the room, a woman on a mission, and I contemplated what all I had to do. I went up to my room and pulled my one good dress from the closet and hung it on the door. Next I found my shoes, both of them, and set them by the dresser. I scrambled around in my bag for a tube of lip gloss and set it on the dresser, then took a quick shower. I was done before Esme even started drawing her bath.

I answered email, read for a bit, then turned off the light and snuggled in under the comforter. Unfortunately, sleep proved elusive. I tossed and turned for a while, then finally switched on the light and opened my laptop.

Lincoln had said Chad Deese claimed a connection to Quinn County. I did a search and found a great-uncle and a smattering of distant cousins, but neither Deese nor his direct-line ancestors had ever lived in Quinn County as far as I could tell. Maybe that had been a ploy, as Lincoln suspected.

I opened the folder I'd set up for information about the fire to check something that had been troubling me. I called up a calendar of 1947 and compared it to a newspaper article. Baby Johnny's death certificate hadn't been issued until almost two weeks after the fire. I wondered what that meant and made a note to look into it further.

I tried again for sleep. As the thunder rumbled and lightning lit up my curtains, I worried about the volume of work we'd taken on and felt guilty about slacking off. Dinah Leigh's case should be simple enough, though the deadline was tight. And the senator and Lenora's case seemed like it should only be a matter of organizing the facts and verifying the official findings. But still I felt a lot of pressure and unease.

I worried it around in my head for a while and had

just fallen asleep, when a bolt of lightning so bright it lit my entire room woke me with a start. The rumble that followed growled on for what seemed like minutes, though it could only have been a few seconds.

I burrowed back under the covers, grateful to be warm, safe, and dry. I remembered a phrase my father had used. It was a night not fit for man nor beast.

four

THE HOTEL HAD PULLED OUT ALL THE STOPS FOR the senator's event. Marble, metal, and glass sparkled and employees bustled about with efficiency and toothy smiles.

"This is grander than the grand opening," Denny said, surveying the activity in the vaulted lobby.

"You came to the grand opening?" Jack asked.

"Professionally," Denny sighed. "Two ladies got into an altercation when one rolled a wheelie-bag full of cosmetics over the other's Jimmy Choos. It wasn't pretty."

"Never a dull moment for you, eh?" Jack said. "I'll stick to planting things and cutting grass, thanks all the same."

In truth, Jack Ford did a lot more than that. He was a landscape architect and owned his own thriving business, no small coup for a guy in his mid-thirties. Plus, he cleaned up real nice.

The scrapbooks were set up in a nicely decked-out display area near the back of the room, and once we reached our table I excused myself to the restroom, which I didn't actually need at the moment. Just coincidentally, I had to walk through that area to get to the bathroom—if you ignored the door *directly* behind our table, which I did. I kept my ears open for comments as I passed through and was not disappointed. I had to resist the urge to start flipping around business cards like a Vegas blackjack dealer.

I literally ran into Lenora, or rather she ran into me. She was craning her neck, scanning the space with squinted eyes. "Oh, Sophreena," she said, patting my arm. "I'm so sorry. Have you seen Lincoln? We can't find him and Stanton wants him to sit on the dais with us."

"No, I haven't seen him today. Would you like me to help look?"

"No, no," Lenora said, smiling and dispensing little waves and greetings as people walked by. "He'll turn up. Just if you see him, tell him. And come to my table when you can. I was feeling very low yesterday because Judith's husband and the grandkids can't be here. But I had a wonderful surprise last night. Be sure you stop by." She rushed off, working the crowd along the way.

I looked for Dinah Leigh's table, figuring if anyone might know where Lincoln was, it'd be Chelsea. I spotted the table but Chelsea wasn't with Dinah Leigh. I stopped by and was introduced to Ken Dodd. He was ridiculously handsome, with thick, wavy blond hair and an athletic build. And he oozed so much charm I felt like an overwatered houseplant. It was too much to soak in.

Patricia was like a different woman today, warm and friendly. The contrast from her demeanor yesterday made me wonder if she was bipolar, but then I realized she was wearing her politician's mask. Her husband seemed about to jump out of his skin and Dinah Leigh dismissed him to "go network, before you bust a gusset."

I glanced at Conrad and Phoebe's empty seats, and Dinah Leigh smiled. "Lovebirds, you know," she said. "They'll be down, eventually."

"I haven't seen Chelsea today," I said, gesturing toward her place card. "Please thank her again for organizing your family memorabilia. It's a big help."

"Poor Chelsea's sick," Patricia said.

"Patricia," Dinah Leigh said, her voice rising.

"I'm not being snide, Mother," Patricia protested. "I mean it, she was green to the gills this morning. I felt bad for her."

"Which should tell you," Dinah Leigh said to me, "how sick Chelsea is if Patricia's being sympathetic. I hung the *Do Not Disturb* sign on her door and let her sleep. If she's not feeling better by nightfall, I'm taking her to urgent care."

I saw that Lenora had apparently given up on trying to find Lincoln and was back at the head table. The food would be coming out at any moment, and I decided now was my chance to find out what her big surprise was. I thought maybe she'd gotten a nice telegram or some flowers or something but the surprise was a human being—two, actually.

"Sophreena, this is my son, J.D.," Lenora said as a thirty-something man rose to shake my hand. He was wearing a loose cotton shirt with ornately embroidered vertical panels down the front. His hair was longer than the current fashion and he had a scruffy beard. But he was attractive and I saw in him his mother's warm smile and easy manner as we exchanged nice-to-meet-yous.

"I wasn't expecting him," Lenora said, which I already knew. She'd lamented the fact that one of her children would be missing the celebration many times over the past months.

"Well, this is a nice surprise," I said.

"Oh, he's not the surprise," Lenora said. "I mean I'm tickled pink he could make it, but the real surprise is that I have a new daughter-in-law. This is Gabriela." She motioned toward the woman seated next to J.D. as he sat back down and put his arm around her shoulders. She had dark, exotic features and without any apparent assistance from the cosmetic industry was hands down the most beautiful woman in the banquet hall. And more lovely still when a radiant smile lit her face.

I offered my congratulations and chatted a moment, and when I walked away Lenora came with me, renewing her search for Lincoln.

"This the first time you've met J.D.'s wife?" I asked.

"This is the first time I even knew J.D. was *contemplating* a wife," Lenora said. "He's always been so devoted to his work he's had no time for serious relationships."

"Are you pleased?" I asked tentatively.

"I'm *ecstatic*," Lenora said. "I've only had a little time to adjust to the news but already I see the changes in J.D. Positive changes. She's good for him, I think. I look forward to getting to know her. Judith loves her already and I value her judgment. Oh dear," she said, looking toward where the senator stood with a small cluster of people. "Stan's gotten buttonholed by Ardeth Wilkins. She'll talk his ear off. I'd best go rescue him."

Reaching octogenarian status did little to dim Senator Stan's ardor for the microphone. Despite Lenora's request that he keep his "speechifying" to a minimum, he'd been running on for more than thirty-five minutes now.

His family was seated on the raised platform behind

him. I was as happy as everyone else to learn that Lily Rose had been able to come. She gazed at her husband with that adoring-spouse smile politicians' wives are required to cultivate. Except in Lily Rose's case, it seemed authentic.

Their only child, Sarah Sawyer Lowell, sat to one side along with her two children. Her son, Damon, was in his late twenties. I'd met him a few times, but hadn't gotten to know him very well. Emma, whom the senator called the "splendid bonus" due to her late entry into the family, had just turned sixteen. Ordinarily I'm not a big fan of teenagers; angst-ridden teens set my teeth on edge. But there was something about Emma. I'd been drawn to her, despite her self-absorption, and we'd become unlikely friends.

I watched as she slipped a smartphone from her pocket and started surreptitiously texting until she looked up to see her mother giving her the stink eye. She turned back toward the podium with what appeared to be rapt attention and let the phone slide back into her jacket pocket.

Esme leaned over and whispered, "Where's Sarah's husband?"

"Couldn't make it," I whispered back. "He's a petroleum engineer and he's somewhere in the Middle East on a sensitive project. The company didn't want him to leave right now."

"Priorities," Denny said, leaning in to join the whispered conversation. "And after all, Senator Stan's got no room to criticize. I bet he's missed a few family events because of his job over the years."

"Speaking of job obligations," Jack said, nodding toward the doorway. "Isn't that Jennifer out there? I think she's trying to get your attention, Denny."

"Oh for pity's sake," Esme said, her whisper turning into a hiss. "Can they not get along without you for one blessed day?"

"I'll just go see what she needs," Denny said, sliding his chair back and leaving the table as unobtrusively as a man his size could manage.

"It better be something big," Esme muttered, "and I mean big. A bank robbery or something."

"Esme!" I scolded. "You're not ill-wishing some poor bank teller, are you?"

Esme sighed. "Well, no, of course not, but it better not be a cat-stuck-in-a-tree case. Or Ida Ruth Butterfield calling in another burglary report 'cause she sees her neighbor's handyman cleaning the rain gutters and thinks he's breaking in."

Detective Jennifer Jeffers was Denny's partner at Morningside PD. She's a capable officer and I didn't think she'd bother Denny at this event unless it was important. From my sliver of a view, I could see they were having an intense conversation and when they finished

Denny walked away with Jennifer instead of coming back to our table. "Definitely not a cat in a tree," I whispered.

Senator Stan finally wound down, though I hadn't taken in much of what he'd said from the time Denny was called away. People began to mill about, laughing and talking and sharing stories about the senator, and a half hour later Denny still hadn't returned.

I could tell Esme was ticked, though she tried to hide it. Jack and I both tried to make plausible excuses for Denny's sudden departure but Esme wasn't placated. She argued that he could've at least done her the courtesy of saying good-bye.

I had to concede her that point.

A few minutes later, a hotel employee told us Detective Carlson would like us to join him in the lobby. Esme was not happy about being summoned and less happy still when we got to the lobby and were left cooling our heels as Denny talked with an older gentleman wearing the hotel's official blue blazer. When he caught sight of us, he broke off the conversation and came to meet us. He had on his grim face and it made my heart race. I wanted to pepper him with questions, but knew that would only delay getting answers.

He steered us to a more private corner and wasted no time with the social niceties. "It's bad," he said. "A murder. Or more accurately, there was a death that will in all likelihood be ruled a murder. The ME's still got to make the call. Newlyweds out for a run spotted the body at the bottom of the overlook off the exercise trail. As you'd expect, the owner of this place"—he jerked his head in the direction of the man he'd been speaking with—"is interested in keeping this as low-profile as possible. And that suits me fine. Fewer people who know about it right now, the better. I'd like to get the investigation going without interference, but I need your help. We're setting up a system for questioning the guests as to their whereabouts last night, but we don't have the manpower. That's a problem because the longer people are detained, the more agitated they'll get. The hotel's getting us a list, but I need you two to screen the people leaving the senator's event. I just need their contact information and to know if they were out on the grounds at any point last night and if so, did they see or hear anything unusual. That's all."

The whole time Denny was talking, Esme and I were both searching for an opening to ask the pressing question. I'm sure we looked like goldfish at feeding time, our mouths opening and closing. Denny was too focused to notice. Finally Esme grabbed his arm. "Denton!" she said, her voice sharp. "Who's dead?"

"Sorry, didn't I say?" Denny asked, reaching up to pull at his tie. "It's Lincoln Cooper, the senator's—"

"Ghostwriter," Esme whispered.

She and I both let loose with questions. When? How? Was he sure it was Lincoln? An accident? Denny put up a hand to stop the onslaught. "It's definitely Cooper," he said. "From what I saw, there was some kind of scuffle, and I'm more than half convinced he was pushed over the railing. I'll know more once we process the scene. Can you help or not?"

"Yes, of course," Esme said. "Does the senator know? Lenora?"

"Jennifer made the notification and is escorting them up to the senator's suite now."

The next two hours passed in a blur. Esme and I were stationed at one exit of the large banquet hall while hotel employees were at the others. Uniformed officers had been brought in to speak with people at the valet queue as cars were being brought around.

I didn't have time to take in the fact that someone we'd worked with and liked was dead. I was on autopilot, but a part of me knew the numbness would wear off soon. I needed to be someplace else when that happened.

We kept the questioning low-key, giving out only that there had been an incident on the grounds and we needed to know everyone's whereabouts for the previous evening in case they might have observed something helpful. Everyone was cooperative, still basking in the good-time-had-by-all glow of the event. That is, until an elderly woman with a Marge Simpson bouffant—which was almost as blue as Marge's—reached the table. She must've been devout about her calcium supplements, because her spine was straight as a rod. She smiled at us in a knowing way and I noticed there was nearly as much lipstick on her teeth as on her lips. I gave her the same spiel I'd given everyone else and she reared back and gave a mirthless laugh. "An incident?" she said. "Is that what they're calling it these days? By that you mean the dead man they found at the bluff?"

"Mrs. Douglas," I said, referring to the contact info she'd given me, "we're just here to help gather information and—"

"Who was he?" she demanded. "Did he die of exercise? God knows he could have. It's hot out, and there's dreadful humidity. People ought not to be exerting themselves in this weather. Or did somebody kill him? *Was* it a murder?"

"Thank you for your cooperation, that's all we need," Esme said, trying to move her along.

But it was too late; the buzz was spreading through the crowd and soon the whole place was humming. The drone was no longer punctuated by peals of laughter or the mellow murmurs of contented conversation. It had dissolved into a worried grumble.

*   *   *

The mood in the senator's suite was somber. Any small hope I might've had that this was all a big mistake was immediately snuffed when I saw Denny talking with the senator's daughter, Sarah. He had on his cop face and was scribbling in his faithful notebook. Sarah was pale and holding on to her mother's hand as Lily Rose softly wept.

Lenora was twisting a crumpled tissue and trying to keep her composure. "Stanton's on the phone with Lincoln's father. It's the hardest call he's ever had to make," she said. "They haven't even moved the poor boy's body. Who could have done such a dreadful thing, Esme?" she asked, clutching at Esme's arm as if she might actually have the answer.

"I don't know, Lenora," Esme said gently, "but I can promise you that Detective Carlson and Detective Jeffers are very good at what they do."

"I'm sure that'll be a comfort down the line," Lenora said. "But right now we're all in shock. Poor Chelsea is so broken up, they've had to sedate her."

"And you, Lenora," I asked, "how are you holding up? I know you were fond of Lincoln."

"Oh yes," she sniffed. "I know people say this all the time, that someone is just like family, but it was true in this case. We'd gotten to know Lincoln so well and spent so much time together, he did seem like one of us."

"We need to speak with Detective Carlson when he's available," I said, "but is there anything we can do in the meantime? Do you need anything?"

"Not that I can think of," Lenora said. "Cyrus Hamilton has been very attentive. He's been sending up food and beverages, and the doctor from the spa attended to Chelsea. As soon as the detective is finished speaking with them, Sarah will take Lily Rose to her room to rest. Poor thing. I daresay she'd come to regard Lincoln as the son she never had. She knew his parents from years ago. She and his mother were fast friends and Lily Rose was very sad when she died a few years back. Now Lincoln's gone and she's heartbroken."

Denny came toward us and I could practically feel Esme vibrating with suppressed questions, but she didn't get the opportunity to ask any of them. Instead, Denny collected Lenora and took her off to a private corner to talk, giving Esme and me a look that begged forbearance.

Damon, the senator's grandson, was sitting in a side chair near the desk scribbling furiously into a notebook as the senator occasionally covered the phone's receiver and relayed information. Emma was staring stonily out the window. She looked peculiar. Not sad, but more a combination of stunned and angry. A subdued J.D. sat on one of the sofas alongside an obviously bewildered Gabriela.

After what seemed like an eternity, Denny pulled Esme and me into the hallway. "I've gotta get back out to the scene," he said. "The wagon's here and they're getting ready to move the body. Jennifer's on-site, but apparently the word's out and the looky-loos are getting brassy. I've called for some uniformed officers to keep them back, but it'll be a few minutes before they get here. Here's what I know: the death will almost certainly be ruled foul play and he died instantaneously. The height of the fall was survivable, but the rock pile below the overlook was not, time of death between midnight and two a.m. I'm going to be tied up on this one no telling how long, Esme. I'll call you when I can."

"Go on," Esme urged.

He punched the button for the elevator, but was too impatient to wait. He jerked open the door to the stairwell and his footfalls on the metal steps faded away within seconds. Just then the elevator dinged and Patricia and Marc Benson stepped out wearing matching frowns.

"What are they saying about what happened?" Patricia asked. "Do they know who did it? This is just awful."

"Do they have any suspects?" Marc asked.

"You know as much as we do," Esme said.

"I doubt that," Patricia said. "You and that detective are a couple, aren't you?" She was unable—or unwilling—to keep the sharp edge from her voice. Marc had an arm around her shoulders and I noticed he gave her a squeeze, which seemed to adjust her attitude.

"I mean, surely he's told you what's going on, Esme," Patricia said.

"The investigation is under way," Esme said. "And Denton is very good at what he does. That's all I know."

"I'm sure that'll be some comfort to the family and to all of us who knew Lincoln," Marc said. "If there's any way we can help, we're available. We've cleared our schedules to stay on with Dinah Leigh for a few days. She's insisting on staying near Lenora and the senator. Please call on us if there's anything we can do." And with that he steered Patricia toward Lenora's room.

"Scariest words a politician can utter," Esme whispered as she watched them walk away, "I'm here to help."

"Well," I said with a sigh, "it doesn't appear there's anything we can do here."

Esme sighed. "I know. Let's go say good night and go on home. We do have work to do, though it doesn't seem as important as it did a few hours ago."

"No, it doesn't," I said as I felt my shield beginning to disintegrate.

I glanced out the window at the end of the hallway

and was surprised to see darkness had fallen. I tapped lightly on the door to Lenora's suite. Emma answered, her phone in her hand and her eyes red-rimmed.

"We just wanted to let your aunt Lenora know we're leaving," I said.

"She's talking to Grandpa," Emma said. "You want me to get her?"

"No, it's okay," I said. "Just tell her if she needs anything she can call us anytime."

"I will," Emma said, glancing at her phone. She started to close the door but as we turned to go, she called after us. She looked back over her shoulder, then slipped out into the hallway. "Do you think it was somebody who knew Lincoln who, you know, did that to him?"

Esme and I glanced at each other. "I don't know, Emma," I said. "Is there a particular reason you'd ask that?"

She pulled the door almost closed, keeping it from latching so she could get back in. "I just can't figure out what would be so bad that a person would kill somebody over it. Lincoln was a good guy. He talked to me like I'm a person. He was like that with everybody. Why would anybody want to hurt him?"

Suddenly Emma wasn't a sullen teenager living in her phone, but a vulnerable girl whose tender feelings were being overlooked in the hubbub surrounding her. Tears were welling in her eyes and as one spilled onto her cheek, she swiped it away with such force it sent her long golden hair swinging in an arc back over her shoulder.

"You've lost a friend and that's a terrible thing, Emma," Esme said. "You don't need to be ashamed of tears, or being mad, or feeling helpless."

The girl burst into great racking sobs and moved into Esme's arms. She cried until she had no tears left as Esme stood and rocked her from side to side. When Emma had control of herself again, she wiped her nose on the sleeve of her sweater, a gesture so childish and vulnerable it made my heart hurt.

"You call us if you need anything, even if it's just somebody to talk to, okay?" Esme said, wiping the last vestiges of tears from beneath the girl's eyes with her thumbs.

Emma thanked us and slipped back into the room. I wondered if anyone would even notice she'd been gone.

As we walked to the bank of elevators, I saw Ken Dodd tapping on Chelsea's door and calling her name in a low voice.

I debated whether to say anything, especially since I'd only met Ken once in passing. I wasn't sure he'd even remember who I was. He knocked again and pressed his forehead to the door, calling her name a little louder this time.

"She's probably sleeping," I said. "They gave her something to help her rest."

"Oh," he said, recognition dawning as he studied my face. "That's good. She must be losing her mind. I know I am."

"I understand you and Lincoln were friends," I said. "I'm sorry for your loss."

Ken nodded. "We went way back," he said. "He was a good guy. Maybe too good."

"How so?" I asked.

"Linc was a principled guy, you know," Ken said, clearing his throat and plainly struggling to keep his emotions in check. "He'd stand his ground for what he thought was right. Good thing, right? Except Linc never learned the art of compromise and that's a premium asset in life."

He ran a hand through his hair. "Do the police have any theories at all about who killed him, or why he was killed?"

"We don't know any more than you," Esme said. "But the investigators are doing everything they can."

Ken nodded and took a couple of steps backward. "Yes, I'm sure," he said, sounding dubious. "I'd better get back to my mother now. She's sort of coming apart, too." He turned and walked the few steps to his mother's door.

"We should just make a little sign that says 'We

don't know any more than you do,' and hang it around our necks," Esme said. She narrowed her eyes as Ken let himself into his mother's suite. "What do you think of that guy?"

"I haven't really talked to him. He seems okay. A little tightly wound maybe. But the work he's doing sounds pretty impressive, don't you think?"

"Mm-hmm," Esme said, continuing to stare, though the hallway was now empty. "Except we all know lots of cases where people do the right thing for the wrong reasons."

"You sound like Patricia," I said. "She's quite snarky when it comes to Ken."

Esme smiled. "She's snarky about a lot of things. Doesn't mean she's wrong, but it makes it hard to listen to her. That poor husband of hers has his work cut out for him. Seems like she goes out of her way to be disagreeable."

"Yet it was Lincoln, the nice guy, who was murdered. Where's the sense in that? Or the fairness?"

"Nowhere to be found," Esme said.

five

THE HOUSE SEEMED PRETERNATURALLY QUIET, AS if the structure had prepared itself for our sorrow. Esme headed for the kitchen to put on coffee and I went into the workroom and turned on every light to dispel the gloom in the room—and inside me.

The landline rang and I squinted at the number on the display. Marydale.

"What in the world is going on back there?" she asked. "We go away for a week and now Morningside is in the national news, and not for something good. What happened, Sophreena?"

I thought of reciting Esme's imaginary sign inscription, but we actually did know more than Marydale and Winston. I filled her in.

"Wait," Marydale said, "is this the boy you've been working with all this time you were gathering the senator's information?"

"Yes, though he isn't—wasn't—a boy," I corrected. "He was about my age, mid-thirties. But I think they all thought of him, affectionately, as their boy. They're in total shock."

"What's Denny saying?" I heard Winston ask from the background.

"Not much yet. It's early. No theories about motive and no suspects as far as I know."

"Do they even know for sure the poor man was murdered?" Marydale asked. "The news is saying foul play hasn't been ruled out, but they didn't say it had been ruled *in* either."

"The medical examiner hasn't issued the official report," I said, "but Denny's saying it was murder."

"Cyrus Hamilton must be terribly upset about this," Marydale said.

"Cyrus Hamilton?" I repeated. "You know him?"

"Yes, I know him. Back when he submitted his proposal for the hotel/spa complex, I was on the citizens advisory committee, remember? He had many, many questions about Morningside and I became his unofficial guide. This was years ago; that spa was a long time in the making. And now, only a few short weeks after the grand opening, there's this terrible tragedy. Why does it always seem so much worse when they're young? All that lost promise, I guess. In any case I feel bad for Cyrus, too."

"I didn't realize you moved in such rarefied circles, Marydale," I teased.

"There's nothing rarefied about Cyrus Hamilton, Sophreena. He's as plain as an old shoe."

When Esme came into the room, I clicked the speakerphone button and we moved on to lighter talk. Marydale regaled us with their tourist activities, then asked for other news from Morningside.

"We've got no idea what's been going on in town since we've been holed up like fugitives working on the senator's project," Esme said.

"Well, you can venture out into the open now," Marydale said. "The senator's birthday has passed. But, oh heavens, what a terrible way to end the celebration."

"It was," I agreed. "But we're still on lockdown." I told her about the two projects we'd taken on.

"What are you two trying to do, invent a whole new profession, forensic genealogist?" Marydale asked. "I wish we were there to help."

"I'd say genealogy is always forensic. After all, we gather and evaluate evidence with every job," I said.

"I guess that's true," Marydale said. "Listen, I know someone who might get you some leads for looking into that fire. She was a first cousin of Martin's. Or should I say *is* a first cousin of Martin's. Does the relationship remain when half of it has passed on?"

"I guess that depends on your belief system," I

said. Martin Thompson was Marydale's first husband; he'd been gone for many years now. She had loved him dearly and had stayed close to his family after his death.

"Well, anyway, her father was a deputy sheriff in Quinn County for a time. He died several years ago. I can't tell you when he was in office, but she might be able to help. I'll send along her number when I hang up and call to give her a heads-up to expect your call. She doesn't answer her phone if she doesn't recognize the number." After a few more minutes of chatting we signed off, wishing Marydale and Winston more well-deserved R & R.

I set up my drawing board with pots of ink, my calligraphy pens, and a large sheet of hot-pressed paper, then took up a sketchpad and started to rough out how I wanted Conrad's tree and the nameplates to look. Esme settled at her computer and took over the search for more info regarding the house fire.

"I must be losing my edge," Esme said after she'd been clicking around for a while. "I saw some of this information on the fire when we were doing the senator's history, but nothing jumped out at me as being controversial or peculiar in any way. It was a tragedy I hope to the dear Lord I'll never know the likes of, but I never even realized it was such a hot button."

"Me either," I said, "but we didn't spend a lot of time on the senator's early childhood."

"True," Esme said. "Still, it seems to me I should've picked up on something just from the fact that they were putting off having a conversation about it until the very end."

"What're you thinking, Esme? Are you getting one of your feelings about this?"

"Maybe," Esme said, letting out a sigh. "For as long as I've been aware of my gift, it's always come in strongest when somebody's died leaving something unresolved, and that sure seems to be the case here, at least the way that reporter was describing the parents' reactions. But nothing's really coming to me except for a distracting buzz in the back of my mind."

"Well, maybe you've just got to let it develop. You're always telling me you have no control over this thing and that it seems to be bestowed rather than bade? And by the way, it's not nearly as useful as you pitched it to me when we became partners."

I'd meant it as a joke but I saw Esme wince. "You want to dissolve the partnership?" she asked. I could tell she was straining to keep her voice light.

"Not a chance," I said. "I'm stuck with you now, fickle gift and all."

I should've known Esme couldn't brook any teasing right now. As the time came closer for her to move, we'd both become more emotional about the pending separation. Esme was dealing by finding piddling reasons to delay and I by picking at her. Neither approach was doing a solitary thing to help with the adjustment.

"Well, anyhow, I'm not finding much more than you did about the case," Esme said. "But now I understand why the senator is so thorny about it—the early articles make the parents look like conspiracy nuts. I did find a few newspaper headlines that look promising, but we may have to go old school and actually go out to the newspapers' morgue to get them. They haven't gotten that far back with their electronic archiving."

"It always astounds me that people seem to think you can find everything in the written history of mankind on the Internet," I said, studying my sketch and making an adjustment to a tree branch. "They don't stop to think about the bazillions of documents that haven't found their way to a scanner yet. Though I do love to fantasize about the day everything will be available from my computer chair. I know my allergies would appreciate it. No more dusty books and papers."

"Alas, not in our lifetimes, Sophreena," Esme said. "And nothing on the Internet will ever displace talking to actual live people, or in my case, some dead ones. I'll call Marydale's cousin tomorrow."

"Good," I said, meaning it both for Esme's plan and the sketch, which I now found satisfactory. I stood and stretched, flexing my hands and shaking out my arm and shoulder muscles vigorously. I knew it looked like I was having some kind of conniption, but Esme was used to my rituals and didn't comment.

I dipped my calligraphy pen and made the first broad stroke to create one side of the tree trunk, trying to manage the tension that comes with concentration against the need to keep my muscles loose and movements fluid. I dipped my pen again and just as I was about to touch nib to paper, my cell phone rang, vibrating across the desktop near my computer.

I knew it was unfair to be annoyed with whoever was on the other end just because they'd almost caused me to ruin a sheet of expensive paper, but still I was irked. I checked the display and saw an unfamiliar number, but with all that had gone on today I decided to answer.

"Sophreena?" came a breathless voice. "It's Emma."

"Emma, what's wrong?"

"Nothing," she said, and I could hear a sniffle. "Everything. Could I talk to you in the morning? Someplace not here; *anyplace* not here. Is there a coffee shop or maybe a park?"

"There's both, Emma, but won't you tell me what's wrong?"

"I just need to talk to someone and everybody around here is, you know, like busy. But if you can't that's okay."

"Of course I'll meet you," I said, wincing as I glanced

around the workroom and considered how much we had to do yet. "Top o' the Morning is our regular coffee shop. Shall I pick you up?"

"No, that's okay, I can take my mother's car. I'll meet you there at eight."

I disconnected and frowned at the phone. "Huh," I said to Esme. "Emma's upset. She wants to talk to me. Why me?"

"Plenty of reasons. You have a sympathetic ear and she admires you."

"Why would she admire me? She's one of those pretty, popular girls. I was a nerd at her age, still am."

"Maybe she's got higher aspirations than just being pretty and popular. Ever thought of that?"

I thought of Emma's sobs when we'd talked this afternoon in the hallway. She was a girl alternately doted on and ignored. "No, I guess I never did," I said softly.

The next morning, Emma was waiting at an outdoor table at Top o' the Morning, her thumbs working little staccato punches on her phone. The place was quiet now, but later the after-church crowd would be jockeying for tables. When Emma saw me, she smiled. It was a weak, tepid smile and it seemed to have required some effort, but I took heart from it.

I offered to go inside for our order and had to ask

her to repeat hers—twice. "Soy latte with an extra shot, cream, light caramel drizzle," I muttered over and over until I got to the counter and regurgitated it. This earned me an eye roll from Kate, the morning barista, who was accustomed to my standard order, which is a *large coffee, light roast if you've got it or whatever*. But as uncomplicated as I am about my coffee, I'm super picky about my pastries. I want my apple fritters at the peak of freshness. I scrutinized them while Kate stood by with a plate and tongs at the ready. "They came out eight minutes ago," she said. "I knew you'd ask if you came in."

"Perfect," I said, and ordered two to go.

Emma couldn't seem to find a way in to what she wanted to say, so we chatted about neutral topics for a bit. My leg was bouncing under the table, but I tried to act like I had all the time in the world. I told her a little about the town and asked how she was coming along with studying for the SAT test, which she was about to take for the second time, hoping to increase her score. We talked about the college campuses she was planning to visit in the upcoming year, though she had her heart set on Chapel Hill already. As we chatted, she relaxed and eventually worked her way toward the purpose of our meeting.

"I have a moral dilemma," she announced. "I know something that will make someone I like look bad, so I don't want to tell anybody about it. And anyhow, *how*

I know will get me in trouble. But on the other hand, it might be important and I probably *should* tell someone. Can you see any way I could tell but not have it come out that it was me who told?"

"I don't know, Emma," I said. "I'd need more information. Can you at least tell me what this is about? Is this something to do with one of your friends?"

Emma sighed. "No, it's not teen drama or anything. This is serious."

"Emma, does this have anything to do with what happened to Lincoln?"

"I don't think so but it might. That's the thing. I don't think what I know would help anything and it'll for sure get me in trouble. *Big* trouble. So I was thinking I'd tell you and then maybe you could help me decide if I have to tell anyone else. But you'll have to agree not to tell unless I say so."

I shook my head. "I can't make that promise, Emma, not without knowing more. I'll try to help you if I can, but I can't promise to keep it to myself if I think it's important for someone else to know."

Emma tipped her cup back and downed the last of her coffee. I thought she was getting ready to leave but instead she drew in a deep breath and let out a growl.

"Fine," she said, "I figured you'd say that. But if I get my phone taken away and I'm locked in my room until I'm as old as you, it'll be all your fault. It's

Chelsea. I like Chelsea; I *really* like her. And she's always so nice to me. I don't want to make her look bad, and after what happened to Lincoln, I worry if I tell what I saw she'll become a suspect or something. But she's so, like, hysterical they're keeping her drugged and I'm afraid by the time they let her come out of it she'll forget everything that happened. And maybe she saw something. Or heard something. Or knows something."

"Saw something when, Emma?" I asked. "Where?"

Emma puckered her lips and again I thought she was going to clam up. When she spoke, her voice was a monotone. "She and Lincoln had a big fight on Friday night, when they say he died. I mean a total blowup. Like epic. But couples fight, right? I mean it's normal to fight and then make up just as passionately, isn't it? My folks never fight, but it's like they were born married to each other. They've got like one brain, so I can't go by how it is with them."

"Well," I said, "I'm no expert but I believe it's normal to disagree, maybe even forcefully, for some couples anyway. But Emma, how do you know Chelsea and Lincoln fought?"

"I saw them," Emma said, her body sagging. "Out on the exercise trail near that overlook where he, you know, fell."

"And when was this?" I asked, my leg now bouncing like crazy.

"Late," she said. "That's the sticky part. I was supposed to be in bed, but I was going stir-crazy up in that room. I wanted to call my boyfriend, but my mom was reading in bed while I watched TV in the sitting area. Mom's got like supersonic hearing and she has some 'reservations' about my choice of boyfriend." She gave the word the two-finger quotes. "She doesn't like me calling him every day, or six times a day," she said with a quick grin. "So I waited until she was asleep and went down to the lobby to call him, but the night clerk kept looking at me funny, so I decided to go outside. Once I was outside I just wandered around while we talked. It felt so good to have a little freedom."

"And you went out on the exercise trail?" I asked.

She nodded. "I didn't mean to go out that far, but I just sort of wandered off. I'd been out there that afternoon, and it's really cool and peaceful and there's nobody around."

"Didn't you get caught in the rain?" I asked, hoping to get a time frame.

"Later on, yeah. It wasn't raining when I went outside, but it had been. Everything was wet, but I didn't mind. Everything looked and smelled fresh, you know? There was lightning, but it was far off and I wouldn't have gone out that far and gotten caught in the rain if I hadn't heard Chelsea and Lincoln. I didn't know it was them at first. I just heard people yelling. I went off the path and into the woods so I could see what was going on. I listened for a while and watched and I thought it was Chelsea and Lincoln but I couldn't be sure, so I moved closer. Then this huge flash of lightning came and for a second the whole sky lit up and I could see them clear as day. They were waving their arms around and screaming at each other. I was worried something might happen." She looked up quickly. "I don't mean like Chelsea killing him or anything, I just mean like, well, I don't know what I thought exactly, but it looked scary, like they were out of control. So I ducked deeper into the woods and moved up even closer to try to hear what they were saying, but by then the thunder was booming and there was more lightning and I was afraid they'd see me if I went any closer."

Afraid of being seen, but not afraid of being struck by lightning, I thought, resisting the urge to do a face palm.

"What exactly did you hear?" I asked Emma.

"Chelsea was saying it'd 'kill her if she found out'— that I remember really clear. Those were her exact words, but the rest is sort of muddled. Something like that she didn't care what *he* wanted, that he gave up his right to have a say a long time ago, after he did what he did. I thought maybe she was talking about her father, that maybe he didn't approve of her being with Lincoln or something like that.

"Then Lincoln said something about how the truth

has to come out and that it had been too many years and that some things shouldn't stay hidden. But then Chelsea started sobbing and really yelling. She said she couldn't do that to her, or to any of them—whoever *her* or *them* is and whatever it was she couldn't do," Emma said with a shrug. "Then she told him she'd never forgive him if he told anybody. Not until she had time to think things over and decide what was right. What do you think they could've been fighting about?"

"I have no idea, Emma," I said, though several possibilities were flitting through my mind. "Tell me what you did after that."

"Chelsea tried to leave but Lincoln grabbed her arm. She was really mad. They sort of tussled. Not fighting," she said, as if fearing she'd said too much. "I mean there was no hitting or anything. He was just trying to keep her there, but it had started to rain and she pushed him away and ran back toward the hotel. He shouted but she wouldn't come back."

"Then what happened?" I prompted.

"He pulled out his cell phone. He was pacing back and forth and even though the rain was coming down hard by then, he didn't seem to notice. I couldn't hear anything he said, but I could tell he was talking into the phone."

I tried to remember if they'd recovered Lincoln's cell phone. At the very least they'd have gotten his phone records by now. Denny was nothing if not thorough.

"You didn't hear anything to let you know who he was talking with?"

She shook her head. "Nothing. Like I said, it was raining and there were these rumbles of thunder and the wind picked up and it was blowing the trees around until they bent over. I was getting scared and wanted to get out of there, but I still didn't want Lincoln to see me. I was afraid he'd think I'd been spying on them, which I guess I was, but I hadn't meant to. Anyway, I went through the woods, but I got turned around and somehow ended up down by the lake. There were people camping down there, like in somebody's backyard. A man was scrambling to take down a tent in the wind and rain and someone else was inside a car. Course, I didn't know then it was my cousin J.D. and I didn't even know he *had* a wife. Nobody did. Don't you think she's beautiful?" she asked, and I could see that she was relieved to have gotten the bit about Chelsea and Lincoln's argument behind her.

I agreed that Gabriela was lovely. "I think your aunt Lenora was really surprised at the news they were married."

"You can say that again," she said, and I got the first fleeting real smile of the conversation. "But happy, too.

She was so annoyed when he told her they'd camped out that night. But J.D. said even though he knew Aunt Lenora would've been happy to pay for a room in the hotel for them, they *chose* to camp. Which I totally get. I'd gladly sleep in a tent if it meant I could just get away from everybody for a little while. Anyhow, I didn't know it was them, so I just watched for a minute as he struggled to get everything back in the car. He was swearing, big-time," Emma said with a giggle. "Aunt Lenora would've been shocked. I guess the tent had a rip in it and they'd gotten soaked. Eventually I figured out where I was and followed the lights back to the hotel. It was really storming by then. I was drenched and I panicked when I got to the door 'cause I thought I'd lost my key card and wouldn't be able to get back in. I knew if I had to call Mom she'd flip *out*. And I didn't dare call Chelsea, not with the mood she was in. But I found the card and went up and sneaked into the room. I changed out of my wet things and went to bed with nobody the wiser."

"Emma, did it not occur to you that it's not such a good idea to wander around in the dark outside a hotel? Not to mention the danger of being out in the open in bad weather."

She shrugged. "It was dumb," she said. "But sometimes I feel like I'm suffocating and other times I feel like nobody would miss me if I got abducted by aliens or something. I won't do it again. The thing is, I know Chelsea didn't hurt Lincoln or anything. She'd never do anything like that to anybody, and especially not Lincoln. She was in love with him. Like crazy in love."

"Did she tell you that?" I asked.

Emma nodded. "I saw them kissing once. She swore me to secrecy, but I guess it doesn't matter now. She was afraid Dinah Leigh would be upset about them getting together. I think Dinah Leigh was hoping Chelsea would end up as her daughter-in-law someday."

"What makes you think that?" I asked.

Emma shrugged again. "I hear stuff. I'm like furniture; people hardly notice I'm in the room."

"I'm sure that's not true, Emma," I said. "But it may feel like it just now. We all tend to take one another for granted at times."

"Yeah," she said gloomily. "Don't I know it! But anyway, I don't want to get Chelsea in trouble. Right now she's like sick and half-crazy she's so upset. I don't want to make her even sadder by clueing in the cops so they'll ask her a bunch of stupid questions."

"I know," I said, and this time it was my turn to sigh. "But I think you're going to have to talk to Detective Carlson, Emma. He needs to know what you saw and heard. You can let him decide if it's important to ask Chelsea about it, and if it is, he'll be kind and fair. I know him and I totally trust him."

"Will she have to know it was me who told?" Emma asked, her blue eyes going dark.

"I don't know," I said. "But if that happens I'm sure Chelsea will understand. She won't blame you."

"Will my mom have to find out?" she asked.

"I don't know about that either," I said. "But you said it yourself, this is a really serious thing. I know you want to do anything you can to help find who killed Lincoln, right?"

"Yes," she said, and I saw her lip tremble. "Even if nobody really cares what I think, I'm sad he's dead, too. He was smart and he could be really, really funny when it was just the two of us. He did all these funny accents and could mimic people like spot-on. He could do Grandpa perfectly. He totally fooled me a couple of times on the phone. But it wasn't like he was mocking him or anything. He loved Grandpa."

I pulled my phone from my pocket and checked the time, surprised to find we'd been here for more than an hour. "Is your mother going to be wondering what's keeping you?" I asked.

"No," Emma said. "I've got my phone on. If she gets worried she calls or texts to check on me. They're all working on arrangements for the funeral. Lincoln's dad is coming this afternoon."

"Would you like me to call Detective Carlson and ask him if he can stop by and talk with you now? Get it over with?" I asked, fearful that what little Emma remembered might be lost if Denny didn't talk to her soon.

"I guess," Emma said with a groan of resignation. She stared off into the mid-distance as I punched in Denny's number. She was muttering and I leaned in close to hear what she was saying. "Chelsea's gonna hate me. She's gonna *hate* me."

six

I CRINGED WHEN I SAW THE DETECTIVES' SEDAN
pull up with Jennifer at the wheel. Denny had said one
of them would be by shortly and I'd hoped it'd be him.

Though things had been a lot better lately, there
was a time when Jennifer had disliked Esme and me
intensely. But after we'd helped her father by identify-
ing the occupant of an ancient casket found buried on
his land, things had been a lot better between us. She
confessed that she'd been jealous of our relationship
with Denny and his habit of discussing his cases with
us. Since our air-clearing she'd learned to trust us—
somewhat—and vice versa, but I wasn't sure she was
best suited for questioning Emma. She's a stickler for
protocol and she's not what you'd call touchy-feely.

Emma asked if I could stay and Jennifer allowed
it. I felt all my muscles starting to bunch in anticipa-
tion of this talk going badly, but Jennifer surprised me

by showing a deft and empathetic touch that elicited more from Emma than even I'd been able to get from her. She'd remembered hearing the woman in the car— whom we now knew was Gabriela—shouting to J.D., "Just let it go, he didn't mean anything by it," as he was wrestling with the leaky tent.

"She just said it like they were kidding around. And she was laughing. It got my attention because she has that cool accent. It wasn't like they were arguing or mad or anything—not like Chelsea and Lincoln." Suddenly she put her arm on the table and plopped her head down on it. "Chelsea's never going to speak to me again."

"Don't know why she wouldn't," Jennifer said, her tone breezy. "She told us they had a fight that night."

"She did?" Emma asked, sitting up and brushing her hair back.

"Yep," Jennifer said, flipping her notebook shut. "But even if she hadn't, you'd still be doing the right thing by telling us what you saw. You never know what little thing might turn out to be important. But do me a favor, Emma, don't go wandering around the grounds alone out there anymore, okay?"

"I won't," she said and plucked her bag from the seat next to her. Her mood had lightened so much I half expected her to float from the chair. "I'd better get back," she said. "I may be needed for important things like licking envelopes for the thank-you notes. Thanks"—she turned to Jennifer and dipped an actual curtsy—"both of you. I feel much better. Except sad still, about Lincoln. He was like the brother I never had."

"But you do have a brother," I said, which got me a smirk.

"I was being sardonic," she said. "You know, like irony. Yeah, I've got Damon, but honestly it's more like having two fathers. He doesn't get me at all. And anyhow, he's such a hypocrite. He's pretending to be all torn up about what happened to Lincoln, but he didn't even like him."

"He didn't?" Jennifer asked. "Huh, I thought just about everybody liked him."

Again I had to admire Jennifer's technique with the girl. She sounded offhand while offering up something to refute, a temptation many teens cannot resist.

"Damon definitely did *not*," Emma said, lifting the strap of her crossover bag over her head. "He was jealous of Lincoln—I mean like jealous down to the bone. He'd wanted to be the one to write Grandpa's book, but Grandpa said it wouldn't look right for it to be a relative. And besides, he wanted Damon to spend the year studying for the bar exam."

"Well, it hardly seems like any of that was Lincoln's fault, now does it?" Jennifer said.

"Not at all," Emma said. "But that didn't matter to Damon. The thing is, Grandpa thought Lincoln was smarter than Damon. Everybody could see that. Damon knows the law, but Lincoln knew how to be with people and all that policy stuff, too. Grandpa eats that up with a spoon. If I learn enough about an issue to talk with him without sounding like a total airhead, he nearly busts his buttons he's so proud of me. That's what he always says, but who knows what it means. I don't even know how or why you'd bust a button. That's just the way Grandpa talks.

"But anyhow, Damon *is* my brother and I love him, so I shouldn't be talking trash about him even if he is being a hypocrite." She gave a little wave before trotting off toward the parking lot.

"Interesting," Jennifer mused, once she was out of earshot.

"May not mean anything," I said.

"May not," Jennifer said, still staring after Emma. "But still interesting. I wonder just how deep that animus ran."

I was wondering how far *our* détente had come and decided to test it. "Did Chelsea really tell you about the argument?" I asked.

"Yep," Jennifer answered. "First thing. She was distraught and feeling guilty and morose about her last encounter with Lincoln being a fight. She made it sound more civilized than the girl described. But Emma doesn't need to know that. She feels guilty enough about ratting on a friend."

"Did Chelsea tell you what they were arguing about?"

Jennifer nodded. "Same rules as with Denny, right? Confidential?"

"Yes," I said, though I thought by now that should be understood.

"She says Lincoln wanted to announce their engagement and she wasn't ready. He was eager to get on with marriage plans, but she couldn't see her way clear to leaving Ms. Dodd just yet."

I frowned and thought back over what Emma had told me. It jibed, for the most part. Dinah Leigh probably would be heartbroken if Chelsea left. She seemed dependent on her professionally and fond of her personally.

"Seems like she's trapped for the foreseeable future if that's the way she feels," I mused.

"Yep," Jennifer said, standing and adjusting her jacket to hide her holster. "I need to go. Thanks for the heads-up with the girl," she said and gave me a smile— a phenomenon I was still getting used to.

"How'd it go?" Esme asked. She was dressed for church, which was a notch up from her everyday chic, and I glanced at my watch. She'd have to leave soon or she'd be late. She was straightening and arranging a series of sticky notes on a whiteboard, her chosen method for organizing tidbits of information.

"It went okay," I said, "thanks to Jennifer."

"Do tell," Esme said with only the slightest whiff of rancor. Although we'd established a truce, Esme still wasn't ready to fully embrace Jennifer. "What got her involved?"

I told her about the conversation and about how Jennifer had handled Emma and put an end to the girl's guilt trip.

"Well, good on her," Esme said. "I suppose she didn't *have* to share that with Emma, and it must have taken a load off the girl's shoulders. But I'm so sorry to hear that about Chelsea. I know just how she's feeling. My last conversation with Roland was a brutal argument. I said some harsh things. They were all true, but nonetheless over all these years I've wished to heaven I could call them back."

I knew Esme didn't like to talk about her husband or the brief, troubled marriage that had left her a young widow, so I let this go by without comment.

"What have you been up to?" I asked, bending to squint at the whiteboard.

"Spinnin' my wheels," she said. "Called Marydale's cousin this morning. Her daddy came into the sheriff's office much later than our time period and she didn't know much about the fire except what she's read and heard over the years. But you know how one thing leads to another."

"Story of our lives. Please tell me that one led somewhere," I said.

"Indeed it did. The cousin put me in touch with the granddaughter of James Ogdon, who *was* the Quinn County sheriff in nineteen forty-seven, the year of the fire. And she would *very* much like to talk with us about that old case. She still lives in Quinn County, but as it happens, she'll be in Durham tomorrow for a doctor's appointment. We're having lunch. Want to come along?"

From the look on Esme's face, I knew there was more than she was letting on. "You know I would," I answered. "What does she know?"

"Well, I told you something was niggling at me—"

"You've heard from someone?" I cut her off.

"No," Esme said, "not that kind of niggling, just a hunch there's something off with this case. I know what Senator Stan and Lenora both said and I know they're convinced beyond a doubt that their brother died in that fire, but I'm beginning to see why the parents weren't ready to accept the findings. This isn't just a bunch of crackpots spouting off grassy knoll theories. This was either such a badly bungled case it was worthy of the Keystone Cops, or something else was going on. The rulings were changed and changed back again and there are a number of conflicts in the official reports.

The sheriff's granddaughter, Nancy Collier, told me a few things that are just plain weird."

"So you're saying you think the baby was kidnapped?" I asked.

"No, no, I'm not saying that," Esme said firmly. "Not *at all*. I think the baby probably died in the fire just as they ruled. But I can see why the parents latched onto hope and wouldn't let go. I might have done the same in their situation. It's a mess. And we've landed right in the middle of it."

"Have you heard anything new about Lincoln's case?"

"I talked to Denny earlier," she said, "but there are no new developments. He's gonna stop by for lunch after church. And Lenora called—poor woman is so torn up. She's worried sick about what this is doing to the senator. Apparently they hope to release Lincoln's body tomorrow. His father is coming in later today to escort the body back to Quinn County for the funeral. She asked if we could stop by later to pick up the testimonials and telegrams that came in on Saturday to add to the scrapbooks, but you can tell her heart's not in it anymore. I told her one of us would be by this afternoon."

I glanced over at the family tree I was working on for Conrad. I hadn't gotten very far with it. "I can go. I've got a few questions for Dinah Leigh or Conrad. Maybe one of them will still be there."

"All of them are, except maybe Judith. She was going home to check on her sick kids. And they're all planning to return here after the funeral. Apparently some of the treatments at the spa are helping Lily Rose and she's going to stay for a while."

"That's good. And Dinah Leigh is staying, too?"

Esme shrugged. "Moral support, I guess. Maybe she's doing it for Chelsea. Anyhow, I take it she's decided to stay as long as the others do."

"Hoping for some answers before they leave, probably," I said.

"Aren't we all," Esme said with a sigh.

After Esme left for church, Jack called and asked if he could stop by. "I won't stay long, I know you're busy. I'm going kayaking with Mike Bennett but I thought maybe you could use a little pick-me-up."

"And you thought you'd be it?" I teased. "A little conceited, aren't we?"

"Well, a guy can hope," Jack said. "But I meant ginger ale. I got you a six-pack of that stuff you like that burns its way down to the belly. Oh, and a package of Fig Newtons, too."

"You sweet-talkin' cowboy, you know me well," I said.

"I should, I've seen you eat a million of those things," Jack said. "I'll be by in a few."

I was arranging my calligraphy supplies when I heard Jack's customary "hey" from the front hall. It was the same buddy greeting I'd gotten for the past few years, except that when he came into the workroom now, he gave me a lingering kiss to go with it. I heartily approved of the addition. I've decided friendship that ripens into romance is the best, most frightening relationship there is. Jack and I knew each other well from our years of being pals. That was good. But we were both nervous about what we had to lose if this didn't work out. Still, the pledge to take it slow had proven surprisingly hard to keep, on my part anyway.

The high-octane ginger ale, the cookies, and the visit from Jack all served to pep me up, until he told me a choice bit of info he'd picked up that morning.

"A guy from town who works at the boat launch told Mike he'd heard the senator's grandson and Lincoln talking the afternoon before Lincoln's murder. Well, not talking exactly, more like taking verbal shots at each other. And Damon said something like 'You're done for,' when he walked off. Anyhow, the guy got to thinking about it after all that happened and called Jennifer to report it. You think the grandson could've had anything to do with it?"

"I don't think there was any love lost between them," I said. "But I never got the impression Lincoln felt threatened by Damon in the times I saw them together. If anything, he seemed to regard him as sort of a lightweight."

Jack shrugged. "Probably nothing."

"Maybe nothing, maybe something," I said, taking another punishing gulp of the ginger ale.

I worked steadily for the next hour, but the drawing wasn't going smoothly because my mind was churning. Lincoln had been a mild-mannered guy. How had he managed to get crossways of so many people?

When Esme came back I told her what Jack had said and she cringed. "I hope to heaven Damon had nothing to do with this bad business," she said. "That would surely break them all."

"I know," I said. "But unfortunately he makes a pretty good suspect."

"He's not the only one," Esme said, going over to her Post-it note array. "You remember you found Chad Deese had some relatives in Quinn County?"

"Yes, pretty distant ones."

"Well, Great-Uncle Russell spent some time in the hoosegow back in the early fifties for beating up his neighbor over a land boundary dispute."

"So? Guilt by association?" I asked. "That's pretty thin."

"Yes, but guess who his lawyer was," Esme said.

"Alton Sawyer, the senator's father. And Uncle Russell got the maximum sentence and later claimed he had incompetent defense. Maybe that's what the family feud was all about."

Denny's deep bass voice called from the front hallway. I was still getting used to that. He'd only recently been given the privilege all our other close friends have of "helloing the house" instead of ringing the bell.

Esme got up from the table, wearing a smile that was exclusively for Denny. "Go on into the kitchen," she called out. "I know you don't have long. I've got your lunch ready." She curled her finger at me. "You, too. There's pulled pork in the slow cooker and fresh rolls from the bakery. Come have a sandwich."

She didn't need to ask me twice and I followed her in to find Denny slumped at the table.

"You look terrible," I said, honesty overtaking tact.

"I'm beat," he said. "Esme, I'm not going to be able to repaint your kitchen anytime soon. We may have to hire it out."

Esme flapped a hand at him. "You think I'm worried about that at a time like this? It can wait."

For the past couple of months Esme had been pushing hard to get the house into shape, but as the time came closer for the actual move, she'd become uncharacteristically patient with every delay and had even put up her own impediments. After the kitchen was painted she'd decided she didn't like the color. That she, in fact, could not *live* with the color. And she needed more moving boxes but couldn't seem to find the time to go get them. Clearly she was stalling.

"Any developments?" I asked Denny.

"Nothing much," he said. "Official ruling was filed. Definitely foul play, which was pretty clear from the evidence of a physical confrontation at the scene. Cooper wasn't a big guy, so just about anybody could've pushed him over that railing. Doesn't narrow our suspect pool much."

"Who's in your suspect pool?" Esme asked, setting his sandwich in front of him.

"Anybody throughout the known world who was alive last Friday night," Denny said. "Though there are a few we're looking at with keener interest. Apparently Cooper was loaded for bear for that reporter, Deese."

"Yes, he was," Esme said and told him about our encounter with Lincoln that afternoon. "As of late afternoon he hadn't caught up with him."

Denton took out his notebook and scribbled a note. "Doesn't mean he didn't find him later. We're checking on the reporter's whereabouts for our time frame."

"Which was when, exactly?" I asked, pouring mugs of coffee.

"ME's sticking with midnight to two a.m.," Denny said.

I told him more about our conversation with Lincoln about Chad Deese and the admittedly tenuous link Esme had found in his family history.

Denny considered. "People have been known to kill for less." He made another notation in his book. "Next on my list is Lenora's son, J.D. Apparently Cooper had some kind of dustup with him, too. I don't think it amounted to much but we'll talk to him anyway."

"What sort of dustup?" I asked.

"I think Cooper inadvertently ruined J.D.'s big reveal about his marriage. Or maybe insulted his wife. J.D. left the new Mrs. Morgan out in the hallway while he went in to prepare his mother. Cooper came upon Gabriela and started questioning her about lurking outside Lenora's door. J.D. overheard it and took offense at his questions and his tone. Cooper apologized and it seemed like it all blew over quickly, but we'd like to know more. What do you two know about J.D. Morgan?"

"We'd never met him before Saturday," I said. "His mother talked about him during our interviews. I had the impression he was kind of an absentminded professor type off in the jungle living off dried beetles and coconut milk. But I never got any hint he was a hothead."

"No, I didn't get that either," Denny said, "but I'd still like to talk with him. I'm trying to retrace Cooper's steps on Friday to construct a timeline. There are some pretty big gaps, but I'm slowly filling them in."

"Did you talk to Jennifer about what Emma told us this morning?" I asked.

Denny nodded again. "Yeah, thanks. Looks like Emma was the last one to see him alive. Other than whoever pushed him over that embankment—assuming it wasn't Emma."

"Surely you don't suspect Emma," Esme said with a huff. "She's not a hundred pounds soaking wet and she's a kid."

Denny shrugged. "Like I said, he wasn't a big guy. It wouldn't have taken much muscle."

"But you aren't seriously considering her or Chelsea, are you?" I asked.

"You know my method," Denny said, "everybody's a suspect until they're ruled out. Chelsea was with him, she admits they fought, and nobody saw her when she came back to her room that night. Yes, she's a suspect. And Emma admits she was there after Chelsea left the scene—again, assuming Chelsea didn't come back and pick up the fight where they'd left off. So yes, they're both suspects."

I wanted to protest, but I couldn't argue with his logic. It was highly unlikely this was a random crime. Lincoln had known his killer.

"In any case," Denny said, finishing off the last bite of dill pickle, "there's one person who's probably relieved by the ME's finding, and that's Cyrus Hamilton.

He was sweating bullets. If this had been ruled an accidental fall, he could've been held liable. Don't get me wrong, the man seemed genuinely saddened about Cooper's death, but he's a businessman, too, and he's got a fortune tied up in that hotel. He's offered free accommodations and services to everyone in the senator's party for an extended stay."

"Generous of him," Esme said. "Though it's hardly his fault this happened."

"Not unless he's the killer," Denny said, draining his coffee.

"Now you're being ridiculous," Esme said.

Denny rose and stretched. "Haven't ruled him out, so he's still on my list," he said, pushing his plate away with an appreciative hum. "And with that, I'd better get back over to the hotel and see if I can knock a few people off this afternoon." He grimaced and shook his head. "No awful pun intended."

After we'd cleared away the lunch things and tidied the kitchen, Esme went back to church for choir practice and I went to the hotel to pick up the testimonials from Lenora. I thought of taking pastries or flowers of condolence, but their room had been overrun with both, so I went empty-handed.

I pulled into the visitors' lot, which was situated at the bottom of a steep incline, and started the hike up to the hotel. Today I found it a pleasure, as it was a perfect North Carolina afternoon. The azaleas were in bloom and created a riot of color around the grounds, the temperature had climbed to around seventy degrees, and there wasn't a cloud in the blue sky. On a day like today, it seemed impossible anything bad could have happened in this place just two nights ago.

The terrace doors on the lakeside of the hotel were open, creating an indoor/outdoor area adjoining the pool, which meant I didn't have to hike around to the front entrance. A number of people were sitting about, sipping fresh juices, reading, chatting, or relaxing. Most were dressed in casual chic, making me feel like a fashion don't, but there was one exception. A man who looked faintly familiar was pacing back and forth at the edge of the terrace. He wore a striped short-sleeved shirt, and a pair of khakis that were a tad too long. As I watched him pace, it reminded me of how Senator Stan had stalked back and forth the day after that article came out. This man had something troublesome on his mind, too. And he moved with the same kind of pent-up tension. He even looked a little like the senator, except for his rumpled dress.

As I started up the steps, the man stopped his pacing and called to me. "Ms. McClure? You're the genealogist, right?"

"Yes," I said, more wary than friendly.

He walked over, thrusting out a hand. "I'm Cyrus

Hamilton. I wanted to thank you for helping out yesterday after the . . ." He hesitated, searching for a word. "After the tragedy."

"Esme and I were glad to help," I said. "We both liked Lincoln Cooper."

"He was a nice young man," Hamilton said, nodding pensively. "I know Stan and the rest of them are broken up about this and I feel just terrible that it happened here. Or that it happened at all. When I asked Lenora and Stan to hold the celebration here, I assured them that everything would go smoothly and it most definitely did not."

"You're not to blame, Mr. Hamilton," I said.

"I know that. At least my brain does," he said, tapping his temple, "but in here it feels different." He put his hand over his chest. "Just don't ever tell my lawyer I said that. I'm waiting for him and my insurance guy to show up. They want to see where it happened now that they've released the scene. They're afraid Cooper's family will sue. And maybe they will. But I knew Samuel Cooper, Lincoln's daddy, way back and unless he's changed in the intervening years, I don't think he's the kind of man who'd do that."

"So you're a Quinn County man?" I asked.

"I didn't grow up there," Hamilton said. "But my grandparents lived there and we visited pretty often, so I knew the Sawyers—my dad made sure of that. I stayed part of each summer with my grandparents start-ing from when I was around ten, so I had the chance to get to know other kids at church or at the ball field or the community doings."

"Why do you say your dad saw to it that you met the Sawyers?" I asked.

"My dad had worked for Stan's father as a farm manager when the Sawyers lived out in the country. He wanted to make sure I met them because he admired Alton and Margaret Sawyer so much. After everything that happened with the fire and losing the baby and all, the Sawyers moved into town and my dad was out of a job but Alton helped him out till he could find work. Even with everything Alton had been through and all he had on his mind, he still made sure Dad landed on his feet. Dad never forgot that. And it wasn't too long till Dad found another opportunity. He moved out to the mountains to run a little hotel my uncle had bought as an investment. I grew up out there."

"So it's the family business," I said.

Hamilton laughed. "I guess it is. That little place was all of eight units. An old-style motor inn where all the doors opened out into the parking lot so you could lift your suitcases straight into your trunk when you opened your door. It had clean rooms and good rates and was situated on a mountainside with a good view. But that's all it had going for it. It was run-down and ugly as sin when my dad took it over. He didn't know anything at all about inn keeping, but he figured if he could run a farm, he could run a motel. And he made a big success of it, so much so that by the time I was grown he'd bought six more small hotels and put me in charge of one. And eventually that led to this." He swept his hand to indicate the seven-story structure. "There now, you didn't expect my autobiography, but you know you can't meet a southerner without learning about his people and his story."

"Considering my profession, you can guess I'm a fan of that southern inclination," I said. "Is your father still living?"

"He is," Hamilton said, fiddling with something in his hand. "And living well for his age. My mother passed twenty-odd years ago, but my father's health is remarkably good for a man in his ninth decade. He travels with me sometimes, though he wasn't up to coming to the grand opening of this place. He hasn't seen it yet."

"I hope he'll get to soon, it's spectacular," I said, but my mind was on other facets of this revelation. The senator had said I was free to talk to anyone about the assignment he and Lenora had given us, so I plunged in. "Mr. Hamilton, do you mind if I ask whether your father was working for the Sawyers when the house burned down?"

"It's Cyrus, if you please, and yes, he was, though

he never liked to talk about it. He was out on the back forty and the house wasn't in sight, but he saw the smoke and knew what it had to be. He gathered up all the farm hands and they ran over, but it was too late."

"Do you think he'd be willing to talk with me about it?"

"I can't honestly say. It's a touchy subject. But I'll ask him, if you'd like."

"Thank you, Cyrus," I said. Using his given name could have felt awkward, but Marydale was right about him being a regular Joe. Or at least he presented himself that way. And if he could get me that interview with his father, I'd call him anything he liked.

We chatted for a few more minutes and Hamilton brightened when I mentioned I was a friend of Marydale's. "What a woman!" he said. "I'll tell you the truth, I was leaning toward a place up in Virginia to put this thing"—he gestured again, taking in the complex—"but after spending time with Marydale, I figured if the folks here were anything like her, Morningside was the place."

As he talked, I kept hearing metallic chinks as he worried something in his hand. He saw me look down and held up a gold Zippo lighter.

"I haven't seen one of those in years. Now I've seen two in the last twenty-four hours," I said, remembering Yvonne's beat-up old lighter.

Hamilton smiled. "This was my father's. It's a classic. I carry it as a good-luck charm. And I guess I use it as a worry stone when I'm nerved up," he said, flicking the cover open and closed again. "I don't even smoke. But back when so many loyal North Carolinians puffed away to support the tobacco farmers, everybody had at least one Zippo in the household."

I smiled. "You're right. My father had one and he didn't smoke either. He kept it in his dresser drawer. It came from his father, who was a pack-a-day man, a habit that unfortunately caught up to him."

"Ah," Hamilton said, "like the old proverb says, we grow too soon old and too late wise, eh?"

I followed his gaze and spotted three men coming onto the terrace, each dressed in crisp business suits with ties snugged around starched white collars. Not exactly dressed for their trek along the exercise trail to the overlook.

As Cyrus excused himself and went over to greet them, I remembered where I'd first encountered him. He'd been the one who wheeled in a cart for us to transport the scrapbooks and stands to the banquet hall. I'd thought he was a bellman.

seven

AS I WAS PASSING THROUGH THE LOBBY, I SAW THE senator come out of the elevator. I started to go over and speak to him, but saw he was approaching a man at the check-in desk. They shook hands and as they talked, the senator's expression was grave. The other man's back was to me, so I couldn't see him. He slumped and Senator Stan embraced him and clapped him on the shoulder. After a moment they walked back toward the elevators. This had to be Lincoln's father, although it could well have been a relative of Senator Stan's. They had the same lanky build and rolling walk, though both were bent now with the burden of grief.

Not wanting to intrude, I waited for the next elevator, and as I stepped out on the top floor Chelsea was coming out of her room, her movements stiff. Her eyes were red and puffy and her skin looked sallow and bloodless.

I stopped to give her my condolences.

"So you knew about Lincoln and me? How?"

"I've got eyes," I said. "It was clear how he felt about you and I assumed it was mutual."

"It was," she said, tears welling. "I was just going out to get some fresh air." She looked toward the elevator with both longing and dread.

"Would you like company or would you rather be alone?" I asked.

"I'd like you to walk with me. Do you have time?"

"Sure," I said, resolving to put everything I needed to do out of my mind.

Once outside, Chelsea drew in a gulp of air as if she'd been underwater so long her lungs were caving. "I know everyone means well, but I feel like I'm suffocating," she said. "Could we walk down to the lake?"

At first I thought she meant she wanted to go to the spot where Lincoln died, but the thought must have showed on my face. "Not there, just down by the boat launch or somewhere. Just so it's by the water."

I veered off the path and beckoned her to follow.

"I grew up in a house beside a riverbank," she said by way of explanation. "I like to be near water. I was happy there once upon a time."

"Where was this?" I asked.

"Out east, near the coast. Our county had the distinction of being the poorest in the state," she said with a sad smile. "And my family contributed to the de-mographic. We were poor—I mean like dirt poor—but the funny thing is, I didn't even realize that until I was twelve or thirteen years old. There was always food. And somehow we had clothes and shoes. Always clean, no matter how threadbare. Our mother was a miracle worker when it came to marshaling what few resources we had. She died when I was fourteen, and things sort of fell apart after that."

"How about your father, what's he like?" I asked.

"He died when I was twenty. He was a good man, quiet and earnest. But he had a stubborn streak about some things and one of them was taking government assistance. When he and my mom first married, he worked at a small manufacturing plant out on the western end of the Piedmont and earned a decent liv-ing. They'd just had my brother back then and life was pretty good. Paycheck to paycheck, but still good. Then in the late seventies the bottom dropped out and the plant got bought. The new owners hauled off everything worth a dime, then shuttered the place. They took all the workers willing to move to Ohio and let the rest go. Dad didn't want to go and he wouldn't take pub-lic assistance and things spiraled down fast. Lincoln was a lot like that. Not about government assistance, but about other things. He had these principles—at least he would've called them principles—and he was unbending sometimes." She choked up and I waited while she regained her composure.

"Anyway, by the time I came along, my folks were living in a tiny little house out east, and that was only through the largesse of a cousin of my mother's. Dad did odd jobs and somehow kept our heads above water, no pun intended." She looked over at me as we walked. "Do you always have this effect on people? Making them blather on about themselves?"

"Only on people who like to talk, or *need* to," I said with a smile. "So you have a brother?"

"Yes," Chelsea said with a sigh. "I visit him once a month. He's in Central Prison in Raleigh. He got tired of being poor and when he was eighteen, he decided armed robbery was the way out. He wasn't good at it. He'll be eligible for parole in another two years. There's hope for him."

"So how did you make your way out of your humble beginnings?"

"Dinah Leigh," she said. "And some others, too. I had a teacher in high school who took an interest in me. She was kind and encouraging and determined that I'd get a shot at college. That seemed like a pipe dream to me, but she kept at me to send in an application for the scholarship Dinah Leigh offered. I had to go for a personal interview and I'd never been so scared in my life. But Dinah Leigh put me at ease and I got through it. And the next thing I know, I'm in college, then I'm in Dinah Leigh's office filing and stapling, then I'm her personal assistant."

"It's obvious she values you," I said. "Do you enjoy the job?"

"What's not to love," Chelsea said. "I've had the opportunity to travel and I've learned so much from her, about business and about life. I never even imagined how people of means lived before. And, most of all, I adore Dinah Leigh. She's very good to me. But she'll be stepping down from the company within the next few years. She's grooming a nephew of Mr. Dodd's to take over the company since neither of their own children is interested. I don't like the nephew much and I have no interest in being just a social secretary to Dinah Leigh, so I'll be looking for other opportunities. But I hope I'll always stay close to Dinah Leigh."

We reached the boat launch and turned to walk across an expanse of manicured lawn toward a mossy embankment. We tested the earth, which was only slightly damp, and sat down.

"Lincoln and I had an agreement," she said, her eyes settling on a tree limb floating a few feet away in the lake. "A five-year plan." She laughed, a small, muffled sound. "He said we shouldn't call it that because it sounded communistic. Anyway, after the senator's book was finished, he'd spend the next year writing his dissertation to complete his doctorate. Then he'd look for a job at one of the colleges or universities around Charlotte and I'd stay with Dinah Leigh through her transition into retirement. Then we'd get married."

"Wow," I said. "That'd be a long engagement." I wondered if Jack and I would take that long to discover if we were in it for the long haul.

"Yeah," she said. "Except I didn't even want to get engaged. I mean not officially, not publicly. I didn't want anyone to know we were even involved. We kept it secret. At least I thought we did; clearly we didn't fool you. It all seems so stupid now, but I couldn't think about telling Dinah Leigh. I was afraid she'd see it as me betraying all her kindnesses if I even *thought* about leaving her."

"She doesn't strike me as the kind of person who'd hold you in forced servitude," I said. "She'd want you to be happy."

"She would," Chelsea said, and now the tears couldn't be held back. "But it's a moot point now. Do you ever think about how your whole life can change in the blink of an eye? How one thoughtless act can bring your whole world crashing down? After what's happened I don't think I'll ever be happy again."

Lenora's suite had become the hub for logistics. Damon was sitting at a desk by the window making phone calls and ticking off check marks on a list, and Emma was helping Lenora with a list of people whose phone calls should be returned. J.D. and Gabriela were sitting side by side on a love seat looking at the scrapbooks we'd made for the senator.

"Thank you so much for coming out to get these, Sophreena," Lenora said, handing me a bag stuffed full of cards and papers.

"No problem," I said. "Is there anything else I can do?"

Lenora sighed. "Not that I can think of, but you're a dear to ask. Lincoln's father just arrived and he and Stan are having some private time together."

"I think I may have seen him downstairs with the senator. Is he about this tall and slender like the senator?" I asked.

"I expect so," Lenora said. "I haven't seen Samuel in years. When we lived out in the country, all the kids went to the same school but he's quite a bit younger, so we wouldn't have had much association even then. And once we moved into town I didn't see much of the Coopers at all."

"I didn't realize you knew them," I said. "I thought it was Ken Dodd who recommended Lincoln to the senator."

"Oh, it was," Lenora said. "But as it happens, Lincoln and Ken were at Duke together and lived in the same dorm. And they were on some sort of intramural team, rugby or squash or something. They became pals and when Ken heard Stan was looking for someone, he told him he thought Lincoln would be a good fit and it all went from there."

"Will Ken be able to stay for a while or is he due back to his posting?" I asked.

"He'll be here until after Conrad's wedding. He was due for his break anyway."

"That's good," I said. "At least he'll have a happy occasion before he goes back. It's hard to lose a friend."

"Yes, he's very sad," Lenora said, "and very concerned about Chelsea. She's taking this so hard. Course, why wouldn't she, she and Lincoln were practically engaged."

"Really?" I asked, surprised this was coming from Lenora.

She nodded. "We all knew they were in love. They both thought they were the very soul of discretion. It was sweet, really, but nobody was fooled. And now he's gone and we'll never have a chance to share their joy in each other. It's just so sad."

I agreed and hefted the bag in her direction. "I'd best get out of your hair. If there's anything we can do, please don't hesitate to call. We're not far away."

"Well, there is one thing. Most of us will be going back to Quinn County for the funeral. Lily Rose isn't up to the trip, so she'll stay behind. If you wouldn't mind, maybe you or Esme could look in on her while we're away? Sarah's going to stay with her, but I'm sure she'd welcome company."

"We'd be happy to," I said. We'd spent a lot of time with Lily Rose Sawyer while preparing the senator's narrative and scrapbooks, and both Esme and I enjoyed her dry humor and lively wit.

"That would be lovely. I offered to stay with her and let Sarah go to the funeral, but she's not willing to leave her mother and she thinks maybe I'd be more comfort to Stan, though I don't know if that's true. I'm not sure there's comfort to be had for him right now."

I asked if she knew where I might find Dinah Leigh or Conrad, and she said she'd seen them down in the restaurant just before I arrived. As I started for the door, Emma gave me a beseeching look.

I felt sorry for her. This surely wasn't the way any sixteen-year-old would wish to spend spring break. Without thinking it through, I asked if she'd like to come to my house to put the cards and testimonials into the scrapbook—a job I could have handled in fifteen short minutes, but which would probably take longer with her help.

"Sure thing," Emma said. "Is it okay, Aunt Lenora?"

"You need to check with your mother, but I suspect it'd be all right," Lenora said.

"You ask your mom and I'll go find Dinah Leigh," I said. "Text me if she says it's okay."

"Check," Emma said.

I berated myself all the way down on the elevator. Since when did I get so maternal? Or at least big-sisterly. I'd probably lose two hours of productive work by having Emma with me. But I'd done it now and there was no going back. Maybe Sarah would say no. I could hope.

Too, I was wondering if I should've pushed Chelsea harder to get information about the night Lincoln died. And what she'd meant by that remark about "one thoughtless act." But she'd seemed so fragile, I hadn't had the heart to push. So we'd simply sat for a few silent minutes, watching as two novice kayakers struggled to find their equilibrium on the lake's placid surface.

I was relieved to find Dinah Leigh and her party in the casual dining restaurant, which was still plenty fancy by my admittedly low standards. Patricia and Marc Benton, Conrad, Phoebe, and Aunt Yvonne were with her. They all looked up as I approached, and welcomed me with undue enthusiasm. I soon learned why—the tension in the little group was tight as a guitar string.

After a little social chitchat, I asked a few follow-up questions pertaining to the information I'd gotten in the interviews with Conrad and Yvonne and verified a few names.

Aunt Yvonne was again disdainful of delving into family history, opining that so much dwelling on the past was unhealthy, a ridiculous waste of time, and a "silly thing for a grown man to be doing."

"Oh, but Aunt Yvonne," Phoebe said, her soft voice placating. "It's important to know who we come from. And it will be important to future generations, which is why it's especially important to Conrad and me right now. We're about to produce a member of that new generation." She leaned over to nuzzle at Conrad's shoulder, a brilliant smile lighting her face.

"I thought we agreed not to share our news just yet," Conrad whispered into the stunned silence around the table.

"Oh, don't be so prudish, Conrad. Babies get started before the wedding vows are said all the time these days."

"It's not that," Conrad said, his expression pained. "It's more that this period of grief doesn't seem quite the appropriate moment."

"Oh, I see what you mean," Phoebe said. "But really, darling, that's even more reason to share joyous news of new life. Don't y'all think so?"

The silence continued for a long moment before Dinah Leigh let out a whoop. "That's fantastic!" she said. "A little Conrad's on the way."

Patricia leaned across the table. "Yes, great and all,"

she said, in a tone that belied the words. "But do you have a good doctor? I mean, you must have concerns? You're kind of an older mom-to-be . . ."

Marc, a smile frozen on his tanned face, put what I'd begun to think of as the inhibitor arm around his wife's shoulders and squeezed. It looked like a loving gesture, but I could see his fingers turning white.

"Patricia!" Dinah Leigh said, turning a palm toward her daughter's face. "This is happy news, and that's something we all desperately need right now. I won't have your snide remarks."

"It's okay," Conrad said. "I know some are going to find this unsettling. And yes, I have visions of shuffling into the child's high school graduation with the assistance of a walker with those little tennis balls affixed to the legs, but I'm over the moon at the prospect of being a father and I have every intention of being around to raise this child to adulthood. I'd imagined this was a gift that had passed me by."

"Me, too," said Phoebe. "But here I am, and here's little Conrad, or maybe it will be a girl. I think Dinah has a nice ring to it, don't you?" she said, nodding in Dinah Leigh's direction. "And while it's early days yet, everything seems to be going fine, Patricia. Thanks for your concern. We have a very good doctor who's monitoring me closely. And speaking of which, she's instructed me to put my feet up for a while each afternoon. I think I'll go do just that." She pushed back from the table, and Conrad hopped up to assist her.

"I'll just go put my feet up, too," Conrad said. "Sympathetic napping. Text me if you hear anything about the arrangements for the funeral, would you?"

Their departure broke the luncheon up, and Dinah Leigh went off to the spa with a grumbling Aunt Yvonne in tow. I hit the ladies' room and when I came back into the hallway, Patricia and Marc were standing between me and the elevators arguing loudly, clearly unaware of how their voices carried.

"For pity's sake, Marc," Patricia hissed. "It's not like I'm courting voters, they're family. And anyway, they're not even in my district. I'm sick of biting my tongue. I should be able to say what I mean *some* of the time. I'm not a robot."

Marc put his head down and pinched the bridge of his nose. "More's the pity, Patricia," he said, his voice mournful. "Then I could have you reprogrammed. You're going to have to file down that sharp tongue of yours, at least until *after* you get elected. I'm not doing all this for my health, you know. Keep in mind you've got to get into this *first* office before we can use it as a stepping-stone to something bigger. Now, get a grip."

He stalked away and she gave his back a look that could've melted plastic, then her eyes shifted and she spotted me. She gave me a rueful smile. "Apparently I lack finesse," she said.

"It was big news; nobody was prepared for it," I said. Then, struggling for something to say, I asked if she was going to Lincoln's funeral.

"Yes. Marc insists it'd look bad if I don't go, so I let him think I don't want to so I can earn points for co-operating. But I want to go and pay my respects. That kind of game playing is my life these days. The truth is, I liked Lincoln Cooper. He was a good guy and uncommonly smart. I learned more about policy from him in a ten-minute conversation than I do from Marc and the assembly of wonks he's sicced on me in a month. I'm really upset about what happened to Lincoln, but these days, my distress seems to manifest in really unattractive ways. Some women claim they cry ugly—it seems I live ugly these days."

Her voice was soft and I could see the words were heartfelt. It took me aback.

"Do you have anyone to talk with about it? How about your brother? I know he's upset as well," I said. "He and Lincoln were close friends from what I hear."

"*Were* being the operative word," Patricia said, the acerbic tone back. "Everybody thinks Ken is such a saint. Well, he's not. This whole doctor-volunteer thing is just to polish his image so he can get on staff at a prestigious research hospital and never have to touch a patient again. And yeah, he and Lincoln were friends. So much so he recommended him to the senator." She laughed but there was no merriment in it. "But there were unforeseen consequences. Contact with the senator meant more contact with us, ergo more contact with Chelsea. I think Ken's plan was to spend his volunteer time deciding if he wanted her or not and if it turned out he did, he'd come back and deign to let her marry him. I don't think it even occurred to him she might make alternate plans. He was shocked when he realized Lincoln had repaid him by poaching his woman. He was *not* a happy camper. I, on the other hand, found it gloriously karmic."

I couldn't think of anything to say to that and as the silence stretched out, Patricia sighed and let her shoulders sag.

"Oh, pay no attention to me, I'm such a harpy. I wasn't always like this, you know," she said, strolling over to a window that looked out on the tennis courts. She seemed to expect me to follow, so I went, trying desperately to think up a good exit strategy.

She gazed out the window for a long moment, then started to talk, her voice almost a whisper. "It's tearing me up that Phoebe is having a baby. I hate her for it. Marc and I went through so much pain and expense to try to have kids but nothing worked. I finally had to accept that it's not going to happen for me. Marc won't even consider adoption, so that's the end of it. I'll never be anybody's mother. That's one reason I decided to run for office. I think I can do some good, especially for kids."

"That's commendable," I said.

She smiled, an honest-to-Pete genuine smile.

"I'm a good person," she said. "I am. I know I'm negative and annoying and, Marc's favorite word, *abrasive*, but I really am working on it. I've got so much to be grateful for. Money isn't a concern for me, thanks to my parents, and Marc is a good husband. I've got my mother and my brother and Conrad and now *Phoebe*"—she said the name as if referring to a skin condition—"so assuming I don't permanently alienate them all, I've got good family support, but the thing I wanted most in my life I can't have."

"I hope you'll find fulfillment in your political career," I said, feeling like the world's most out-of-her-depth counselor.

"I hope so, too," she said. "I want it, more than anything right now. So I guess I've got to work on the charm thing."

"You have a nice smile—maybe you could use it more often," I blurted, and immediately wished I could take it back.

Patricia laughed. "Marc should put you on the payroll," she said, turning toward the elevators. "You going up?"

I checked my phone and saw that Emma had gotten the okay to go with me. "Yep," I said. "Seems I've acquired an assistant."

*   *   *

As it turned out, Emma was a tremendous help. And, despite my concerns that she'd be bored out of her gourd, she was actively interested. She helped me scan, trim, and mount the testimonials and she had a deft hand and a good eye. When I told her so, she smiled. "I'm on the yearbook staff," she said. "Course, we do most things digitally, but sometimes we do layouts on paper. I kind of like this old-school stuff."

"Me, too," I said. "But technology marches on. We often do video scrapbooking, and sometimes the clients want digital slideshows, but more and more people are requesting the heritage scrapbooks. I guess it's considered retro now. I like working with paper and enjoy telling a family's story through the scrapbooks."

"Hm," Emma said, "I never thought of a family having a story. I mean, a family is lots of different people, right? Doesn't each of them have their own story?"

"Yes," I allowed, "but a family has an identity, too. Your family's reputation, their standing in the community, their talents and personalities, their habits and customs—all of that sets them apart from other families. Like if someone says about you, 'Oh, Emma, she's a Sawyer,' that would mean more than just telling your mother's name. It would mean you belong to all the things the Sawyers stand for."

"OMG, I hope not all of it!" Emma said, frowning. "I mean, I don't agree with a lot of things Grandpa stood for. And what about people who have families that have crappy reputations to begin with? That wouldn't be fair."

"You're right. And the flip side is if you come from a good family, sometimes you get credit you might not have earned just for the luck of having been born to those people."

"It's pretty complicated, isn't it?" Emma said. "I love my grandpa and I'm proud that he's a senator and all, but sometimes I'm embarrassed because I don't believe the same as him about everything, and people think I do just because I'm his granddaughter. Like that bill he sponsored way back in the day, the one Lincoln was doing his dissertation on. It was terrible for the environment. Lincoln and J.D. used to get into really fierce arguments about it. I didn't understand it all, but I know it allowed terrible things to be done to the planet. I was on J.D.'s side. But then I'd feel disloyal to Grandpa 'cause I love him."

"As you say, it's complicated."

Just as we finished up I heard the front door and Jack's customary "Hey, Soph." That sparked new regrets about bringing Emma home with me. I called back to direct him to the workroom and his answer brought red to my cheeks. "Esme's car's gone, does that mean we've got time for—" He stopped abruptly as he reached the doorway and saw Emma.

I made introductions and avoided his gaze, trying to get the blushing under control. Honestly, you'd think *I* was the one who was sixteen.

"How was kayaking?" I asked.

"Good, good," Jack said. "I just stopped by to see if there's any chance of catching a quick supper tonight?"

"Maybe," I said, my gaze wandering to the sparse family tree meant for Conrad. It looked like Charlie Brown's Christmas tree. "I'll call you later."

Once he'd left, I did some high-level bargaining with myself. If I could get the frame illuminations done and two generations of nameplates drawn, I could take a couple of hours off to go to supper with Jack. *That* was motivation. But I needed something for Emma to do. I can work on calligraphy projects while someone is in the room with me, but not if they're just watching me.

I asked if she'd enter the inventory of the materials Dinah Leigh had given us into our system.

"Sure, I can handle that," she said. "I helped Chelsea when she sorted and scanned the stuff for you, so I already know what some of it is. But she made you a list, you know."

"I know, but we've got a special system and we need it in our own database."

Emma was a quick study. She followed directions to the letter and understood the importance of handling the things gently.

"I saw Jack with you at Grandpa's birthday," she said as she began typing into the database. "So he's your boyfriend?"

"Yes," I said. "I guess he's now officially my boyfriend, but we've been friends for a long time."

"He's cute," she said. "And you don't mind that he's kind of, you know, short?"

I laughed. "In case you haven't noticed, I'm not exactly an Amazon. He's taller than me, and even if he wasn't, I like him just as he is."

"That's cool," she said.

"Tell me about your boyfriend," I said. "I mean, if you want to."

"Sure," she said, carefully transferring the postcards she'd just entered to the spot reserved for them on the opposite tabletop. "His name is Justin and everybody says we look really good together."

"And that's important to you?" I asked. "How you look together?"

"Of course," she said, "really important. Like I'd never go out with anyone who's not taller than me or who was chubby or had black hair. We wouldn't look good together."

"You might be eliminating somebody really terrific with those parameters," I said, concentrating on keeping my arm muscles loose as I drew the long, sweeping lines of the tree's branches.

"That's what my mom says," Emma said. "And honestly, when I say it out loud it makes me sound like such a poser. But it's just always been that way. You know how you were talking earlier about your family's identity or whatever? Well, I've got one, too. For me it's that I'm the pretty one."

"Well," I said, "you are pretty, but that's certainly not all of you."

"It seems like it sometimes. Damon is the smart one with the bright future and I'm like the pretty little shiny thing. Nobody expects much from me. And I'm not being conceited. I know I'm not drop-dead gorgeous. I'm just kind of ordinary pretty, like my mother."

"Your mother is a beautiful woman," I said, "but I'm sure she has other admirable traits as well."

"She does," Emma said. "And really she's done everything she could possibly do to make sure I'm not shallow or vain, but it seems like it's happening anyway. She used to work at a textbook publishing company, but when Dad started getting these jobs that took him away for months at a time, she quit so she could stay home with me. She was afraid I'd get in trouble if I had too much unsupervised time. And I probably would have. No, I definitely would have. It's not like I'm wild or anything, but I get bored."

"So I take it your mom's not a big fan of your boyfriend," I said.

"Nope. She doesn't hate him and she's not mean to him when he comes over or anything like that. But she says I'm not my best self when he's around, whatever that means."

"Maybe she sees changes in you that she doesn't like," I offered, leaning back to study the tree. Having Emma there to talk to actually seemed to be helping me relax into the work.

"Duh, of course there are changes. I mean, I want him to always see me like perfect, so I pay attention to my clothes and I make sure I don't snort when I laugh like I usually do. Really, it's a disgusting sound. I can stop it if I really try, but I have to be on top of it. I'll bet you don't do disgusting things around Jack."

"I hope I don't do disgusting things around *anybody*, but I've got a few less-than-sterling qualities. I chew my cuticles, especially when I'm driving, and I'm messy—except in here, where I'm super fanatical about order. Oh, and Esme lets me know every single day that I'm a terrible dresser and that I need to do something about my hair, which is always a hot mess."

"Yeah," Emma said, scrutinizing my thatch of auburn hair, which I'd twisted into a bun with a number-two pencil. "It's totally out of control, but that's okay. It's your look."

"My point," I said, "is that I don't feel the need to act differently around Jack, or change my dress or my hair to suit him, because then I wouldn't be myself. I'd be tired and nervous all the time trying to keep up the false front."

"Maybe it's different for you; you're older and I'm sure once you get to be your age you don't care anymore."

"Okay, first off, I'm not shopping around for a rest home just yet, and second, Esme is older than me and believe me, she cares a lot about her appearance. But her getting gussied up isn't for Detective Carlson or anybody else. She does it for herself. She doesn't have to do anything apart from being one hundred percent herself to earn his admiration."

"That's kind of like what Chelsea said about Lincoln. I asked her straight out why him. I mean, she's really pretty. She could have any guy she wants. Lincoln was okay in the looks department, but she could definitely have done better. But she said he was a prize and she felt very lucky."

"I think that says a lot about a relationship when both of the people involved think they've got the best end of the deal."

"Lincoln was really nice," Emma said, and I glanced up to see that she was close to tears. "But he was a hopeless nerd."

"So he was *my* people," I said. "No wonder I liked him. I'm a nerd, too."

"Well, you don't have to act like you're proud of it," Emma said, sniffling.

"Oh, but I am. It's the nerds who change the world."

"Can I tell you something?" she asked.

"Sure," I said.

"I had a crush on Lincoln," she said. "When I was younger, I mean. When he first came to work for Grandpa, I tried to kiss him once."

"You did?" I asked, trying to sound casual, though the revelation was setting off an alarm that was making my skull rattle.

"Yeah, I mean I was just a kid and I wanted to try kissing. But he said it wasn't appropriate. He was really nice about it and I could tell he was trying not to hurt my feelings. He told me never to do anything like that again 'cause some people might get the wrong idea."

"He was right about that," I said.

"Was he ever!" Emma said. "I get it now, but it wasn't skeevy or anything. He didn't do anything wrong. He didn't even know I was going to try to kiss him and he didn't kiss me back, he nearly fell out of his chair trying to get away from me. But Damon was always lurking around spying on people and eavesdropping and he saw the whole thing. He freaked *out*! They had a big fight and Damon threatened to tell Grandpa and get Lincoln fired. I got really mad and marched off and told Grandpa myself. I told him exactly what happened, even though it was so embarrassing. Grandpa said I was right to tell him and that I should never do anything like that again and for me not to worry, that Lincoln wouldn't be fired."

"I'd say you handled that well," I said, leaning back to study my work again. I was pleased, because it looked good and, more important, because now I could play hooky for a guilt-free dinner with Jack. I glanced at the clock. "I'd better get you back to the hotel soon," I told Emma. "It's almost four. Your video chat with your dad is at five, right?"

"Five thirty. I only have this one little pile left to go, so let me finish up."

"I never refuse free labor," I said, impressed with her diligence. "So did Damon and Lincoln argue a lot?" I asked.

"Damon argued," Emma said. "Lincoln mostly just ignored him, especially in front of Grandpa. But I'm sure he got sick of Damon's crap."

"Do you know what they argued about?"

"What didn't they argue about," Emma said with a laugh. "Damon could not *wait* for them to finish the book. He was always telling Lincoln that once the book was finished, Grandpa wouldn't want him around anymore. That he was just hired help. I don't think that was true, though. I think he and Grandpa would have kept in touch. Okay, that's it," she said, placing the last stack of artifacts on the back table and looking over the array. "Everything's entered. But wait, where's that blue letter?"

"Blue letter?" I asked.

"Well, a blue envelope. There was a letter or something in it," she said, looking over the table again. "It was in the box of stuff."

"I didn't see any blue envelope," I told her. "Are you sure?"

Emma shrugged. "Maybe I'm wrong." She stood for a moment, frowning as she scanned the items again. "No, I'm sure; it was in this box. It fell out of a baby book—Conrad's, I think, though it didn't have much writing in it. I remember handing the envelope to Chelsea. It was a letter, I think, pages and pages of spidery handwriting. I don't know who from or who to, but it was a bunch of pages. Chelsea looked over it, then crammed it back into the envelope without scanning it. I thought it was because it was so many sheets, so I offered to scan it for her but she said she'd do it later and that it wasn't important, but she acted kind of weird about it. Maybe she forgot to put it back in the box or it wasn't supposed to be in there in the first place. Who knows."

"I'll ask her about it," I said. "But if she said it wasn't important, I'm sure it wasn't."

Yet I was irritated that whatever was in the blue envelope hadn't been included. I like to personally examine everything I can get my hands on. One never knows where a seemingly insignificant artifact can lead.

eight

I DELIVERED EMMA TO HER ROOM AND SARAH thanked me for spending time with her. I could see she recognized the girl was feeling ignored, and that made me feel better. Through the opening in the doorway I spotted Sarah's laptop set up for the video chat with her husband and declined her invitation to come in. I wished them a happy virtual visit and went down the hall to Lenora's room to drop off the scrapbook.

I tapped softly, hoping I wasn't disturbing anyone who might be managing a much-needed nap. Gabriela opened the door a crack and smiled a question at me. I held up the book and explained why I was there.

"Come in, please," she said, opening the door wide. "Ms. Lenora is with the senator, and the others are out, but you can leave it right over there." She motioned toward the desk. Her English was perfect, heavily accented and musical on the ears.

I placed the book where she'd indicated and turned to find her looking at me expectantly.

"I'm so sorry your first meeting with the family was amidst all this," I said.

"I'm sorry as well," Gabriela said, "it's a terrible thing." She motioned for me to sit and I glanced at the clock. I could stay a few minutes if I met Jack at our favorite eatery.

"I know Lenora is very happy about your marriage," I said. "Though I think she's still in shock."

Gabriela laughed. "I think J.D. and I are still in shock, too. We'd agreed to have a long engagement, and I was going to come and meet the family and we'd all have a chance to get to know one another. But then one day we suddenly decided we didn't want to wait any longer and we got married that very afternoon. I know Ms. Lenora is probably disappointed that we didn't have a big wedding, but nonetheless she's been very good to me. And Judith has made me so welcome I feel we are sisters already. I feel close to the family despite this tragedy, or maybe because of it. You can tell a lot about people by how they act in hard circumstances."

"So are you staying here for a while?" I asked.

"You mean here in the States or here at the hotel?" she asked.

"Either," I said.

"We'll be in the country for at least two weeks, but

J.D. can't stay away from his work any longer than that. And we aren't staying at the hotel, or at least only for a little while to visit during the day. We're camping down by the lake."

"But I understand the owner of the hotel has offered free rooms to anyone in the senator's party. That certainly applies to you—you're family."

Gabriela smiled. "Yes, but it's not what we're used to. Everything is so, how do you put it? Clipped?" she asked, mimicking the motion of scissors, then pointing toward the window.

"Manicured," I said. "The grounds are all very manicured."

"But the lake is so beautiful," she said quickly, "and we are enjoying being under the stars at night. We can't see the stars much where we are deep in the rain forest. There is too thick a canopy. We love it by the lake—well, except for the night J.D.'s friend died. It rained so hard that night we had to get into the rental car and sleep there. It was so muddy we were afraid we'd be washed right into the lake. Everything we had with us got soaked. In fact, J.D. left me in the car and came up here to borrow some towels from the pool house so we could at least dry off. I got a little worried because he was gone so long and it was really storming. When he came back he ran the heater in the car and we dried a change of clothes on the vents." Her eyes came up to meet mine.

"We brought the towels back the next day, he didn't steal them."

I put up my hands. "I'm not the towel police. So where you're staying is nearby," I said.

"Oh yes, very nearby," she said. "We were so close to the place where that poor man died, we might have heard something if we hadn't been inside the car. J.D. is feeling a lot of guilt about it all."

"Guilt?" I asked. "Why guilt?"

"He and Lincoln had an argument that afternoon. It was all so silly. J.D. brought me here. I thought it was a bad idea, but he couldn't wait for me to meet his mother, so we came. He left me in the hallway while he prepared his mother and sister for the news. Lincoln saw me standing out there and asked what I was doing loitering. Is that the word, loitering?"

I nodded and she went on. "Yes, loitering around Ms. Lenora's door. And as I was trying to explain, J.D. came out and was very angry that Lincoln was speaking to me in that way. It was all just a big misunderstanding, but J.D. was still angry about it that night. He thought Lincoln had disrespected me, but I didn't feel that way at all. He was just being protective of Ms. Lenora."

"J.D. shouldn't feel guilty; they were both looking out for people they cared for," I said. "And as you say, it was a misunderstanding."

"Yes, that's what I tell him," she said. "But he says that the last conversation he had with Lincoln before he left for Peru was also an argument. They argued often, mostly about environmental issues, I think. But usually respectfully. J.D. says their last argument before he left the States got out of hand. And now Lincoln is dead and they can never reconcile about it."

"I guess we all have regrets when we lose someone," I mused.

"Yes," Gabriela said. "Most people think J.D. is really laid back, but he is not. He feels things deeply. That's good, especially for me," she said, stacking her hands over her heart with a demure smile, "but sometimes I worry. Once he gets something in his head, he doesn't want to let it go."

As I exited the hotel, again via the terrace, I passed the three suits who'd been meeting with Cyrus Hamilton. They wore serious faces. Then I saw the senator talking with Hamilton. They exchanged a few words and I was struck again by the similarities in their mannerisms. Hamilton headed back into the hotel, nodding to me with a forced smile. The meeting with the suits must have been stressful.

I'd almost made my getaway when the senator called out. "Sophreena, would you have a few minutes?"

I dashed off a quick text to let Jack know I'd be late and joined the senator as he started down the exercise trail. I had a hunch about where he was headed and he quickly confirmed it.

"I feel the need to see the place where the boy met his end," he said, his voice hoarse. "If you find this ghoulish, you may go on your way, Sophreena."

"No, I don't find it ghoulish, Senator. I think it's natural to want to know *how* a thing like this could possibly have happened."

"It's a poor substitute for knowing *why* this would befall a young man with nothing but bright promise ahead, but I suppose we must commence our attempts to understand somewhere."

I told him about my conversation with Cyrus Hamilton earlier. "I think knowing how would be a comfort to him at least. He seems to be feeling some responsibility in Lincoln's death."

The senator nodded and I concentrated on calculating how to match my stride to his. He was old, but his lanky legs covered more real estate in one stride than I could in two, and he wasn't even winded. Lucky for me, Esme had given me plenty of practice at this pace and I was able to keep up and still carry on the conversation.

"Cyrus does feel partly responsible," the senator said, "though his lawyer and his insurance people have assured him that all proper safety precautions were in place at the lookout. I feel responsible because Lincoln was here because of me. And I'm guessing others are playing what-ifs of their own. I'm a believing man, but on this one I can but wonder what the Almighty was thinking when he took Lincoln in the prime of his life."

"I suspect if Detective Carlson was here, he'd tell you it had more to do with what the killer was thinking. And that even when you find that out, it still won't make any kind of sense; these acts of violence seldom do."

"I expect he's right. You have confidence in the detective?"

"He's a good man and an excellent detective," I said. "I have the utmost confidence in him."

"I hope Lincoln's father will take comfort in that. The man is destroyed. His wife passed more than a decade ago and four years ago he lost his daughter, Lincoln's only sibling, in a car crash. Now Lincoln is gone. I cannot imagine the depths of his despair, yet I am keenly attuned to this particular loss. Over the years I've had many young people work with me—interns, aides, and staffers. I was fond of many of them, but the relationship with Lincoln was on another plane. We had a kinship, if not of blood, then of the mind, the spirit, and at the risk of sounding hopelessly corny, the heart. Lily Rose felt it, too."

"Where is Lincoln's father now?" I asked.

"Resting," Senator Stan said. "I didn't want to bring him out here unless he asks." He stopped at the bottom of the slope that swept upward to the bluff's overlook. "So there yonder is the place where evil came to ground."

We took the hill slowly and neither of us spoke until we reached the top. The overlook was a man-nature collaboration. The bluff was stone and jetted out over the lake, but to allow for safe viewing, a bowed concrete pad had been put down and safety railings installed, not only around the immediate overlook, but running down the slope at least twenty-five feet in each direction.

We walked over to the railing, each of us lost in our own thoughts, and almost in unison we drew in breaths and looked over the side. I saw immediately what Denny had meant. The distance of the fall might have been survivable, but the rocks at the bottom almost ensured fatality. They were mounds of boulder-sized jagged rocks and they covered almost every square inch of shoreline directly below the bluff.

"I understand this was an old rock quarry," the senator said. "Years ago, before your time, they dredged for this lake and as a tip of the hat to history, or perhaps to some civil engineering purpose, they left this one rock ledge of the original quarry."

He ran his hands along the rail, then shook it. He waited a moment, then shook it harder before letting his hands drop. "The faith I profess calls on me to believe there is a hereafter. I expect I'll be seeing Lincoln again not too long from now, in whatever form our souls manifest in the sweet by-and-by. I suppose I must take succor in that."

I fantasized about telling him that, in that eventuality, it would be nice if he or Lincoln could say hello to Esme and let us know how they were getting on. But I couldn't do that, so I simply stood with him until he was ready to go back.

As we walked I told him about our scheduled luncheon with Nancy Collier the next day, and the senator slowed his pace, frowning. "The name sounds familiar, but I can't seem to recall how I know it."

"She's the granddaughter of the man who was the sheriff in Quinn County at the time of the fire."

"My, you have been busy. Still, I can't imagine she'd know anything that could be helpful. She'd be far too young. James Ogdon's own children hadn't even been born then."

"Well, it's a place to start. That's often how it happens with these things—you talk to a person who has a little info and they tell you about another person who might know more and you keep talking to folks and connecting the bits until you get a clear picture. Esme says it's like working a jigsaw puzzle, but without the box for guidance. We have to make our own picture."

"And what picture have you formed of the sheriff?"

"A very vague one at this point," I admitted.

"James Ogdon was young to have been elected sheriff. It was the first office he'd ever held. Everyone called him Big Jim, both for his enormous size and because he had a big presence. He was a thoroughly decent man. But he was not a skilled investigator and some of the things he did, or didn't do, caused unintentional harm. We can talk more of that in the days to come," he said as we reached the terrace. "For now, my mind must dwell on the loss of Lincoln. Thank you for taking that walk with me."

"Good night, Senator," I said. I couldn't honestly say I'd been glad to go with him—I'd have the image of those lethal rocks stuck in my head for weeks. And now my psyche was trying to construct a soundtrack to go along with it.

Jack wasn't in the least annoyed by my tardiness. That was yet another benefit of having been platonic friends for so long. He knew I was never late without a good reason, though good reasons seemed to crop up fairly often in my life. I apologized anyway and explained the delay.

"No problem," he said, stowing the paperback he'd been reading into his backpack. "I imagine that was pretty awful."

I could only manage a nod, trying to get the image of those rocks out of my mind. My hand was shaking as I reached for my water glass.

"You'll feel better after you eat something," Jack said, knowing also my tendency to forget to eat. "I ordered for us, food'll be out soon. Tell me, is Esme still planning to move next weekend? I want to make sure I'm available to help."

"No, there's no telling when that'll happen." I went on to tell him about the kitchen repaint.

"I could do it for her. I'm a really good painter."

"Nice offer," I said. "But then she'll just come up with something else. She's stalling."

Our food came and as Jack had predicted, after a few bites I felt better. He asked what Emma had been doing at my house.

"I felt bad for her," I said. "I haven't even had a chance to tell you about what she overheard the night Lincoln died."

I had no reservations about talking this through with Jack. Our group of friends has an uncommon bond. We'd come together years ago in a genealogy class I taught through Marydale's papercraft shop. When the class ended we weren't ready to give up one another's company, so we formed an informal club. And since we were dealing with private family matters, we agreed to keep anything we shared strictly confidential. And in the years since, there's never been one breach of that agreement. So I told him Emma's story, trying to stick to exactly how she'd told it to me and Jennifer.

"Oh man," Jack said, "that's gotta be rough. Did Chelsea and Lincoln fight a lot?"

"I don't think so. Emma made it sound like this was an unusual thing; that's why it made such an impression on her. She asked if it was natural for couples to fight like that. I didn't know the answer. Is it?"

"For some couples, I guess," Jack said. "In any human relationship there are annoyances and negotiations, but it seems like some couples need more drama, big blowout fights once in a while to clear the air."

"Will we have blowouts?" I asked.

Jack shook his head and stole an onion ring from my plate. "Not our style," he said. "We'll have wobbles."

"Wobbles?"

"Wobbles," Jack repeated. "Those times when things aren't quite in balance. Then we'll figure out how to get things leveled out again and go on. That's the way we've always done it."

"I don't think Chelsea and Lincoln had a wobble. And the more I think about what Emma told me, it seemed like the relationship was hanging in the balance."

"Over?" Jack asked.

I told him what Chelsea had related to Jennifer.

"She thinks quite a lot of herself, doesn't she?" Jack said, pursing his lips. "Nobody's indispensable. I imagine there'd be a line of young people waiting to become Mrs. Dodd's personal assistant."

"Yeah," I said, "but Chelsea already knows Dinah Leigh's business, not to mention her personality and her habits."

"Still," Jack said, frowning. "Let's think about this. What *exactly* did Emma overhear?"

I pulled out the notebook where I'd scribbled it all down.

I went through the things Emma remembered with certain confidence and some of the phrases she thought *maybe* she'd heard. "Then at the end she heard Chelsea scream at him that she'd never forgive him if he betrayed her and disclosed it."

"Betrayed her? Disclosed it? That's a weird way to talk about an engagement."

"Well, that's what they were arguing about."

"Assumption," Jack said. "Aren't you the one always preaching against assumptions?"

"Yes," I allowed, "but in this case we have verification from Chelsea herself."

"You have what Chelsea *said* they were arguing about," Jack corrected.

"Why would she lie?" I asked.

"Ah," Jack said. "There she is. My skeptical Sophreena is back. And she's asking a very good question."

nine

On the way to our lunch date with Sheriff "Big Jim" Ogdon's granddaughter, Esme was optimistic we were about to find out something so compelling it'd wrap this up and we could write a report and be done with it.

"Weren't you the one telling me never to say a thing like that just a few short days ago?" I asked, wagging my finger at her.

"Yes, and I meant it—still do. But after talking with Nancy Collier on the phone, I expect we'll be able to learn a lot from her. She tells me she's been bustin' to tell somebody what she knows for years and never could get anybody to listen. She's tried to contact Senator Stan several times over the years but she always got a polite note from a staff person saying thanks, but no thanks, for her interest."

"How solid do you think her information is?" I asked.

Esme shrugged. "I don't imagine it'd hold up in court, if that's what you're asking. And her information is secondhand. But it may be enough for our purposes. We'll see."

"I've been thinking about what Denny said about how different things would've been back then as far as investigative tools and techniques. And fire investigation, too. It really was a different time. Nineteen forty-seven," I said, and Esme rolled her eyes.

When we do our scrapbooks, I always do an intro page to set the context for the political and social culture of the times. Doing that for so many years had embedded historical tidbits in my brain, and at the mention of a date, they sometimes come spewing forth.

"Nineteen forty-seven," I repeated, more firmly. "An average house went for sixty-six hundred dollars, which doesn't sound like much, but when you consider the average salary was below three thousand dollars a year, it was a lot. And a postage stamp was only three cents, so people wrote a lot of letters, which is very good for us. Let's see, grocery prices? Bread was around thirteen cents a loaf, tomato soup, twelve cents a can. Throw in a little sliced cheese and a pat of butter and you could have a nice soup and grilled cheese for under half a dollar."

"Yes, but as you say, let's look at the value of the dollar back then," Esme said. "What was it worth in today's dollars? Five bucks?"

I did some mental calculations. "Closer to eleven," I said.

"So, not such a cheap meal after all. Now do tell, what else was happening back in nineteen forty-seven?"

I knew she was being cheeky. Esme isn't particularly enchanted by these little eruptions of factoids, but I ignored her and went on. "Germany was getting divided, Israel was getting created, and here at home, according to some very interesting folks, we had our first UFO land at Roswell. Oh, and *The Howdy Doody Show* premiered. You think maybe there was a connection?"

Esme laughed, despite herself. "Could be," she allowed.

"Chuck Yeager broke the sound barrier, the first instant camera was presented to the public and so were the first long-playing records—that's what LP stands for, did you know that? And that was also the year Bing Crosby dreamed of a White Christmas. Okay, I'm done."

"Thank the Lord," Esme said.

"Yeah, you say that now, but someday when you find yourself in a red-hot trivia contest with real money on the line, you're going to wish you'd paid closer attention."

"No doubt," Esme said as she slowed to make the turn into the parking lot at the Morningside Cafe. We were early, but Nancy was already waiting for us. She looked to be in her fifties and I pegged her as the out-doorsy type. We made introductions, the waitress came for our order, and Nancy wasted no time on chitchat. "I'm happy you called." She waved both hands in front of her face and lowered her head. It looked like she was about to cry and I glanced at Esme. Had she set us up with a kook?

Esme shrugged and we waited.

"Sorry," Nancy said. "It's just such a relief. Nobody ever cared to talk about this with me, not even my husband or kids. Emmett is sort of a bygones-be-bygones kind of guy and the kids have more pressing things on their teenage brains than their mother's old family stories."

"You mentioned on the phone that you'd written down your granddaddy's recollections about the Sawyer house fire," Esme said. "Is that it?" She motioned toward a notebook on the table beside Nancy's coffee cup.

"Yes," Nancy said. "There's a lot of other stuff in here, too, but he talked most about that case. I think it really haunted him. Daddy Jim was the sheriff of Quinn County back in the nineteen forties and early fifties. He served for six years, and I mean that literally; he really saw his job as a service. And he had a good record—until the fire. After that he served out his term, but he didn't run for re-election. He took a job as a security guard at a new fabricating plant and worked there for the rest of his working life. When I was four, my grand-mother died. Apparently Daddy Jim didn't have a clue how to live on his own. He didn't know how to cook a blessed thing and taking care of a household was be-yond him. He was getting ready to retire anyhow, so he came to live with us. That was the year I started school, and with him there to take care of me after school, my mother went back to work. Both my parents were high school teachers."

"So you two were close," Esme said.

Nancy smiled, but it seemed forced. "We were," she said, "only now I realize maybe it wasn't entirely appro-priate how he was with me."

A gasp escaped my lips and Nancy turned to me and frowned, then put up a hand and fanned it back and forth.

"No, no, not that," she said. "Never *anything* like that. Oh, I'm making a mess of this." She slumped back in the booth.

Esme gave me a scowl and an almost imperceptible jerk of her chin in Nancy's direction, which translated to *You did it, you fix it*.

"You're doing fine," I said. "I apologize, I jumped to conclusions. Go on, please."

"Okay," Nancy said, scooting forward and pushing her coffee cup out of the way. "What I meant to say was that Daddy Jim talked to me about some of his old cases and sometimes the subject matter, *nothing* sexual," she said, glancing at me, "wasn't appropriate for a child. As I said, he was haunted by the Sawyer case and as he sank into old age he dwelled on it more and more. He didn't have anyone he could talk to about it. Anyone who'd listen, anyhow."

I dug my fingernails into my palms, determined not to interrupt again, but I was itching to ask questions.

"He couldn't ever talk to his colleagues because he'd ruined his reputation with them, and he surely couldn't talk to my grandmother because of how she felt about the senator's mother. She blamed Margaret Sawyer more than she blamed Daddy Jim for how things went for him."

"How's that?" Esme asked.

"Daddy Jim had courted the senator's mother for a time back when she was really young, but her parents disapproved because of the age gap. He was seven or eight years older than her. But according to my grandmother, he was still pining for her when she decided to marry Alton Sawyer. Her name was Margaret, but most people called her Meg. I suppose you knew that already. Anyhow, I understand she was quite the beauty in her day. She and Daddy Jim parted ways and went on with their lives, but my grandmother always believed he carried a torch for Meg. All this I got from my mother. I don't remember my grandmother much, but I think she must've been a bit of a shrew."

"And you said your grandfather had ruined himself with his colleagues—what did you mean by that?" I asked.

"Because of what he did after the fire," Nancy said, looking at me with wide eyes.

When I gave her a blank stare she shook her head. "Of course, how could you know? I'm sure it's not in any official records. It wasn't even in the newspapers but I think lots of people in the community knew about it at the time."

"What happened?" Esme asked, softly but firmly.

Nancy sighed. "It pained Daddy Jim so badly to see how Meg Sawyer was suffering. Her husband, too. Alton was a good man; Daddy Jim said so all the time. He didn't bear him any grudge. But he did have a soft spot for Meg, Grandma had been right about that. I could hear it in his voice when he talked about her. I'm not sure how much you know about all this, but they never found any remains of the baby. That's pretty uncommon, at least from what I've learned. They usually at least find bone fragments, even when the fire is intense. And in this case, I'm not sure how hot it could've gotten; the Sawyers' house didn't burn all the way to the ground. Have you seen the pictures?"

"Only the one from the paper," I said. "It sure looked like it burned down."

"Yes, from that angle it did, but if you see the ones

in the official fire marshal's report," she said, reaching into her bag, "it looks a lot different." She handed me a sheaf of photocopies. "I hope I can trust you. Technically, I'm not supposed to have these. Or, I should say, Daddy Jim wasn't supposed to have them. It's all the reports from the investigation into the fire. I don't know how or when he got them. He didn't take them with him when he left office. They didn't have office photocopiers back then—I checked."

The pictures were grainy and low contrast, but I could see what Nancy was trying to tell us. The house, while collapsed in the front, humped up in the back, and in the rear views there was still a good portion of the structure standing. The shots of the interior were even muddier, but I could make out what probably had been the parents' bedroom. It was bizarre. Some things were completely charred, like the bedposts and the dresser, yet the chenille bedspread looked to be untouched by the flames. A wooden bureau stood upright and a plump side chair had lost its legs, but the upholstery was intact and the white antimacassar draped over the top stood out stark against the ruins.

"Look at the ones of the nursery," Nancy said. "The crib wasn't burned, and the curtains are still in the windows behind it. They look sooty, but they didn't burn. The rest of the room is burnt, though—look at this angle back toward the interior doorway. That's completely burned up and it fell in when the front of the house went down."

"So where do they think the baby died?" I asked. "Clearly not in the crib."

"They think he crawled out and tried to go out the door but succumbed to smoke inhalation there in that area near the doorway."

I shivered as goose bumps rose on my arms. Nancy noticed.

"I know," she said, "it's a gruesome thought. That's what I meant when I said Daddy Jim talked to me about inappropriate things."

"So am I to take it your grandfather didn't agree with the findings?" Esme asked.

"Oh, don't misunderstand, he was convinced the baby died in the fire. What he disagreed about was that the lack of evidence in the official report left the door open for the parents to question. So he made up his mind to do something about that. That's what ruined him."

"What did he do?" I asked. "What *could* he do?"

"Nothing officially," Nancy said. "The reports came from the coroner and the fire chief."

"And unofficially?" I asked.

Nancy sighed. "You have to understand, he wanted the parents to have some peace. That was his only reason for doing it. He found one of the barn cats dead one morning and he got the idea of burning the cat's carcass and planting some of the bones at the scene so they could be 'discovered' by the coroner when Daddy Jim put in a request for a second sweep of the scene. It sounds horrible, I know, but he had the best of intentions."

"Surely the medical examiner wouldn't have been taken in by that," Esme said. "Your grandfather had to know that."

"Coroner," I corrected. "They had the coroner system back then. It was an elected office, and some of them didn't have any medical training at all. They did, however, have the power to call an inquest if a death was suspicious."

"Exactly right," Nancy said. "But the coroner was a dentist in town and he knew enough about human anatomy to know the bones weren't human. He and the fire chief grilled Daddy Jim until he confessed what he'd done. They about ran him out of town on a rail."

"And you say this was public knowledge?" I asked.

"Well, they tried to keep it close to the vest," Nancy said. "None of them wanted it to get out, but you know how things like that go. Some folks were saying what Daddy Jim did made matters worse, that it bolstered Meg Sawyer's conviction that Johnny had been kidnapped and that somebody in authority was trying to cover it up. There was already bad blood between the Sawyers and some of the officials because Meg didn't think they were taking what she had to say about that day seriously. It got really ugly after what Daddy Jim did. That's the thing that haunted him, that he made an already bad situation for the Sawyers even worse."

"Why didn't the coroner call an inquest?" I asked. "It seems like this was surely a case where it would've been warranted."

"I've always wondered that, too," Nancy said. "I have no idea. I'm guessing after he'd made his ruling he didn't want to back down. Daddy Jim said he was a stubborn man and kind of a know-it-all. And he and the fire chief were brothers-in-law, so maybe the coroner didn't want to contradict him? I don't know."

"But just to be clear," I said, "your grandfather believed that John David Sawyer died in that fire, correct?"

"Absolutely," Nancy answered with a decisive nod. "Daddy Jim was certain the baby perished. He believed that with every fiber of his being, but it haunted him that he could never find the proof to give the Sawyers closure. He believed they ruled too quick. He would have kept at it but after what he did, they wouldn't let him anywhere near the case again."

Esme and I spent the evening examining copies of the purloined reports Nancy emailed to us when she got home. It was clear the case had been mishandled, but at the end of the day all of the officials involved in the case at the time concluded that John David Sawyer died in the fire. The problem was that they hadn't submitted the proper evidence in the proper form to substantiate their findings. So now we were sifting through every scrap of documentation trying to locate any solid bit of evidence presented to give the findings proper weight. It was tedious work and heartbreaking to think about. I promised myself we would never take on anything like this again, particularly a case involving a baby.

Denny dropped by at the end of a long shift looking as if he hadn't slept for weeks. This time he took Esme up on her offer of scrambled eggs and toast. I followed them out to the kitchen feeling hypocritical since I complain, in my head at least, about not having any private time with Jack, and here I was intruding on their alone time. But I wanted to talk with Denny about something that had been bugging me since my conversation with Jack the night before.

"Who was that parked out in front of your house?" Denny asked as he settled at the table.

I glanced out the window. "I don't know. We haven't had visitors. There's nobody there now."

"They left when I pulled up. Maybe I scared 'em off. I didn't recognize the car, an old Toyota, a little worse for the wear?"

I shrugged. "Probably somebody parking to make a phone call or something."

"A good practice," Denny said. "I'm just suspicious by nature."

As Esme whipped up the eggs, Denny told us about progress on the case, or rather the lack thereof. "I've collected a lot of everybody's little everythings and it adds up to a whole lot of nothing," he said, his voice sounding as weary as the rest of him looked. "For such a nice guy, Lincoln Cooper sure generated a lot of conflict—that day, anyhow. He picked up Ken Dodd at the airport that morning and according to a witness from the parking garage, they had their own little row. It was serious enough that the witness called security. She was afraid to go to her car 'cause she was parked close to where they were having their shouting match and she thought it was about to get physical."

"I bet I can guess what that was about," I said.

"Mm-hmm," Esme echoed. "*Cherchez la femme.*"

"So I understand," Denny said. "Dodd says they were just horsing around and the woman misinterpreted."

"Do you believe him?" Esme asked.

"Nope," Denny answered. "The witness was clear about what she saw and heard. I think Dodd's ashamed of his behavior and afraid it puts him in a bad light, which it does."

"So is he a suspect?" Esme asked.

"Of course. He was supposedly asleep in his room,

alone and jet-lagged, during the window when Cooper died. That's no alibi, so he remains on my list. Then there's J. D. Morgan. Seems the run-in he and Cooper had that day wasn't the trifle he let on. A couple of people in adjoining rooms called the front desk. But it was over with by the time somebody got up there."

I told him what Emma and Gabriela had both told me about the past friction between the two. "The thing is, I don't think they disliked each other. It was just the nature of their relationship to debate, maybe a little overzealously sometimes."

Denny nodded, then smiled broadly as Esme set a plate of steaming eggs in front of him. "That was my take on it, too. But still, you can't get into a dustup with a person who gets murdered that very night and not end up on a cop's radar."

Feeling a bit like a fink, I told him what Gabriela had said about J.D.'s foray to the spa to pillage towels on the night in question.

"There you go," Denny said. "Even more reason to home in on him."

"Then I guess Chelsea's still on your screen, too," I said. "That's what I wanted to talk to you about, the argument she and Lincoln had that night."

"You mean you *didn't* want to talk to him about it," Esme said, snatching the bread the toaster ejected and spreading a liberal coating of butter on it.

"That's right, I didn't," I said. "I told Esme this earlier and she said we should go over it with you, but like Emma, I don't want to cause Chelsea any more pain than she's already in because I like her and can't imagine a scenario where she'd kill somebody. But when it comes down to it, I just met the woman a few days ago and I don't really know her."

"You're rambling, Sophreena," Esme said. "Get to it."

"Fine, here's what's bothering me. Some of the things Emma overheard don't mesh with what Chelsea claimed the argument was about." I opened my notebook and went over it with Denny point-by-counterpoint, as I'd done with Jack.

"First off, if Emma is remembering clearly, Lincoln said the truth had to come out and that it had been too many *years*. He and Chelsea had only been seeing each other for a little over a year."

"Maybe it seemed like years to him," Denny said. "Sometimes waiting to be with a person you care about can seem longer than it is. Or so I've heard." He cast a sidelong glance at Esme, who pointedly ignored the comment.

"Okay, well, Chelsea said she 'didn't care what he wanted.' Who is 'he,' and what is it he wanted? That doesn't seem to fit if this was a dispute about announcing their engagement."

"I'm thinking maybe she meant Ken Dodd," Esme

said. "It sounds as if he thought he had a prior claim on Chelsea's affections."

I tilted my head to the side, considering. "Maybe," I allowed. "And that could fit with another thing that's bothering me." I glanced at my notebook again. "If Emma has it right, Chelsea said 'he,' whoever this he is, gave up his right to have any say 'after what he did.' Let's assume for a moment that she means any say in her life. But that still leaves the 'after what he did' part to ponder over. Maybe that's about Ken as well. Maybe he insulted her or deceived her, or something worse."

"Interesting," Denny said when I'd finished my exegesis. He drew out his notebook and scribbled. "I'll follow up, but I have to be careful about how much weight to give it. Earwitness testimony is even more unreliable than eyewitness testimony. People mishear, misremember, and misinterpret things, and that's with the parties sitting in a quiet room all together. These three were out in a howling storm at midnight. And Emma was yards away when she caught what she believes she overheard. Plus, she's a teenager. Kids that age don't have the maturity to interpret things right."

"I thought of all that," I said. "But, honestly, Emma's not a typical teenager. She's got a sharp memory, and I mean sharp. You can tell her a list of complicated instructions and two hours later she remembers everything you've said, *verbatim*."

"I second that," Esme said. "The child has a roach motel for a brain. And she's really attached to Chelsea. If anything, she'd probably downplay things so Chelsea comes out looking better."

"Okay," Denny said, throwing up his hands. "I'll talk to Bremer again when she gets back. The funeral is the day after tomorrow and they're all leaving early tomorrow morning to go back to Quinn County. It's my understanding they'll all come back here and stay at the spa until Conrad Nelson's wedding. Bet that's gonna cost a pretty penny."

"I don't think money's an issue for the Dodds, and of course Cyrus Hamilton offered to put up the senator's party gratis," I said.

"Yeah, he must be more worried about liability than I thought," Denny said. "Way I hear it, there's a waiting list, and with those rooms occupied he's sacrificing a lucrative revenue stream."

"I don't think it's the liability issue," I said, telling Denny about my conversation with Hamilton. "Not legal liability anyway. I think he's just trying to be a friend. His and the senator's families go way back."

"Huh," Denny said. "Funny, he never mentioned anything about that to me."

I shrugged. "Maybe he thinks it's common knowledge or not relevant."

"At this point everything is relevant," Denny said.

"That's one problem, too much information and no context for any of it. Speaking of which . . ." He reached into the messenger bag he'd plopped onto the chair beside him. "I got the records on that fire. I had copies made for y'all, but let's not go bandying that about. They're mostly public, but there might be a few internal memos in there, purely by mistake, you understand."

"But we—" I started and Esme kicked me under the table with her size 10 shin-bruisers.

"—appreciate it so much," she finished, reaching over to rub Denny's arm. "Thank you, Denton. We'll be discreet."

". . . because he went to a lot of trouble getting those reports for us," Esme said, continuing the scolding she'd started the moment the door closed behind Denny. "And I don't want him to think we're ungrateful."

"Okay," I said. "You're right. I wasn't thinking. And Denny's feelings aside, we promised Nancy we wouldn't say anything to anybody about where we got the ones she shared with us."

"I think she's hoping something we find will end the rumors and put the parents' behavior in perspective," Esme said. "And if we manage to accomplish that, she'll want the senator and Lenora to know it came from her grandfather. It's her way of making amends for what he did back then to sully the investigation."

"That was the impression I got, too," I said, opening the folder Denny had brought. Many of the records were duplicates of what we had from Nancy, but some we hadn't seen before. I stacked up all the materials we'd been perusing earlier and carefully distributed the ones Denny had given us down the length of the table, a blue sticky note affixed to each so we'd know the source. I matched them up with the items we'd printed out from Nancy's set, which each got a yellow sticky note. When we had things sorted, I unspooled two yards of paper from a big roll I keep for making timelines for family histories. This is how I always begin making sense of the information we've gathered on each job.

I drew a long line bisecting the paper down the length and measured out increments for weeks at the far ends and hours for the day of the fire.

I looked over the first record, a written statement from the farmer who'd been the Sawyers' closest neighbor. According to him, he'd "looked over east along about three o'clock and saw black smoke. I knew it weren't no trash fire or nothing, but I reckoned it might be the barn. I took off over that way and afore I ever got up close I saw it was the house afire."

I put the first tick on the timeline at 3:00 p.m. with

a fifteen-minute bracket on either side and labeled it
House in flames/witness statement.

"We're in it now, Esme," I said. "And we're gonna
take it wherever it leads. *Wherever*. Agreed?"

We both stared down at the bright white paper
inscribed with a thin black line that, we hoped, would
eventually lead us to the answers.

"That we will," Esme said. "Tell the truth and
shame the devil."

ten

LILY ROSE WAS SITTING ON THE TERRACE TALKING with Cyrus Hamilton when we came to visit the next morning. She looked better than I'd seen her since we'd first met months ago. She had color in her cheeks, and her wheelchair was nowhere in sight, though she had an intricately carved wooden cane hooked on the arm of her chair.

"How good of you to come," she said, stretching out one hand to Esme and the other to me. "It's such a beautiful day and yet such a sad day. I'm glad for your company. But where are my manners, Cyrus, are you acquainted with these ladies?"

"Sophreena and I have met," Hamilton said, getting to his feet and giving a slight bow in my direction before extending his hand to Esme, "but I haven't had the pleasure."

I saw a frown cross Esme's face as she shook his

hand. I'd need to remember to ask about that later. She doesn't normally get any more of a read off living people than I do, but she'd given Cyrus a peculiar look.

After the introduction he excused himself, but not before urging Lily Rose to summon him personally if she needed anything. "Any little thing at all," he said, "do you promise?"

"I'm perfectly content," Lily Rose said. "But if a need arises I will let it be known."

After he left, Lily Rose let out a sigh. "Ah, poor Cyrus. This is surely not the way he intended Stanton's birthday celebration to go. I wish I could have gone to Lincoln's funeral. Had I known I'd be feeling so well today, I would've ventured it, but yesterday wasn't so good. That's one of the things this condition steals from you. I've got no capacity to plan my daily life anymore."

"Isn't Sarah here with you?" I asked, wondering if Lily Rose's improved condition had convinced her she could leave her mother for a time.

"Yes," Lily Rose answered. "She's up in our room working on thank-you notes, a job that should rightly fall to me. I don't like her to hover and she tries to grant me what little freedom I can claim, especially on days when I *can* do for myself. I can't tell you how annoyed I am that this old body has failed me. It's confounding. But today I am rather feeling my oats. After all the physical therapy and injections and pills and what-all

I've had, who would've thought lying in a vat of warm mud could give me such relief. But you didn't come here to hear me complain about my ailments. Tell me, have you been able to spend any time on the report Stanton and Lenora asked you to prepare? I know they're most eager to set up the foundation and they want the way absolutely clear to that."

"We've made a start," Esme said. "As I recall, you didn't know the senator back when the fire happened, is that right?"

"That's correct. I knew of the family, of course. It seemed everyone in Quinn County either knew, or knew *of*, everyone else. But I wasn't personally acquainted with any of the Sawyers. Our families were of differing religions, schools, and most importantly, political affiliations. Politics was a blood sport back in those days and one did not consort with the enemy."

"Ah, the more things change, the more they stay the same," Esme said. "So how did you two overcome those barriers?"

"Love finds a way," Lily Rose said with a smile. "As I believe I told you during our interviews, we met at a community dance; a friend of Stanton's introduced us."

"Yes, that much we know," I said. "But we never got any of the particulars of how you came together."

"Well," Lily Rose said, "I came to find out later that Stanton had hectored his friend into introducing us because he'd had his eye on me all the while. And after talking to him for only a few moments over punch and pound cake, I, too, was smitten. Don't misunderstand; I was no tender young thing. I was twenty-one when we met. I was getting ready to graduate from NC Teachers' College and I had aspirations of my own. I'd dated a few promising fellows, but none of them had impressed me much. Stanton did."

"And how long before you married?" I asked.

"Six months," Lily Rose said. "And that engagement was several months too long in Stanton's estimation, though my parents thought it unseemly haste."

"Did both sets of parents give you their blessings despite the differences?" I asked.

"Eventually," Lily Rose said. "Honestly, you would've thought it was the Paris Peace Conference. If it hadn't been for our mothers, we'd never have gotten through it. They formed an alliance and worked at softening up the menfolk, who came around in the end."

"So did you have a good relationship with your in-laws after all that?" Esme asked.

"I respected Stanton's father, Alton, tremendously. But I can't honestly say we were close. And I suspect if you ask Lenora, she'd say the same. It was hard for men of that generation to find their way in a relation-ship with a female after they passed the daddy's little princess stage and became young women."

"And your mother-in-law?" I asked.

"Ah," Lily Rose said with a sigh.

She was silent for so long, I thought maybe she was trying to order her words carefully to avoid saying what she really felt, but when she spoke I saw that it was a welling of emotion that had made her pause.

"I won't dishonor my own wonderful mother by saying that Mother Meg was like a mother to me. But I believe Mother Meg understood me better and supported me more earnestly in the things that were important to me. Meg Sawyer was the very antithesis of the stereotypical mother-in-law. I loved her fiercely and I've missed her every single day since she passed on."

"And you didn't find their refusal to accept the baby's death . . ." Esme's voice trailed off as she searched for the right word.

"Peculiar?" Lily Rose offered. "Crazy? Delusional? Don't worry, Esme, we've heard it all through the years. All I can say is I've never known two more astute and sensible people."

"I don't mean to put you on the spot, Lily Rose," I said. "But are you saying it wasn't irrational for them to hold out hope the baby was still alive?"

Lily Rose frowned, staring down at the stone terrace. She held her silence a long while and when she turned back to us, she was clearly troubled.

"Since Stanton and Lenora have asked you to take on

this task, I feel I should speak about it openly. But I must ask you to hold what I tell you in confidence, even from my husband and Lenora, though I know they're your clients and perhaps that would be a conflict for you."

Esme and I exchanged glances, and I could tell she was as perplexed as I was.

"We can promise not to reveal the source of what you tell us," I said, "but we may have no choice but to reveal the information if it turns out to be relevant to our task."

"That satisfies me," Lily Rose said. "It's not as if I have exclusive information. A number of people who you'll likely talk with may tell you similar things. I just don't want Stanton and Lenora to know it came from me. Please know, I do not withhold things from my husband, never have in all our married life." A small smile creased her face. "Oh, maybe now and then the exact cost of a new dress or how much I spent on Christmas presents for the grandchildren, but nothing important. So you can appreciate how difficult this is. I do not like to go behind Stanton and Lenora's backs to say things to you that I would not say to them, but this is an extremely painful subject for them. The loss of John David was like a malevolent fog that moved in and hovered over everything for their whole lives. Even in moments of what should have been utter joy it was always there in some dark corner. Not that Daddy Alton and Mother Meg were gloomy. They weren't. They were warm, caring people who tried their best to carry on, but I think Stanton and Lenora sometimes felt neglected by their devotion to baby Johnny."

I was getting antsy with this preamble, but I made noises of encouragement to keep from interrupting.

"Mother Meg was a meticulous woman. Her house was always neat as a pin and she was careful with things, very organized and observant. She told me about the day the fire took John David many times over the years, usually on a day when it was heavy on her heart— the anniversary of the fire or John David's birthday or when a new call came in claiming to have information about him."

"I imagine those were hard days," Esme said.

Lily Rose nodded. "Very hard. I've never repeated any of this to a single soul. But here's what I think you should know about Mother Meg's account. That day she put baby Johnny down for his nap, his nursery was on the ground floor at the back of the house, as I'm sure you've learned. She took Lenora with her up to the sewing room on the second floor, where she set her to sorting buttons from a jar while she worked on a new dress Lenora was to wear to a birthday party. Mother Meg had one of those old pedal-type sewing machines and it made quite a racket. A couple of times when the machine was quiet she thought she heard something odd and stopped her work to listen, thinking it was baby

Johnny waking up, but she only heard the noises of a summer afternoon, men in the fields shouting to one another and the far-off putter of a tractor. At one point she went to the doorway, certain she'd heard something, and was poised to go investigate, when Lenora spilled the buttons. They went everywhere and Lenora started to cry. Mother Meg went back into the room to soothe her and help pick them up. When she checked at the doorway again, everything was peaceful."

"She thought there was someone in the house?" I asked.

"She didn't think that *then*," Lily Rose said. "If she had, she'd have descended those stairs like one of the Furies of ancient mythology. She was very protective of her children. And if that had been all of it, I'd say it was a tiny peg to hang such a big hope on, but there's more. When the smoke started to curl up the stairs and Mother Meg realized there was a fire, her first thought was to get the children out. She grabbed Lenora's hand and ran down to find the thick wooden door at the bottom of the staircase closed. She was certain she'd left it open so she could hear if the baby cried. When she pushed the door open the flames were already licking up the walls. She thrust Lenora toward the front door and told her to run as far as the woods and wait there and she'd come once she got the baby. Lenora was crying and didn't want to go without her mother, but Meg shoved her and watched as Lenora pushed open the front screen door and ran outside. It struck Meg at that moment that she'd latched that screen door when she went upstairs and it shouldn't have swung open without being unlatched. They had a scoundrel of a cat who'd learned to let himself into the house to hunt for food, so she'd formed the habit of setting the little hook and eye latch."

"Maybe she just forgot that day or maybe the fire had already damaged it," Esme said.

"Maybe," Lily Rose allowed. "But then there was the chair. They had a wing chair in their front room that had been her grandfather's and she kept it in a certain spot, away from the window so the sun wouldn't fade the upholstery. It was directly in front of the window."

"Well," Esme said, "I understand it was a hot day. Maybe someone raised the window for a breeze and moved the chair over to take advantage of it."

"Could be," Lily Rose said. "I understand these all sound like trifling things. But if you'd known Mother Meg, you'd give them more weight. As I say, she was a fastidious woman and these things all came to her, little by little, in retrospect. At that point she had only one thing on her mind and that was getting to baby Johnny. She made it into his room, but by then the floor was already aflame and she caught her skirt on fire and had to beat it out and move back, but she got far enough to see into the crib and she swore Johnny wasn't there.

And the other thing is the window was up. She never put the window up in that room because there was a hole in the screen and she didn't want the flies to get into the baby's room. She looked around desperately for him, but by then the smoke was so thick she couldn't breathe and she was forced out. Once she got her breath, she tried to go back in, but the men who'd come running when they saw the smoke held her back. And then the whole house caved in and it was over."

"During all this did she ever hear the baby cry?" I asked.

"No, not a peep. And there was one more thing, and this is the one that has always given me the chills. After everything was over with and she'd had time to turn everything over in her mind, Mother Meg became certain that she'd recognized the sound she heard just before Lenora knocked over that button jar. It was the sound of a cigarette lighter, a Zippo. Do you know what that is?"

"Yes," I said. "In fact, I was just having a conversation with Cyrus about those lighters the other day. I have my grandfather's."

"Then you know they make a very distinctive sound, a click when you open the lid, a sort of hiss when the flint hits the strike wheel, then a clack when the lighter closes. Each sound in the sequence fits together like the percussion to a familiar song, and Mother Meg knew it well since her father was an avid smoker. She was convinced that's what she heard."

"Lily Rose, let me ask you straight out, are you persuaded the baby was kidnapped?"

"No," she said softly. "I'm not trying to make a case for that. Stanton and Lenora were there, they surely know better than me what happened that day. I'm telling you all this because I want you to understand that Meg Sawyer was not off her rocker like some folks have tried to make her out to be. She told all these things to the authorities and they either ignored her or condescended to her, but they never really considered anything she had to say as worthy of investigation. Nobody listened to her but Alton. I admired the way he stood by her. He never gave her one speck of an indication that he doubted her. Not even when she did that foolish thing a few months after the baby died."

"Foolish thing?" I asked.

"They got a ransom demand, a note slipped under the door at their house in town," Lily Rose said. "She didn't tell anyone, not even Alton at first, and she delivered the money herself. She took it from a small inheritance her parents had left her. Five thousand dollars. That doesn't sound like much now, but it was a good sum in those days. She left it under a fallen tree in the woods near the burnt ruins of the house where she was told to leave it. The money was gone the next day and that was the end of it. Some terrible person took advantage of her state of mind and robbed her as surely as if they'd held a gun on her. But even then Alton didn't scold or blame. She had her reasons for believing as she did, and they were plausible, sensible reasons, even if they didn't quite stretch to her conclusions. Still, her holding on to that hope, she and Alton both, it took a lot of things away from Stanton and Lenora over the years. Every time they went by that billboard it was like opening up a wound."

"I'm beginning to wonder if we're doing the same thing," Esme said.

Lily Rose shook her head. "It was that magazine article that stirred it all up again. And poor Lincoln took that upon himself. He was the one who'd arranged for the senator to give that reporter, Chad Deese, an interview. I say reporter, but he's not a political reporter. He's a freelancer who writes human-interest pieces and Lincoln expected him to do a nice profile piece for Stan's birthday. He felt blindsided when that article came out. I'd never seen him in such a temper. I dreaded to think what might happen when he caught up with that Deese fellow. Funny, isn't it; now I wish I had that worry back."

We chatted on about more pleasant things for a few more minutes and as we were getting ready to leave, Conrad came out to join us. "Am I interrupting anything?" he asked.

"Not at all," I said. "We were just saying good-bye; I've got work to do on someone's family tree."

"Then you must go," Conrad said. "I wasn't sure if you knew, Lily Rose, that we've lagged behind the others. Phoebe isn't feeling well."

"Oh, I'm so sorry to hear that, Conrad," Lily Rose said. "Nothing serious, I hope."

"Just one of those pregnant lady things, I think. To be expected, the doctors tell us. I hope she'll be feeling better in the morning and we'll drive over for the funeral then. And Aunt Yvonne's stayed behind, too. She'll go over with us. Aren't we lucky? In any case, I thought I'd meander down and keep you company for a while."

"Sarah sent you, didn't she?" Lily Rose said with a laugh. "So much for my sovereignty."

"She might've mentioned you were down here," Conrad said with a smile, "but truth be told, I've been kicked out of our room while Phoebe naps, so I'd love your company."

"Delighted," Lily Rose said with a nod. "Today, of all days, I'm glad to have company."

"And how, might I ask, are you progressing on my wedding gift?" Conrad asked, settling his lean frame onto the wrought iron chair next to Lily Rose.

"Very well," I said, hoping he didn't detect the slight flinch as I thought of how much was yet to be done.

"Despite her feelings about the project, your aunt Yvonne's information was a big help."

"And it was such a joy to extract it from her, wasn't it?" he said with a laugh. "Though you managed to get more than I did. I don't understand her. I've never come across anyone so virulently anti-genealogy before. People who think it's a bore, sure. People who give it a halfhearted try but just can't get into it, those aplenty. But she acts like we're dabbling in the black arts."

"You'd be surprised at the attitudes we get," Esme said.

"It's true," I said, "sometimes people aren't exactly proud of what they find out about their ancestors. And some are foresworn never to speak of the black sheep to outsiders. Sometimes that gets inculcated into generations, even when the big secret doesn't matter anymore. We've had people request that we destroy all the research we've done for them when we unearth something not to their liking."

Conrad laughed. "I hardly think Aunt Yvonne could have any deep dark secrets. She's lived a very circumscribed life, in the same town, with the same small circle of friends, most of whom she's outlived, and up until her retirement, the same civil service job pushing papers around for thirty years."

"Speaking of papers," I said, suddenly remembering

a loose end I'd meant to follow up on, "do you happen to remember a blue envelope with maybe a letter in it that was stuck in the back of your baby book?"

"I had a baby book?" Conrad asked. "I don't remember ever seeing one. That surprises me. My mother wasn't the sentimental type."

"It's the preprinted kind and not a whole lot is filled out," Esme said.

"Now, *that* sounds like my mother," Conrad said, chuckling. "But what is the significance of this letter?"

"None that we know of. We're just trying to make sure we have everything that could help us plot your family line."

"What I showed you the other day is all I've got. I was living out west when Dad died and only came back for the funeral. It fell to Dinah Leigh to clear out and sell the house. She collected any personal things we'd want to keep. I guess there wasn't much. As I say, my mother was a minimalist."

"We don't like minimalists," Esme said with a smile. "We much prefer the packrat mentality. Every artifact, every piece of ephemera, every letter, photo, card, or bill—they're like bread crumbs we can follow."

"Well, I'm afraid you'd be lost in the piney woods forever if you depended on my mother's feeble collection of keepsakes to lead you anywhere."

"I think that's our signal to get back on the hunt,"

I said. "We'll drop by to see you again soon, Lily Rose.
And I hope Phoebe feels better."

"Oh, I trust she will," Conrad said. "She's pampered
here in this lovely place. She's going to feel quite let
down when we go back to ordinary life."

We were headed down the broad flagstone steps toward the visitor lot when, out of nowhere, a young man
stepped in front of us. He was a redhead and looked
to be in his thirties. And if I'd had to guess, he'd spent
most of his life beanpole skinny. But he'd bulked up and
now his black T-shirt stretched across a muscular chest.

"You're Esme Sabatier and Sophreena McClure," he
said, a statement, not a question.

We admitted that we were, exchanging brief glances
that confirmed neither of us knew the guy.

"I understand Senator Sawyer hired you to look
into the investigation of the fire that *supposedly* killed
his younger brother all those years ago. What have you
discovered about the mystery of the child's disappear-
ance? Are you confident you'll find baby Johnny? Will
the parents be vindicated?"

I saw he had a lavalier mic clipped to his shirt and
the dime dropped. Chad Deese.

Esme stiffened. I recognized the danger sign, but
Deese didn't.

"Do you have anything to share with my readers?"
Deese persisted.

I knew engaging him would only make him harder to shake. Even a *No comment* would be incentive.

I went to move around him and he sidestepped into my path. "Anything?" he repeated.

I looked at him closer and saw he had a purple ring under one eye. He'd tried to disguise it with makeup but it was still swollen and the bruising showed through.

"Where'd you get the shiner?" I asked, moving a step closer to him. "Did Lincoln Cooper find you? What do *you* know about Lincoln's death?" I stepped closer still.

That usually worked to back a person down, but Deese wouldn't be cowed.

"I had nothing to do with Cooper's death. I hardly knew the guy. I've been questioned by the police and cleared," he said calmly. "But okay, let's go with that one. What can you tell me about the Cooper investigation?"

"Nothing," I said and tried to step around him again.

"Okay," he said, blocking my way again. "Back to my story, then. Why reopen the inquiry now? Has new evidence come to light on the John David Sawyer case? Was the family hiding something all these years?"

This time it was Esme who crowded into his space, and he did step back. "We have no comment about anything. But I would like to know what's got a burr under your saddle when it comes to Senator Sawyer? Is this about your uncle Russell?"

Esme was now nose to nose with Deese, though she had to bend down to accomplish that.

"Uncle Russell?" he said. "Who is Uncle Russell? I just want a statement. Anything you can tell me. Was the fire intentional?"

I looked back at the hotel and saw a man wearing the hotel blazer watching us as he spoke into a walkie-talkie. I raised my hands slowly as if in surrender.

Within seconds security guards came charging out and suddenly Deese was the one answering questions. *No, of course he wasn't trying to rob us. Freedom of the press, yada yada.*

Esme and I demurred when asked if we'd like to press charges and went on our way, leaving the guards to deal with Deese.

"How did he hear about this?" I hissed once we were out of earshot.

"Lots of people know," Esme said. "I mean aside from those we've talked with, they discussed it with us in the middle of a crowded restaurant. Anyone could've overheard. The question is, what's this guy's deal? Either he's a good actor or this has nothing to do with his distant kin in Quinn County."

"Well, you heard what Lily Rose said, he's just a stringer. He's probably trying to parlay the interest he stirred up with that story on the senator into a staff job somewhere."

"Maybe, but it seems more personal," Esme said.

I opened the door of Esme's SUV and prepared to climb in. This was no challenge for Esme but it left me wishing for ropes and pulleys or maybe a small catapult. Just then Patricia Benson came roaring into the parking lot in a silver Jaguar, hardly slowing as she whipped into the space behind us.

She didn't notice us until she was out of the car, jerking at the strap of her handbag, which seemed to be caught on something inside the car.

"Oh, hey," she said, wresting it loose with a grunt.

"You don't use the valet service?" I asked.

"I'm going out again in a little bit and it takes more time than it's worth," Patricia said. "I'm going stir-crazy."

Esme turned her gaze to the hotel, then looked back at Patricia. "I can think of worse places to go crazy in."

"I know, I know," Patricia said. "Who complains about staying in a place like this? It's wonderful, lovely, expensive, extravagant, all those good things, but I just need to get *out*. I'm so desperate I volunteered to take the thank-you notes to the post office."

"Have you changed your mind about going to Lincoln's funeral?" I asked.

"No, we'll go over in the morning. Aunt Lenora would expect us to stay with her and it's nice of her to offer, but she has a houseful and I'd rather have cabin fever here in the lap of luxury than sleep on a futon in her den."

We looked up to see Chad Deese crossing into the parking lot at the far end. He caught sight of us and turned abruptly to take a meandering path to his car. I wasn't much surprised to see it was a beat-up Toyota. He drove past us, rolling down his window. "Nice trick," he called. "I'll be in touch."

"Who's that?" Patricia asked as Esme muttered under her breath, giving Deese the death stare.

"The guy who wrote that piece that upset the senator and Lenora," I said. "He's somehow found out we've been hired. We were trying to figure how he got wind of it."

"Well, don't look at me," Patricia said. "Marc won't let me talk to reporters unless he's there to pull my foot out of my mouth. I don't have much tolerance for imbecilic questions. That's another thing I'm trying to work on."

"I expect you'll have to build up a tolerance if you want to be in public life," Esme said.

"I know," she said with a sigh. "I'm a work in progress. Hey, I'm glad I ran into you. There are a few things up in Mother's room that got left out of that box of family stuff. We were looking at them when Chelsea boxed everything up and they didn't get put back in. Do you want to come back up and get them now or shall I bring them to you later?"

I glanced at my watch. "We'll come up with you," I

said, hoping whatever I could glean from the missing items might wrap up the job we were doing for Dinah Leigh. Maybe Emma's missing blue envelope would be in this batch. I hate loose ends.

We followed Patricia, chatting along the way. It struck me how different she was when she was away from her family. She was friendly, engaged—and likable. *This* Patricia could be a very appealing candidate, at least as far as campaigning was concerned. I knew nothing of her politics.

Once in the suite, we heard sounds coming from the adjoining room, Chelsea's. Patricia frowned and went to investigate. The door was open a crack and when she swung it wide, Marc stood abruptly and slammed a desk drawer closed.

"What are you doing in Chelsea's room?" Patricia asked.

"Looking for a highlighter," Marc said. He came back into the suite, closing the door behind him. "I was working on the talk you're giving to that men's club." He gestured toward the table. "I wanted to highlight the important points you should cover."

We all glanced toward the papers. The top page was striped with neon yellow and a highlighter was beside it on the desk.

He looked over to where we were staring and lifted a shoulder. "It went dry," he said.

Patricia picked up the sheaf of papers and thumbed through them, a neon glow lighting up every page.

"Well, Marc," she said, "you certainly know how to sort out what's important and what's not."

"Wish I could say the same for you, Patricia," he said, grabbing the papers and stalking from the room.

"Alas, no blue envelope," I said once we were back in the car and I'd had a chance to look at the items Patricia had given us. "Three snapshots, a couple of Christmas cards, and a receipt for a new car, a nineteen forty-nine Ford. The Nelsons paid $1,652 for it. They got a whole car for what we'd pay in taxes and fees these days. Oh, and here's a photo of their father, Herbert, standing next to the car. This is the first one I've seen of him standing. He was short. And their mother, Marie, was petite, too. Conrad obviously got a recessive tall gene."

"It happens," Esme said. "I'm taller than either of my parents."

"You're taller than almost everyone. Works in reverse, too. Dad was a six-footer, Mom was average height, and I'm a shorty."

"You're quality, darlin', not quantity," Esme said. She took a hand off the wheel to reach up and rub her temple. I recognized this gesture well enough.

"Esme, are you getting something?"

"Something from someone about something," she said. "Or maybe I've just been studying everything we've collected about that fire too hard. Or maybe it's got nothing to do with that. I keep seeing a man's hand, a rough, work-hardened hand. It's reaching for something, and then there's terrible pain."

"Pain in the hand?" I asked.

Esme nodded. "Just unbearable pain. Kind of sums up both of these jobs we've taken on. Except our pain is in a different body region."

"Do you know that even when bodies are burned for two hours at two thousand degrees there are still bone fragments left?" Esme asked.

"No," I said, uncurling from my hunched position over the family tree. "But that's a really horrifying bit of info, thanks for that."

"I know," Esme said, "but it's got me bothered up. I read through all the reports and it doesn't seem like the fire at the Sawyer house lasted nearly that long. And another thing, do you recall what Lily Rose told us about Margaret Sawyer keeping the window in the baby's room down 'cause there was a hole in the screen?"

"Yeah," I said, warily. "What about it?"

"In this picture here," she said, getting up to bring a printout over, "you can see there's no screen on that window, none at all. But there's one over here propped against the pump house. You can make it out even in these old grainy photos."

I shrugged. "Maybe the people fighting the fire took it down. Or it fell off when the heat distorted it or something. What are you thinking?" I asked.

"I don't know. Mostly I'm just thinking we're in a strange position with this job. We're essentially *hoping* to find out the baby died in that fire. It's wearing on me."

"Oh, Esme, we're not hoping for that. We're simply looking for the truth. Just like we always do."

"Yes," Esme said, "but in this case we've been hired to prove that baby died and at the same time that the parents weren't mentally unbalanced for claiming he didn't. We're walking a tightrope. And I feel my legs starting to tremble."

The doorbell saved me from having to answer, which was good because I had nothing. I pulled the door open with the intention of dispatching whoever it was so I could get back to work, but I was dumbstruck to find Dinah Leigh's aunt Yvonne standing on our front porch and a taxi idling in our driveway.

"I need to talk to you," she said. "He'll wait." She jerked her head toward the cab.

It took me a moment to find my manners. "Of course," I said. "Please come in."

"The other one, too. Your partner, that tall drink of

water, I need to talk to both of you. I'll make it quick," Yvonne said.

I ushered her into the family room and went across the hall to get Esme. I was wondering how I might've offended this old woman since she was clearly put out about something. I couldn't come up with anything other than the fact that she didn't like what I do for a living, which she'd already made quite clear.

I offered tea or coffee and Yvonne waved the offer away, but lifted her cigarette pack and trusty Zippo in our direction. "Mind if I smoke?"

"Yes," Esme answered. "It gets in the upholstery and stinks to high heaven. If you need to smoke, we'll move this out onto the patio."

"Lead the way," Yvonne said, not at all fazed by Esme's less-than-gracious hospitality.

We settled around the patio table and waited as she lit up. "Okay, here's the deal," she said. "You've got to keep Conrad from doing that DNA crap."

"Well, first off, I can't prevent him from doing whatever he wants," I said. "But is there a particular reason?"

"Yes," Yvonne said. She fell silent, her lips set in a hard line. She sat still as a stone for a long while. Finally she picked a bit of tobacco off her tongue with her fingertips and let out a long, forlorn sigh.

"Conrad's adopted," she said. "It was a closed adoption. *Very* closed. Nailed-shut-forever closed. At least it was supposed to be before all this techno-mumbo-jumbo came along."

"Well, that's interesting, but not earth-shattering," Esme said, waving away the smoke curling in her direction. "Times have changed. There's no stigma on adoption anymore."

"Maybe not," Yvonne said. "But his mother didn't want him to know and I promised her he never would. And I know what's going to be your next question. Dinah Leigh's not. They got her the natural way. But my sister couldn't hold on to another baby. Three miscarriages in four years. That's the reason they moved up next to me. Herbert was worried about Marie—she got so bad off in her mind he was afraid she'd hurt herself. And he got the idea if they'd adopt a baby that would fix everything."

"Okay," I said. "But why all the secrecy? It must've been obvious to anybody who knew them that they had a new baby. Where did people think he came from?"

"Marie faked being pregnant. Well, she didn't fake it exactly. She was pregnant when they came to live with me, but she lost it right afterwards. She just went on pretending she was carrying. That's how bad she wanted everybody to believe whatever baby they got was hers and Herbert's," Yvonne said. "But it needed to happen quick if Marie's story was to hold up."

"And where did they find this baby?" Esme asked.

"Back in those days there was a little general store just down the road from where I lived. It was owned by a family named Leggett, a shoestring operation if ever there was one. There was a whole mess of those Leggetts, most of 'em was no-accounts. Total white trash. Anyhow, Marie and Herbert didn't have but the one car and Herbert needed it to get to work. So Marie would walk down to that store every morning and buy a soft drink or get something to make supper or whatever, and she got friendly with the Leggett daughter that minded the counter in the summertime. She was about fifteen at that time, and lo and behold, the little slut was bloomed-up pregnant. So you see where this is going?"

"But it doesn't jibe with what I've found in Conrad's records," I said.

"Records are just pieces of paper," Yvonne said. "The thing is, Herbert and Marie never wanted Conrad or Dinah Leigh to know he was adopted and the parents have rights. That doesn't end 'cause they're dead and gone now. I want their wishes honored. And besides, the adoption wasn't exactly on the up-and-up, and there might be those willing to make trouble about it, even all these years later. So you've got to talk him out of that DNA test."

"We are in no position to tell Conrad what to do," I said. "He's a grown man. And in terms of the DNA test, unless Dinah Leigh has hers run, too, there'd be nothing to compare his to, so it might not come to light at all. But now that we have this information, we're obligated to tell Dinah Leigh and Conrad."

"Well, you can't," Yvonne said, stubbing out her cigarette on the wire mesh table I'd just repainted. "I don't give my permission to reveal anything I've told you."

"We don't need it," Esme said. "You're not our client."

Yvonne jutted out her chin and stared at Esme for a long moment, then reached into her handbag for her wallet. She took out a dollar bill and slammed it down on the table. "There," she said, "that's my retainer. Now I'm your client, so you have to do as I say."

"That only works on TV lawyers," Esme said.

"So you're saying you're going to tell them?" Yvonne said, her normally growly voice rising to a phlegmy screech.

"We'll have to think about it and do some more investigation," I said, not at all sure I believed her story.

"In that case, everything I told you just now was a bald-faced lie. Conrad is the natural child of Herbert and Marie Nelson. Period. And you won't be able to find a scrap of paper that says anything different. And thanks for the tip—I'll make sure Dinah Leigh doesn't get her DNA unscrambled. Otherwise, thanks for nothing and mind your own damn business."

"This is our business," I said.

She huffed and lit another cigarette, and as she

pulled a long drag, she started fiddling with the lighter, opening it and snapping it shut with her thumb. Clearly it was a nervous habit for her as it was for Cyrus Hamilton. The sound sequence was almost hypnotic.

"Listen, you two, if you tell anybody about this, I'm going to say I was testing you to show Conrad what a crock this all is. You can't go back and relive the past. No matter how much some folks wish they could." She got up abruptly and snatched her bag. "There are things that happen in this life that need to be taken to the grave, not put out for all the world to gossip over. Now you two keep your noses out of our family business." With that, she marched around the corner of the house and a moment later we heard a car door slam.

"What in the name of all that's holy are we supposed to do now?" Esme asked.

"Our jobs," I said, suddenly feeling exhausted. "I hate sketchy adoptions."

Esme patted my arm. "I'm sorry, darlin'. This hits a little too close to home, doesn't it?"

It did. My mother had been adopted under unusual circumstances. At least that's the way everyone who knows about it describes it. A better description would be highly illegal, grossly exploitative circumstances. My mother had conflicting feelings about this all her life. On the one hand, she'd had loving adoptive parents. And because she was here, and not back in the

Marshall Islands where she'd been born to an impoverished young mother, she'd had many opportunities in life. She'd met my dad, the love of her life, and they had me. She'd been happy and felt grateful for all that. Yet she knew nothing at all about her birth culture, or the family she came from, or how her adoption came about, and she'd been hungry to know those things. Her parents had refused to discuss it with her, telling her it was best to look to the future and not dwell in the past, which had only inflamed her need to know. She'd spent her entire adult life trying to find information about her birth family. That's what drew me to genealogy in the first place. When I was in high school she died with her questions left unanswered. As a tribute, I picked up the challenge. But even with all my training and the tools available to me, I hadn't been able to crack the wall—not yet. Not for my mother or for myself, but maybe I could for Conrad.

I pinched the discarded cigarette, lifting it by the rolling paper to avoid touching the filter.

"Get me a baggie, would you, Esme? I think we'll hang on to this."

eleven

Esme and I tried to get back to work, but both of us were too agitated to concentrate. What was our obligation here? Technically our client was Dinah Leigh. She was the one who'd hired us. Most likely she'd be unhappy with this outcome—if it was true. But was it? What possible motive could Yvonne Bayley have had to tell us Conrad was adopted if it never happened? And why was she so sure we wouldn't be able to prove it with a paper trail?

"I can't sit still," Esme said. "I'm gonna walk down to my house. I want to look at the color of the kitchen in the daylight. Come with me and tell me what you think."

It was a glorious spring afternoon and getting out into the fresh air helped clear my head for a reality check. We might have to concede defeat on at least one of these projects, now maybe both. "Esme, remember you scolded me that morning at the spa about jinxing us? I think I did it. We're snakebit on both these jobs."

"You said that, not me," Esme said, transferring a box of cookbooks she had braced against her hip from one side to the other. She'd made it a habit of taking something to her new house each time she went there so on final move-in day there wouldn't be so much to handle. I was initially pleased to see her carrying the awkward box since I thought it would slow her down, and honestly, you'd think the three-inch wedges she was wearing would have been enough to ease the pace, but I was still forced to double-time.

"So what's our obligation on Conrad's job?" I asked aloud, though I was really only talking to myself. "First we need to investigate Yvonne's claim and see if there's any substance to it." Then I remembered something Conrad had said that afternoon. That his aunt Yvonne couldn't have any deep secrets because she'd only worked a civil service job all her life. Maybe that's how she knew there'd be no paper trail. Maybe she'd made sure of that.

"Since we're thinking out loud here," Esme said, "I'm still trying to figure out why Yvonne is so all-fired set on keeping the adoption a secret. It might be a little jolt, but for pity's sake, it's not like they're little kids. They've lived as brother and sister for all these years; I'd say they're bonded by now. What if Yvonne's concern is for herself? What if Conrad is actually her child?

Wouldn't be the first time a woman has taken a sister's or a daughter's uh-oh baby and passed it off as her own. She might have invented that whole story about the storekeeper girl as a cover."

"That's a thought," I said. "She never married and if she was anything back then like she is now, I don't think motherhood would have appealed to her. And aside from any fear she might have about them being hurt by the deception, there are other, more practical, considerations. Dinah Leigh and Conrad look after her now, financially and in other ways. Their devotion might cool if they found out she'd been lying to them all these years. I think I'll hold off on finishing Conrad's tree and go back to digging. I don't suppose you've gotten anything about this from your back channel."

"No, it's just me playing what-if. Nothing from beyond."

"Speaking of which, this afternoon when you met Cyrus Hamilton, there was a strange look on your face. Were you getting something then?"

"No, it just struck me that he looked familiar and I couldn't figure out where I'd met him. In fact, I was pretty sure I hadn't. Then I realized it was something about the way he put out his hand, like a politician, and his speech pattern that put me in mind of Senator Stan. He even looks a little like him, though he's heavier and fuller-faced. I guess it must be the Quinn County look."

"Except he's not from Quinn County. He's from out in the mountains. Though he's got roots there. His grandparents are from Quinn County and that's where his father and mother both grew up. I can't believe I forgot to tell you this right away, but it's been a busy day. Cyrus's father was the farm manager for Alton Sawyer for a short while. He was there the day of the fire. Cyrus said he'd ask if he'd be willing to talk with us about it."

"An actual eyewitness? Other than Lenora and Senator Stan, I mean. But he's got to be elderly; how's his memory?"

"Cyrus claims it's good. We'll find out if we get a chance to talk with him."

When we got to Esme's house, Denny's car was in the driveway. We found him in the kitchen propping a freshly painted slab of scrap plasterboard against the kitchen wall.

"Oh, hey," he said. "I picked up the new paint and made you a sample. You can look at this for a couple of days and make sure it's what you want."

"What are you doing with this silly business?" Esme asked. "Aren't you on duty?"

"Yep, on my lunch break. I'll grab a burger later. I just needed to get out of my own head for a little bit."

"Denton, leave this be," Esme said, "it can wait till the case is solved."

"That may be a long wait," Denny said. "I don't have

a motive, or a reasonable pool of suspects, and we have scant physical evidence. And almost no one we've questioned has a reliable alibi, so until we know *why* Cooper was killed, I can't even rely on the process of elimination. I'm still just harvesting information and hoping something will eventually click."

"Have you learned *anything* helpful?" I asked.

"Maybe. Cooper's phone records came in. The number he tried to call after Emma saw him and Chelsea Bremer fighting belongs to J. D. Morgan."

"How long did the call last?" I asked.

"Three calls. Not long ones. It may be he only connected with voice mail but Cooper called the number three times in a row, about half past midnight. So it must have been important."

I told him about our earlier run-in with Chad Deese. "According to him, he's one suspect you've been able to check off your list."

"That what he says?" Denny asked. "He's a little premature. He claims he was with some people from over in Chapel Hill, but they've been hard to track down. That's where I'm headed when I leave here."

"Did you notice his black eye when you talked to him?"

"Jennifer's the one who questioned him, and yes, she asked about it. He claims he got it at the gym when a hand weight slipped."

"I'm betting a hand weight named Lincoln Cooper," Esme said.

"Haven't ruled that out," Denny said.

"I think that was him parked outside our house yesterday, too."

"Now, I don't like the sound of that one bit," Denny said. "If he shows up again, call me."

"We can take care of him," Esme said.

"Don't underestimate him, Esme," Denny said.

She gave him a dismissive flap of her hand.

"I mean it," he said. "The guy may look harmless, but he's got a reputation for having a bad temper."

"We'll call," I said.

Esme tilted her head while her eyes went from the paint sample back to the wall. "You know, now that the paint is dry and I see it in natural light, I think I like the original color fine."

"You'd better be sure," Denny said, "because I am not painting it a third time."

"I'm sure," she said decisively. "We'll leave it alone."

"That's the best news I've heard lately," Denny said. "So you can move in anytime."

"Not so fast," Esme said. "There's still a leak in that upstairs shower and I'm changing out a couple of the windows in the back that have wood rot. It'll be a while yet. And besides, we're knee-deep in two troublesome jobs of our own."

"You making any progress on the fire report?"

"No," I said, "we're finding out more, but everything we hit on seems to take us further from our goal. If I didn't dislike the idea of disappointing the senator and Lenora, I think I'd bail on that one right now."

"Except your curiosity would kill you, little cat," Esme said.

"True," I admitted. "What do you think about it, Denny? Did you look at those records you got for us?"

"I skimmed them. It was poor work," Denny said, "but I don't know if it was incompetence or something worse. I know the Sawyers lived out in the country, but lots of people showed up there during and after the fire. Seemed to me the witness statements were too sparse. And the ones that were taken didn't get much follow-up. But it's easy to criticize from the vantage point of all these years later. Maybe it was just good people, without much training or many resources, trying their best to do their jobs. And speaking of which, I'd best get back to mine right now."

When he got to the doorway he turned. "I know I don't need to say this, but I trust you two will let me know if you pick up on anything you think I should look into, even if it makes people around the senator uncomfortable."

"It goes without saying, but you said it anyway," Esme said dryly.

"In this case, I felt the need," Denny said. "You're on the inside and I'm outside looking in. Just keep your ears open, will you?"

I assured him we would before Esme had a chance to snip at him again. He came back to plant a kiss on her cheek and as he turned to go, he gave her a firm pat on her behind.

She gasped as if her dignity had been affronted, but I saw the smile.

We walked through the house so I could see the progress that had been made since the last time I'd been over. I found it easy to imagine Esme living here. It was the perfect place for her, and I loved the fact that it was so close by.

As she closed the kitchen door behind us and wrestled with the still-unfamiliar lock, my cell rang. I was surprised to see Cyrus Hamilton's name on the display.

"Hope you don't mind," he said. "I got your number from Lily Rose. I just wanted to let you know I spoke with my father and he'll talk with you about the fire. But he warns he doesn't think he knows anything that can help with what they've asked of you."

"I look forward to talking with him," I said. "You never said where he lives. Is he within driving distance, or could we arrange a video interview?"

"He's in an assisted-living place in Quinn County. My cousin lives nearby, and with me traveling so much,

I wanted him near family. But there's no need to drive out there. I'll pick him up after the funeral tomorrow and bring him back to the hotel for a couple of weeks. As I think I mentioned, he hasn't seen the place yet and I want him to have some time here with me. Let's plan for late morning the day after tomorrow," Cyrus said. "Dad's at his best before noon. You know, it's funny, much as he esteems the Sawyers, he's never wanted to talk with me much about his time with them, especially about the fire."

"They say time heals all wounds," I said.

"Yes, well, I don't know if Stanton and Lenora would agree with that," he said.

Back at my house, I gathered everything we had on Conrad and Dinah Leigh's family and spread it all out on the table. Then I set in on an Internet search on Yvonne Bayley, which yielded very little.

"Conrad was right," I told Esme. "She's lived a pretty quiet life. And her civil service job? Guess where. The health department. And guess who issued the birth certificates in that county. No wonder she's so sure we won't be able to follow a paper trail to find Conrad's biological parents. She created the trail."

"She doesn't know you, sweet pea. She may think she's thrown you off, but she's only put you on the scent."

"Yeah, well, I like a challenge as much as the next person, but I was planning on this being a quick, clearly defined job. Now, not so much."

"What else have you learned?" Esme asked, nodding toward the computer.

"I know she lived in the house her parents left to her. I guess they figured Marie was set since she was married, so they left what little they had to Yvonne. And there *was* a little general store nearby run by a man named Leggett. But I only found that because he was cited for operating without a business license—twice, actually. And he did have a daughter who would've been fifteen the year Conrad was born. She's now deceased, as are her mother, father, and two older brothers. No record she ever had a child."

"Which proves nothing," Esme said. "If it happened the way Yvonne claims, I'm betting the baby wasn't born in a hospital."

"Maybe that's all this is about for Yvonne. She thinks she'd get in trouble for whatever she did to doctor the records, and maybe she would. There might be some prosecutable offense there still, and old woman or not, they might decide to hold her accountable."

"If they knew her personally I suspect they'd be happy to throw the book at her, her being so charming and all," Esme said.

"I hate the idea of bringing all this to Conrad right

now. His wedding is so close and he's so happy. I don't like to be the one to rain on that. And I wonder how Phoebe would react. What's your take on her, Esme?"

"I only talked to her briefly," Esme said. "But she seems nice enough."

"Patricia seems to think she's a gold digger," I said.

"Patricia is a harsh critic of everything and everybody," Esme said. "Dinah Leigh likes Phoebe fine and she's very protective of Conrad. That tells me something."

"I wonder if it'd make any difference to Phoebe if she found out he was adopted."

"I don't know why it would," Esme said.

"Unless she *is* a gold digger," I said. "And a very calculating one who orchestrated their whole romance to get near the Dodd fortune."

"But that's the thing," Esme said. "Dinah Leigh and Conrad grew up as brother and sister, and they're both way along in life now. It wouldn't change Dinah Leigh's feelings toward him. Oh, she might be devastated at first, but—"

"Yes, she might be," I said, sitting up straighter in the chair, "she might be *devastated*. Esme, could this have been what Chelsea and Lincoln were really arguing about the night he was killed?"

"How would they have learned about it?" Esme asked.

"Maybe the same way we did, through Yvonne, or maybe something in that box. The blue envelope! Emma said Chelsea reacted funny when she read whatever was in that blue envelope. Maybe it was something to do with the adoption."

"If there was an adoption, Sophreena. We still don't even know if Yvonne's story is true. You know, that's the thing I like best about dead people. I may not always understand what they're trying to tell me, but they never lie."

We spent the day of the funeral examining and ordering the facts we'd already found out about the fire, and as Esme was searching for more, I dug deeper into Conrad's family history, wallowing in the quandary of what to do about Yvonne's revelation. Obviously I couldn't conceal it. That would be a breach of professional ethics. It'd kill us professionally if it came to light later that she'd been telling the truth and that we knew about it. And if that came to pass I was sure the lovely Aunt Yvonne would gladly volunteer our guilty knowledge.

But perhaps I could delay it, until after the wedding. Maybe give Dinah Leigh a sealed report and ask her not to read it until after the wedding.

And I *could* leave the tree as it was. After all, the records were all in order. I'd scrutinized them down to the last jot and tittle and nothing seemed amiss. I had no way to prove or disprove Yvonne's contentions with what was available to me.

I'd halfway talked myself into that plan. Maybe with a nice accompanying greeting card: *Congratulations on the marriage of your not-quite brother*.

Not an appealing prospect.

After mulling it over for hours I'd realized this wasn't about adoption, it was about deception. If it came out that Dinah Leigh and Conrad weren't blood siblings, they would adjust to the idea, but coming to grips with their parents' lies might prove more difficult. And since Aunt Yvonne was the only one left who had a part in it, they could turn their ire on her. That was probably what she feared.

So what could Yvonne's motive be to tell us that story unless there was at least some truth to it? I was really warming to Esme's theory that Yvonne might be Conrad's biological mother. That would be a secret worth protecting, given the circumstances.

I could only think of one way to get more answers. I retrieved the bag with the cigarette stub from my desk drawer and filled out the form to send it in for testing. I felt not one twinge of apprehension where Yvonne was concerned. She'd raised all these questions and she'd unwittingly given us the means to an answer.

I sealed the envelope and checked the calendar.

There was no way the results would arrive before the wedding, even if I paid the exorbitant fee for rushed processing. So I still had the dilemma of what to do about the family tree.

I'd spent the morning tracking down every Leggett I could find who could be related to the storeowners and had spoken to three of them by phone. All were too young to have any memory of the relatives I asked about, much less any adoption shenanigans. One was gracious and apologetic that she couldn't help, another seemed hopelessly confused by my questions, and the third told me to take his number off my calling list or he'd report me to the Do Not Call Registry and hung up on me.

I was tired and irritable and sick of this job. Esme and I talked it over and made the decision that we'd finish the tree as the information stood so Dinah Leigh could give it to Conrad on his wedding day, but we'd give her the verbal caveat that we were still investigating some irregularities. Then when the DNA report came back we'd give them all the info we had.

I looked over the tree. It would take me maybe two more hours to finish it up. It was visually beautiful, if I did say so myself, but as family history it was very likely counterfeit. Every fiber of my being hated the idea of delivering it as authentic, but it seemed the only viable plan.

Now if we could only make progress with our other

nettlesome job. As Esme continued the search online, I reviewed everything again and prepared a list of questions for Cyrus Hamilton's father. This did nothing to improve my mood. At mid-afternoon Esme had to go to her house to let the plumbers in and I wandered aimlessly around the empty house, too frustrated to work. I made a halfhearted attempt to tidy my bedroom, putting away the folded clothes that had been sitting in a laundry basket for more than a week. I stuffed my T-shirts into a dresser drawer and nudged it shut, then opened the top drawer reserved for miscellaneous junk and rummaged through until I found the Zippo that had been my grandfather's. I clicked it open and thumbed the striker, but it didn't spark. I shook it. No fuel, probably no flint either. I closed the lid, using two fingers to flip it shut. Then I cupped it in my hand and tried to flick it open as I'd seen Cyrus do. It took a little practice, but once I had the motion down it was very satisfying. And Lily Rose was right; the sound was very distinctive. *Click-hiss-clack.*

I decided to visit Lily Rose again. I had the feeling we were going to fail at this job and it was important to me that she knew we'd given it our best and that neither Esme nor I took defeat lightly. I wanted her to hear that from me.

*   *   *

Sarah let me into the room and spoke softly. "She's not doing as well as yesterday."

"I can come back another time if she's not up for a visit."

"No, please," Sarah said. "She'd love to see you and when you called, I made an appointment downstairs. With all that's happened I haven't even been down to the spa since we arrived. I could really use a massage. Will that be okay? Can you stay that long?"

"If she can't, I'll be fine," a voice came from across the room where Lily Rose sat by the window. "My legs don't work very well today, but my ears are dandy. Please, Sarah, go on, and take your time. You've hardly left this room in days. Sophreena and I will have a nice visit and if she has to leave, I will distract myself with mindless television until you return. I can't get into any trouble with that agenda."

"How I wish I could spare her worries about me," Lily Rose said as the door closed behind Sarah. "She doesn't need that on top of her struggles as a temporary single parent, and to a teenager no less! Emma's a good girl at heart, but she can strain against the traces with the best of them."

"Emma's a delight," I said, and meant it.

"You surely can't believe a grandmother would disagree," Lily Rose said. "And Damon is a handsome, smart fellow, but he's got much to learn about how to get on gracefully in the world. He, too, can still give Sarah gray hairs, even if he is a grown man."

"I understand he's to head the foundation," I said.

"Yes," Lily Rose said with a sigh. "I hope he's up to the task. I think that's one reason Stan is so set on having everything absolutely beyond challenge. He doesn't want to give the boy a handicap out of the gate on his first big job."

I told her about my planned meeting with Cyrus's father the next day.

"Well, that'll be lovely. So he's coming here? I haven't seen Luther in years. He was always faithful to come by and say hello to Stanton if we were there when he was back in Quinn County to visit his folks, but after they passed, the visits became less frequent and finally just stopped altogether."

"He's agreed to talk with me about what he remembers. Cyrus says his memory is still sharp, so maybe I'll learn something new," I said, feeling like a fraud, since I sincerely doubted we were going to find anything of use.

"Maybe," Lily Rose said. "He would've been a very young man back then, so the memories certainly won't be fresh."

"Yes, a very young man," I said, frowning as I did the math. "But he was the farm manager, right? Not a hired hand."

"That's right," Lily Rose said. "He was a pretty

remarkable young man. I'm told Alton gave him almost complete autonomy in running the farm. Which was unusual because, first off, Alton Sawyer was a very hands-on kind of man. He was slow to delegate and always imagined he knew how to do things best. And secondly, Luther didn't even come from a farming family. His folks had both been teachers. He knew little about farming when he came to work for Alton, but he was a quick study and a natural-born manager. He was soon running the whole operation with Alton's complete confidence."

"Did he live on the property?" I asked.

"No, he had a little house about three or four miles as the crow flies. He was a married man by then, though not a happily married one."

"Oh?" I asked.

"This is all gossip, you understand. Mother Meg spoke of it to me; she was very fond of Luther and distressed about how his wife acted. Luther had married a young woman who made it clear she felt she'd made a bad match in hitching herself to a farm manager. She'd come from a family of means. I don't know what they did or anything else about them except that Mother Meg thought they looked down on Luther. As it went, I guess Luther told her he wanted to stay on with the Sawyers for a few more seasons and she up and left him without a by-your-leave and went back to her folks. I forget where they lived—down in Tennessee, maybe? Anyway, Luther was crushed when she left him, but he had his pride and he didn't go after her. Everybody thought it was the end of the marriage. But then the tragedy struck and the Sawyers moved away and Luther went west to manage that little motel for his brother. Nearly a year later his runaway wife showed up on his doorstep with a curly-haired toddler she'd never even deigned to let him know he'd got on her."

"Cyrus?" I asked.

"Cyrus," she said. "They patched things up and apparently lived happily ever after, especially after Luther started to prosper in the hospitality industry. Mother Meg was always so impressed with how well Luther treated his in-laws, even after their harsh judgment of him in the early years. She saw that as a real testament to his character. And I do, too. I've always liked that story about him."

"I like it, too," I said.

"Is something troubling you, Sophreena?" she asked, and I realized I'd gone silent and was staring out the window, probably with a frown on my face.

"Yes," I said. "Things aren't going real well with the job. I'm afraid we're not going to be able to give the senator and Lenora what they asked for and I feel we're failing them. And you."

"Nonsense, Sophreena," she said. "Both Stanton

and Lenora have lived with this conundrum. They appreciate how tangled it is. Do what you can and don't fret over it."

Easier said than done, I thought, but Lily Rose's kindness disarmed me. "I'm just discouraged right now because we've got two challenging jobs at once. This job for Dinah Leigh is turning out to be quite complicated, too. I'm having some trouble tracking down some things their aunt Yvonne told me."

"Yvonne," Lily Rose said with a huff. "You'll think me a terrible person for saying so, but that woman would try the patience of a saint. I think that must be where Patricia got her acid tongue. I never knew Dinah Leigh's mother, but those who did say she was a nice lady, nothing at all like Yvonne."

A nice lady who may have been quite willing to take advantage of a young girl's dire circumstances, I thought. Or fake a pregnancy to hide an illegal adoption.

"Did you know Dinah Leigh's father?" I asked.

"I met him once. He was sort of a morose man. Course, I don't know what he was like when he was younger. He was an elderly man by the time I met him and quite ill. Cancer, as I recall. It was a lingering death, something I don't really care to think about given my prospects."

I knew better than to speak pretty, empty words to Lily Rose on this subject. She understood her own situation and faced it with stalwart resolve. I searched my mental databank on Conrad's family tree. "So his wife predeceased him by almost twenty years," I said. "Did he live alone after that?"

"For a while I think he did. He was in pretty bad shape by the time he went to live with Dinah Leigh and Preston. He was there for some time, but eventually, given the level of care he needed, they decided it was best to move him to a facility near their home. He was there until the end."

"Conrad tells me he doted on Dinah Leigh," I said. "She must've taken it hard when he died."

"She did," Lily Rose said. "She loved her mother, too, of course, but I think she was especially close with her father. I never witnessed it myself, but they say Marie wore the pants in that family. Back then they would've called him henpecked. I am so glad you young people have evolved to the point where a young man can appreciate a strong woman and not be threatened by her."

"Your lips to God's ears, Lily Rose. I'm not sure we've quite completed that evolutionary process, but we're moving in the right direction."

Lily Rose laughed, then abruptly her laughter died away and she fished in her sleeve for a tissue. "I feel guilty being lighthearted about anything today as they prepare to put Lincoln to rest. I think of his poor father and wonder how he can bear this burden alone. Though I think he and Stanton are very alike in that way; they prefer to keep their feelings inside. In fact he and Stanton are alike in many ways. I hope they'll keep a good friendship now that they've endured this shared loss. It would help both of them."

I thought of the morning I saw Senator Stan greeting Lincoln's father and how they'd walked away, two proud tall men, a decade apart in age, both bent with grief but so attuned to each other. I had the feeling it was a bond that would endure.

twelve

I ARRIVED THIRTY MINUTES EARLY FOR MY APPOINT-
ment the following day with Cyrus's father, Luther. I
was hoping for a chance to talk with Chelsea. I wanted
to see how she was holding up, but I also wanted to ask
about that blue envelope. It was bugging me that an artifact was missing, especially given the train wreck this
job had become.

I was told she'd gone for a walk, and I knew where
I'd find her. Sure enough, she was sitting on the same
mossy embankment where we'd talked before. She assured me I wasn't intruding and I settled down beside
her, regretting my decision to wear khaki pants instead
of jeans.

"Everyone was wonderful to me," she said in response to my question about the funeral. "I'd only seen
Lincoln's father a few times, but he treated me like
family. They certainly raise some wonderful men out

in Quinn County. Mr. Cooper reminds me so much of
Senator Stan, courtly and kind. Lincoln had told him all
about us, so he knew what Lincoln's loss meant to me.
Seems practically everyone in the universe knew about
us. How could we have been so oblivious? We thought
we were so discreet."

"And how do you feel about them knowing?" I
asked.

She picked up a pebble and threw it in the water,
watching the disturbance spread into a circle. "I guess
it makes it easier to grieve because I don't have to hide
anything anymore, but really, what difference does it all
make now? All the things I feared about revealing our
relationship don't apply anymore. Lincoln's gone. And
so are our plans for the future."

I wanted so badly to ask her about the argument
they had the night Lincoln died, but even if I'd been
able to explain how I knew about it, I could see this
wasn't the time.

"I know this is a terrible time to be asked about
work details," I said, "and this is a trivial thing, but I
was wondering if you remembered seeing a blue envelope with a letter or some papers inside the box of
Dinah Leigh's that you inventoried for us."

"Blue envelope?" Chelsea asked, turning to pick up
another pebble. She took a long beat before she went
on—too long in my estimation. "No," she said, drawing

out the word. "I don't remember seeing a blue envelope. What was in it?"

"Not sure," I said. "Emma thought she remembered
seeing it when she was helping you go through the
things."

"Did she say what it was?" Chelsea asked, throwing
another pebble into the lake.

"I don't think she knows," I said. "She said you
looked it over and set it aside. I thought maybe it was
something you wanted to talk with us about."

There, I'd given her every opportunity to walk this
back, but she didn't take it.

"No, I don't remember anything like that," Chelsea
said. "But if it comes to me I'll let you know."

And with that she stood and swiped at the seat of
her pants. "I'd better go see if Dinah Leigh needs anything," she said.

I studied her as she walked away without a backward glance. I dusted off the back of my khakis, the
second brush-off I'd experienced in the last thirty seconds. So there *had* been a blue envelope. And it had
contained something important enough to lie about.

Esme had stayed at home because elderly people who
have the tendency to tell meandering tales are not well
matched to her patience reservoir. I, on the other hand,

love old stories and am generally quite fond of old people—Aunt Yvonne being a notable exception.

Luther was just getting back from his tour of the facilities. "We took a golf cart," he said with a laugh. "From that little wayside inn to this." He swung his arm in an arc to take in his surroundings. "In that first little motel we could see all the grounds from the office window, all twenty-five feet of 'em. Now we need a golf cart. We've come a long way, son."

The man was not what I'd expected. He was more slender and shorter than I'd imagined he'd be, given Cyrus's height and bulk. His back was still straight and he was groomed and dressed fastidiously. His hair was clipped close and he wore horn-rimmed glasses that were so retro they were in again. He had on faded blue jeans, a white Oxford button-down shirt, open at the neck to reveal a blue T-shirt underneath, and brown boat shoes without socks. It threw me that he wasn't the wizened old man I'd been expecting.

After Cyrus introduced us, he excused himself to go take care of hotel business and I became acutely aware of my less-than-tailored appearance. But Mr. Hamilton put me immediately at ease.

"Cyrus tells me Stanton and Lenora have hired you and your partner to write a report on the fire that took the baby," Luther said. "I doubt I can tell you anything you don't already know, but he said you wanted to talk with me and I rather like the sound of my own voice, so what is it you'd like to ask me?"

The stopper now out of the bottle, I plowed right in. "I know Cyrus says you don't like to talk about it, but you might know something helpful that you don't even know you know."

"Ah, well," Luther said, "Cyrus knows I don't like to talk about that time in my life. He thinks it's because of the tragedy of the baby dying like that and the parents going just crazy with grief. And that's all true enough. But what he doesn't know because it's still hard for me to talk about, even all these years later, is that for a time they thought the fire was arson and I was considered the prime suspect. Big Jim Ogdon put me square in his sights and accused me of setting that fire. That was a hard thing for me to take."

"Why would he think that?"

"The two of us had a history. He'd arrested one of my farmhands after a bar fight. There was a roomful of witnesses, all of them saying the other guy started it, the other guy being the son of a major contributor to Big Jim's campaign, don't 'cha know. Anyhow, my guy, a kid without two nickels to rub together, was the one who finished it, giving the guy the whooping he deserved. I stood up for the kid and it got ugly, with accusations being thrown in both directions. So the sheriff and I weren't exactly on howdying terms when that fire happened. I spent an uncomfortable couple of weeks getting ground under Big Jim's boot before they finally ruled the fire was caused by an electrical defect. Then they issued the death certificate for the baby and that was that. Except it wasn't, of course. Rumors just kept flying."

"That must've been hard," I said.

"Everything about my life was hard right along in that little stretch," he said. "But it got better and here I am near the end of a long and mostly happy life. Still, no man likes to tell his son he was a suspect in an arson, or a kidnapping, or whatever it was Big Jim imagined had happened in the early stages of that investigation."

"Would you mind telling me the story of how that day unfolded for you? Just tell it how you remember it."

"I can do that," he said. "But let me think on it a minute. That was all so long ago." I waited as he studied the ceiling, gathering his thoughts. "It was hot that morning, even before the sun rose. We were pulling corn on the back forty of the farm, which was at a lower elevation than the house and the outbuildings. There was a rise and a thicket of trees between us and the house. Corn was still pulled by hand back then, so workers walked alongside the tractor, twisting off the ears and tossing them into the trailer. We generally had two tractors operating and staggered them so that one could make the run to the barn and unload while the other was still in the field."

"So they would have been coming to the barn every so often through the day?"

"That was the idea," Luther said, "but that day we had flat tires, one on a tractor, the other on a trailer. We ended up with just one hauler. Half the crew worked pulling corn and the other half getting the tires on the tractor and trailer. I thought about that a lot after what happened. If we hadn't had that streak of bad luck, somebody might've been at the barn and sounded the alert sooner, in time to put the fire out. Maybe baby Johnny could have been saved."

"So what was going on when you arrived at the house?"

"It was blazing, big flames shooting out of the windows and the doorways. There were neighbor men doing their best with garden hoses and buckets of water, but it was too far gone. You couldn't see anything, the smoke was so thick. And despite what got into Miss Margaret's head later on, there was no way the baby could have survived that inferno."

"Did you personally know all the men trying to fight the fire that day?" I asked.

Luther frowned. "No. There was noise and confusion and eventually the fire department with its half-functioning rust bucket of a pumper truck showed up.

Those men came from miles around, so I didn't know all of them. You need to understand what it was like back then. Coventry is a proper little town now with pizza parlors, coffee shops, bagel places, and fake Irish pubs. But back then it was a scruffy little crossroads with scarcely any resources, and out in the country there were even less. Neighbors depended on one another in times of emergency, but your closest neighbor might be a mile away and not everybody had a telephone. And no family I knew back then had more than one automobile. They were lucky to have one."

"Eventually the fire marshal ruled the fire was caused by faulty wiring. You were familiar with the house—would you have any reason to question that?"

"No," Luther said, sitting back in his chair and lacing his fingers over his chest. "No particular reason other than the fire marshal was a horse's ass, pardon my language, with a brain the size of a hummingbird's."

The gentle delivery of such blunt words startled a laugh from me and he looked up and smiled.

"I'm old, Sophreena," he said. "I don't have the energy to parse my words anymore. Truly the man was incompetent. But as I say, it was a volunteer fire department and I doubt he had much training. In his defense, there were a lot of house fires caused by faulty electrical wiring in those days, so it was a good guess. Rural electrification came late to those parts and most of the old houses, like the Sawyers', were retrofitted, sometimes in ways that weren't the safest. Codes, such as they were, got wink-and-a-nod compliance. Now, if you're asking if I saw anything specific that I regarded as dangerous, the answer is no. I'd have done something about it if I had. And Miss Margaret would've been more likely to notice than me. She kept a close eye on every aspect of that household. That didn't make her popular with some of the help. She wanted things done the way she wanted. I liked that about her, but not everyone was as enlightened as me." He looked at me over his glasses and again came the slow smile.

"Others have mentioned that Mrs. Sawyer was a particular woman," I said. "And we've learned that after she'd gotten over the initial shock, she brought up several things she thought were out of place in the house when the fire started."

"I heard that, but not until long after it happened. The Sawyers moved into town after the fire and Alton decided to rent out the land. I finished out the fall harvest but I didn't see much of Miss Margaret during that time. Then I went out to my brother's place to learn to be an innkeeper. The next time I went back to visit my folks, nearly a year after the fire, was when I learned the Sawyers were saying they thought little Johnny had been kidnapped and was still out there somewhere.

God bless 'em. I thought it was just their passage through it all and they'd come to accept it after a while, but they never did."

"May I tell you the things she thought were amiss?" I asked.

"I'd like to know." Luther nodded.

I ran through the list—the noises, the closed door, the unlatched screen, the open window, the chair out of place, and, finally, the sound of the lighter.

At the last one his head came up. "Alton didn't smoke but he did carry a lighter."

"But he wasn't home," I reminded him.

He nodded. "And from that you're thinking, the fire might have really been arson?"

"I'm definitely out of my depth here, but I can see where the theory got traction," I said. "It doesn't seem the fire could have gotten going so quickly without a boost, but according to the fire marshal's report, they didn't find any accelerants."

Luther huffed. "The sniff test, that's what they had back then. I imagine he rubbed some char between his fingers and smelled it and if he didn't smell anything he concluded it wasn't there. And I doubt his nose was any smarter than the rest of his head. There were lots of things to hand that could serve that purpose back then that wouldn't have left much odor. Even moonshine worked, and that was easy enough to get."

"Can you think of anyone else connected with the Sawyers who might have owned a Zippo lighter?" I asked.

This drew an outright chuckle. "Yes, the answer is *everyone*. I had one my wife gave me for a wedding present. Cyrus carries it around now for a good-luck charm. Most every farmhand would have had one. Every neighbor, the preacher, the storekeepers, the butcher, the baker, and the candlestick maker," he said, making his voice a singsong. "As I say, even Alton carried a lighter. He didn't smoke, but he used it when we were burning brush or for lighting the wash kettle. Lots of us smoked in those days. Disgusting, unhealthy habit. I had a devil of a time quitting."

He turned to stare out the window for a moment, then put a hand up to rest his fingertips against his temple, a frown creasing his forehead. "All the other things you listed—the doors, the baby's window, and the chair—well, those seem like things you could dismiss. There were other people living in that house and maybe Stanton or Lenora moved the chair or opened the windows without Miss Margaret noticing. But she wasn't a woman to let her imagination run away with her, and what you're saying about her thinking she heard the sound of the lighter disturbs me."

"Me, too," I said. "Esme and I were hired to validate the findings that the baby died in the fire, and everything we're learning just seems to open up more doubt."

"And I surely haven't helped your cause by spouting off about the ineptitude of the fire marshal. My apologies for that."

"I appreciate your honesty," I said. "In the end we'll have to submit an honest report that may leave things muddier than we found them. But so be it. Is there anything else about that day? Anything you remember that was out of the ordinary?"

"Only one small thing, and I seriously doubt it has anything to do with the fire. I had to go two towns over to get the tires for the farm equipment, and I came back along the road on the west side of the farm closest to where we were working. It had been a dry couple of weeks and it was a dirt road, so I was kicking up a storm of dust. As I came along a straight stretch near the field, I saw a girl I didn't recognize walking along the roadside. At least I thought it was a girl. The dust was so thick I only got a glimpse but I had the idea she was wearing a headscarf. She stepped off the road and went into the thicket of trees. I felt bad because it was my dust that drove her off the road. I looked for her when I got to the spot where I thought she'd be, but she was gone. If she was even there in the first place, and I'm not a hundred percent sure of that."

"And you didn't think that was worth reporting?" I asked.

"It wasn't unusual. As I said, most folks had only

one vehicle, and seeing folks afoot was a common thing. We'd cut across fields and make trails through woods to get from one place to another by the quickest route. But I *did* report it. I told Big Jim, but he didn't give it much credence, especially since it came from me. And I didn't honestly believe it had anything to do with the fire. I still don't believe that."

"Probably not," I said with a sigh.

"This was all so long ago," Luther said, shaking his head. "I don't know what difference any of it makes now. Alton and Miss Margaret are gone, Stanton and Lenora are on the downward slide of life, even baby Johnny would be getting on up in years himself if he'd lived. Whatever happened back then can't be undone."

"Still, maybe knowing the truth would be a comfort."

"Maybe," Luther said, "though sometimes I think the truth is highly overrated."

I spent the rest of my visit with Luther Hamilton hearing about his own career and listening to him brag about his son's successes. "My wife and I weren't blessed with more children, but Cyrus is everything I could hope for in a son."

"Then you're both very lucky," I said.

*   .   *   *

As I went down on the elevator, I felt more and more downcast. Though I'd enjoyed my chat with Luther, nothing he'd told me had added much to what we knew and we'd run out of avenues to investigate. The reports and the internal memos we'd gotten hold of reflected ineptitude and infighting among the investigators, but solid evidence of baby John David Sawyer's death was nowhere to be found in any document we'd unearthed.

When the door opened to the lobby, I pushed the button to go back up. Esme had left the call up to me and I'd decided it was time to have a talk with Senator Stan and Lenora. I knew they were back because I'd overheard Cyrus tell Luther they'd arrived.

When Lenora came to the door she must have seen something in my face, because she immediately asked if there had been a development in Lincoln's case.

"No, not that I know of," I said. "I just needed to speak to you and the senator."

"Surely," she said, motioning me inside. "Let me call Stanton's room and see if he's available."

J.D. rose from the sofa, where he and Gabriela had been having a room service lunch. "Could we offer you something?" J.D. asked.

I thanked him but declined, and my eyes roamed to the side table on which sat a plastic zipper bag filled with rice.

"Cell phone mishap?" I asked.

J.D. nodded. "It got soaked that night we got caught in the rainstorm. I'd just gotten the thing, too. My old one died on our trip back to the States. Tech guy said not to turn it on and to put it in a bag of rice for a week."

"So you wouldn't have known if anyone tried to call you around midnight the night of the storm, would you?"

"Well, you didn't try to call me, did you? We hadn't met at that time."

Lenora hung up the phone. "Stan's waiting for us in his room. Shall we?"

I quickly scrawled a number on the pad by the phone and ripped it off and handed it to J.D. "Give Detective Carlson a call and tell him about your phone," I said. "He'll explain."

A look, half puzzlement and half irritation, came over J.D.'s face, but it only lasted a moment. "Sure," he said. "I'll call him right now."

When we got to the senator's room, it was clear he and Damon had been working. There were papers scattered over the tabletop and Damon was clicking away on his laptop. I wondered if Damon was going to step into Lincoln's place to finish the book. The senator stood and herded us toward the sitting area. "If this is about your report, Sophreena, I'd like Damon to stay and hear what you have to say. Since he'll be heading the foundation, he should be in the loop."

"It's fine with me," I said, "though I don't think what I have to tell you will be very encouraging." I proceeded to describe to him how everywhere we probed seemed to be opening up more ambiguity instead of nailing down the conclusions. I gave him a few examples and at first he tried arguing them down, point by point, but eventually he gave up.

"This was not the news I was hoping to hear," he said.

"Nor the news I was hoping to deliver," I said. "But I felt obligated to let you know where things stand in case you want to call in someone else who might be more qualified in law enforcement investigation to take over. I know time is a factor."

"I think not at this juncture," the senator said. "Do you agree, Lenora? Damon?"

"Oh, Stanton, I don't know why we started down this road in the first place," Lenora said. "It was unfair to Sophreena and Esme. We certainly knew how complicated this all was. We've lived with this since we were children."

"Indeed," he said, wringing his hands. "I suppose it was wishful thinking on my part to believe that you and Esme could set things all to rights after all these years."

"We're finding a lot of information," I said. "It just doesn't seem to be moving us in the direction you wanted."

"Still, one never knows, but that something you learn can be useful. I'm on the fence. What say you, Damon?"

Damon shrugged. "I say they're done for. Cut our losses and ax 'em. I'll bat down any claimants that come and send 'em packing They'll learn not to mess with me."

"Damon," Senator Stan said with a sigh, "your eloquence is inspiring. As is your gung ho attitude."

Damon smiled and nodded.

"That was sarcasm, son," the senator barked. "Having to ward off claimants is the very thing we are trying to avoid."

"We'll keep going if you want," I said. "I've got my teeth into it now. But I felt I owed you an update."

"No," Damon said. "You're done. You're fired, don't you get it?"

The senator held up a hand. "This is not your meeting, Damon, and not your call. You're here as a courtesy." Then he looked at me. "I don't think I'm quite ready to *ax you* just yet," he said. "I'd like you to stay on it for a while longer. Let's say you give it another week. Is that agreeable with you, Lenora?"

"If they're willing," she said with a sigh.

"Damon?" the senator asked.

"I don't know why you're asking me," he said with a sulk. "It seems I don't get a vote."

"No, you don't," the senator said, "not until you earn one. But it's good form to give your support once a thing is decided. Let that be your lesson for the day."

As I was leaving, I spotted Emma with her grandmother at one of the tables on the terrace. I went over to say hello.

Emma surprised me by jumping up and wrapping me in a fierce hug. "I have to say good-bye," she said. "Mom and I are leaving in the morning, I've got school on Monday. Will I see you anymore now that you're done with Grandpa's birthday stuff? I will, won't I? You'll still come visit?"

"I hope so, Emma," I said, laughing at her exuberance. "Maybe you'll end up at one of the universities in this area, then we can see a lot of each other." I returned her hug and whispered in her ear, "And stay out of thunderstorms."

"Did you have a nice chat with Luther?" Lily Rose asked.

"I did," I said. "He's a really nice man."

"Helpful?" she asked, noting my evasiveness.

I made a face. "Not so much."

"I'm gonna walk Sophreena to her car, okay, Grandma?" Emma said, grabbing my arm to move me along.

"I guess I'm going," I said, turning to wave good-bye to Lily Rose.

"Okay," Emma said when we'd gotten to the edge of the terrace. "Here's the deal. I feel like I'm telling on Chelsea all the time now, but honestly, she's ticked me off and I don't even feel bad about it anymore. She asked me this morning if I'd been snooping around her room. That's the way she said it, *snooping*. I mean, I don't deny I've been guilty of like looking in people's medicine cabinets at parties or maybe a quick glance into their closets, but I'm not a snooper. So I'm mad at her."

"Understandable," I said, wondering where this was going.

"Anyway, a little while ago I was helping Marc and Patricia with some campaign mailings in Dinah Leigh's suite, and Dinah Leigh asked Chelsea to take some of her jewelry down and put it in the hotel safe since they're staying on a while. I was kind of hoping to get a look at the jewelry. Dinah Leigh has such pretty stuff. So I went to Chelsea's door to ask her if she'd show it to me. The door wasn't closed all the way and I saw her put something inside the jewelry case and zip it up. It was that blue envelope I told you about, I'm sure of it.

She said it was nothing when she set it aside that day, but if that's true, why would she put it in the safe?"

"I don't know, Emma, but I'm sure Chelsea had her reasons," I said. Though inside I was getting a little hacked off at Chelsea myself.

When Esme got home from the grocery store I was lying on the hardwood floor in the workroom memorizing the cracks in the ceiling. I think an occasional moan might have been emanating from deep within me.

"What on earth are you doing?" Esme asked.

"Trying to figure out why in God's name we ever took on either of these jobs," I said.

Esme kicked off her heels and lowered herself to the floor beside me. "Does this help?" she asked, wiggling to get her shirttail untwisted.

"Not very much," I said, "but it helps a little if you whimper."

I told her about my day.

"Okay, let me recap," Esme said. "Your talk with Luther Hamilton only confirmed one thing for us—unfortunately, that was the fact that the officials in this case were dunderheads. And on the other case, Chelsea lied right to your face about that blue envelope, which means it was something she doesn't want us to know about or get in our hot little hands."

"That about covers it," I said.

"So we're continuing to pedal backwards," Esme said. "On both jobs."

The front door opened and I started to get up, but Esme grabbed my arm. "That's Denton, he's come for supper." She shouted for him to come to the workroom—right in my ear, thank you very much.

Denny stopped in the doorway to survey the situation. "Lose something?" he asked.

"Besides our minds, you mean?" I asked. "We're pondering the universe and wondering why we can't get a break on anything we're working on."

"Okay," Denny said, striding into the room and looking down at us. "I'm in. How does this work?"

"It doesn't," Esme said.

"Honest to Pete, I'm ready to try anything at this point," he said, helping us to our feet.

"No developments?" I asked.

"A few nuggets here and there, but still no beacon shining down on the perpetrator."

"Anything on Chad Deese's alibi?"

"Yeah. You know that saying about what happens in fight club staying in fight club? Well, apparently Deese's friends didn't get the memo. He was with two guys and two young women at a gym over near Chapel Hill. They go there after-hours to do some kind of martial arts training, and Deese was there the night Lincoln died.

Apparently this was recommended by his therapist to help with his anger management. The friends couldn't wait to give their account of how Deese got his black eye. One of the women gave it to him."

"So he's in the clear?" Esme asked, sounding disappointed.

"Tentatively," Denny said. "He was away from them for about an hour when he was supposedly in the weight room. We'll look at security footage before we rule him out."

"Did J.D. call you?" I asked.

"Yes, right after you left him. His phone's been out of commission since the night Lincoln died. He gave it to me to see if our tech guys can do anything. He swears he's got no idea why Lincoln was calling him unless it was to patch up the little fuss they had that afternoon. But he doesn't think that was it 'cause they'd already smoked the peace pipe. Though he admits he was still a little vexed about it."

"And you think he was telling the truth?" Esme asked. "That he had no idea why Lincoln would have been calling him?"

"Either he's a good actor or he was really stumped," Denny said. "And he handed over the phone without hesitation."

"Anything else?" Esme asked.

"Well, I met the lovely Aunt Yvonne today," Denny

said. "Jennifer talked to her before, so the pleasure was all mine this time. She believes she's solved the case for me and indicated I'm an idiot for not figuring it out already. She says she overheard Chelsea and Lincoln arguing that afternoon and she's convinced Chelsea killed him later on that night, evidence being optional as far as she's concerned."

"She's accusing Chelsea?" I said. "Dinah Leigh wouldn't like that."

"Aunt Yvonne is clearly not a fan of the assistant. She says Chelsea doesn't know her place and that Dinah Leigh needs to get rid of her."

"Or maybe she's trying to do it for her by accusing Chelsea of Lincoln's murder," Esme said.

"How does one woman grow old as delightfully as Lily Rose and another turn into Aunt Yvonne?" I asked, not expecting an answer.

"Nothing about growing older," Esme said. "Some people are just born sour."

"But I don't think she was always that way," I said, walking over to the table where we had the Nelson family artifacts assembled. I picked up a stack of photos, an amazingly thin stack compared to most families of this era, and dealt them out onto the cleared area of tabletop. "See here, in these old photos she's smiling and looks like a happy-go-lucky girl. Look at these of her and Dinah Leigh's mother from one of those old photo booths. Look how happy they both look. And here's Yvonne in an evening gown. Prom maybe? She's smiling and she looks adorable. And here—" I stopped abruptly as I noticed Esme's expression.

She was staring at the pictures and she had that look. "What is it?"

She pinched her lips, giving Denny an almost apologetic look. Then I understood. While she'd told Denny about her gift, he'd not yet seen it in action. "His hand," she said. "Remember I've been telling you I kept seeing a hand? In every one of these pictures, Herbert Nelson has his hand in his pocket, or hidden behind his leg."

"Is there anything unusual about this hand you see?" Denny asked, with no hint of skepticism in his voice. "A birthmark or a deformity?"

"No," Esme said, drawing out the word. "No, it's a man's hand, I know that, and it's tanned and work hardened, but there's nothing beyond that. It's reaching for something . . ." She paused and I saw her eyes widen. "And then there's just terrible pain."

"I think I might know what that's about," I said. "I asked Dinah Leigh about that new car after Patricia gave us those pictures the other day. I couldn't figure out how they could afford it. Dinah Leigh says after he was laid off from the graphite plant he was hired on a temp crew to close the plant down. There was an accident when they were dismantling some of the machinery and he was hurt, his hand and arm were badly injured. There was a settlement and that's how they got that new car," I said, pointing to the photo of him with the 1949 Ford. "Dinah Leigh said he never thought the settlement was fair and he was very bitter about it. Maybe he still is."

"Well, I'd say that qualifies as unfinished business," Esme said. She let out a sigh and looked up at Denton warily. He pulled her to him, kissing the top of her head. She swatted at his midsection. "You're dead on your feet. Go have a quick nap on the couch while I get supper ready."

Jack ended up joining us for chicken fajitas that Esme had whipped up, and by unspoken agreement, we all honored her work by not talking business at the dinner table.

"I talked to Coco this afternoon," Jack said. "She and River are on their way back from that sustainability workshop. I'm issuing fair warning; she is on fire about this and will be preaching at you at every available opportunity. I already got an earful about how I can change my business practices to be more friendly to Mother Earth."

"Couldn't hurt," Denny said. "Right here at this table we're soon to be four separate households—for now." He slipped a sidelong glance at Esme, who refused to look at him. "That's a pretty substantial foot-print for this number of people."

"Oh, yeah, I agree," Jack said. "I have no doubt I'll learn a lot from her, but you know Coco. When she gets excited about something it's like getting hit by a tornado."

"She and River make a good pair," Esme said.

"Matchmaking?" Denny asked.

"Not I," Esme said. "But if something were to develop, well, maybe they'd have one less household to impact the environment. And speaking of environmental issues . . ." She turned to me. "After I move out you're going to need to remember to only run the dishwasher when it's full, and always run it first thing in the morning—that's when we get a break on our utility rate—and anyway, elsewise you won't have enough hot water for your shower at night. And you need to put a timer in the bathroom to remind you to get out after a reasonable time. You stay in there way too long."

"I like long hot showers," I said. "That's where I do my best thinking. It's a business expense. And I can offset it by only running the dishwasher once a week. I won't be cooking that much."

"You have to eat, Sophreena," Esme said.

"I will," I said with a grin. "All I have to do is step out on the patio and I can smell what you're cooking for supper. I can be there in under two minutes."

"And she can call me and let me know what we're having," Denny said, pointing his knife at me.

"Me, too," Jack said. "Or maybe I should set up a website so you can post the menus."

Esme laughed. "Fine, my mama always said I was bad to feed strays when I was a girl. At least now I'll have a bigger kitchen."

"In a color you love," Denny said.

After Denny went back to work and Esme had shooed us out of the kitchen, Jack and I tried to watch a movie. But I couldn't concentrate. Jack finally flicked off the set.

"Let's play Puzzle-Me-This," he said, settling in on the far end of the couch, out of cuddling range.

This was the term he'd come up with for the talking-aloud sessions we sometimes do in our group to try to figure out how things we've learned about our family histories might fit together. Sometimes the group-brain could unravel things the individual brain only managed to wind into tighter knots.

I moved to sit cross-legged on the other end of the couch. "Okay, job number one, the Sawyer family fire. Everything we learn takes us further away from the proof they're asking for. Now we're working on borrowed time, and if Damon had his way, we'd be off the job already."

At Jack's quizzical look I explained how he'd been included in the meeting this afternoon and why.

"Well, Sophreena, I can't say he's wrong. I mean, it might be a pain to have to ward off people claiming to be John David Sawyer, but with DNA testing it'd only be a nuisance, not a real threat."

"True," I said. "But that wasn't the only reason they want this settled. You'll recall what set the senator off in the first place was how their parents were portrayed in that article."

Jack frowned. "So essentially, they wanted you to show that without a doubt the baby died in that fire, while at the same time showing their parents were not crazy for refusing to accept that?"

"That's pretty much it," I said. "And honestly, I can see both sides of things as equally plausible at this point. The baby couldn't have survived that fire. He was just beginning to crawl and even if he managed to get out of the crib as the investigators claimed, he couldn't have gotten out of the room because the doorway was blocked by fire. He must have perished, so why didn't they find remains? That's assuming the baby was in the room in the first place, and there are a whole bunch of little things that make the theory that he'd already been taken out of the house seem viable. And the lack of physical evidence coupled with the total botch-up of the case makes it even harder to nail anything down."

"So what's the next step?"

"That's the thing—I have no idea. I feel like this one has us beat. I've interviewed the only other eyewitness we're likely to find and that didn't help. In fact he threw in a bit that's got me even more conflicted." I told him about Luther Hamilton seeing the woman cutting through the woods.

"Yeah, but like he said, that wasn't unusual back then. People walked. Now, if he'd seen her, say, carrying a screaming baby, then we might have something to talk about."

I sighed. "He barely saw her at all. And the sheriff didn't even find it important enough to include in his reports."

"Maybe with good reason; maybe he discovered who it was and it had nothing to do with anything. Maybe it was Little Red Riding Hood cutting through the woods to her grandma's house."

I laughed, despite my frustration. "Well, Esme and I will give it a couple more days and if we don't find anything solid, we'll withdraw. I feel bad about taking their money."

"And you'll continue to work it on your own time because you hate brick walls."

"You know me well," I said. "I probably will, but at least I won't feel like I'm robbing the senator and Lenora in the meantime."

"No one's ever going to accuse you of being a ruth-less businesswoman," Jack said.

"I should hope not, and speaking of which, we come to troublesome job number two, Conrad Nelson's family tree. Supposed to be an easy one. Tight deadline, but straightforward. Now the wedding date is coming up fast and we've gotten ourselves into a big mess."

I told him what I planned to do about the family tree and the report. "It's kind of a bait and switch, but I don't want to break the news before Conrad's wedding, and I can't verify what Yvonne told us anyway." I told him Esme's theory about Yvonne being Conrad's biolog-ical mom and about the mystery of the blue envelope.

"Let's try out a scenario," Jack said. "What if that blue envelope contained some kind of proof that Con-rad was adopted? Let's say, just for the sake of the game, that Herbert or Marie Nelson had an attack of conscience and wrote it all down and put it in the baby book, figuring that wouldn't get thrown out."

"But why wouldn't they just tell Conrad?" I asked.

"I don't know, maybe they couldn't find the right time, or just didn't want to admit they'd lied to him. Then jump forward. Chelsea's doing the inventory for you and comes across whatever this proof is of Con-rad's birth status. She knows this will be upsetting to Dinah Leigh. She doesn't know what to do. Who does she turn to? The man she loves, of course," Jack said, reaching over to pinch my toe. "And from what you've told me about Lincoln, I gather he was a tell-the-truth-and-let-the-chips-fall kinda guy. He'd want her to lay it all out. She'd want to protect Dinah Leigh. So I'm with your theory. Sounds to me like that fits better than an argument over their engagement. I say you fake it. Hit Chelsea with it like you already know all about it and see how she reacts."

"I knew I kept you around for a reason," I said, crawling over to give him a kiss. Then I pulled my cell phone out of my pocket and tapped in Chelsea's number. She wasn't happy to hear from me, judging by the fact that I could almost see frost forming on the screen of my phone. And when I asked her to meet me at the coffee shop the next morning, she rattled off a list of reasons why she couldn't.

"Fine," I said. "Well, I'm almost done with the job for Dinah Leigh, and I can tell you right now she's not going to want to give this to Conrad as a wedding present and I think you know why."

She said she'd be there at eight.

thirteen

"THIS IS A RISKY PLOY," ESME SAID AS WE POWER walked to the coffee shop the next morning. "We don't have anything but Yvonne's word, and I trust that about as far as I could throw her, which I'd be happy to do except Denny would have to arrest me for assault and that'd be hard on him."

"I don't see any downside to giving it a try," I said. "Like Jack said, eventually we're going to have to tell Dinah Leigh and Conrad what we've learned, whether we can prove it or not."

Chelsea was waiting for us, sipping her coffee and looking around like somebody might attack at any moment. Esme went inside to get our coffee and I sat down and started right in.

"Thanks for coming, Chelsea. I think maybe you can help us figure out what to do about this fine mess we're in. You and Lincoln weren't arguing about your engagement that night, were you? You were arguing about whether to tell Dinah Leigh about the circumstances of Conrad's birth."

Chelsea tried to look confused, but involuntarily drew in a sharp breath. "How did you find out?" she asked. "Lincoln swore to me he'd hold off. He promised me," she said, hiccupping a sob.

I was already feeling bad about ambushing Chelsea and now I felt even worse. "I'm sorry," I said as she fished around in her bag for a tissue. "Lincoln never told us anything, he never had a chance—" I stopped abruptly, realizing I was only making matters worse.

"Aunt Yvonne told us," Esme said, sliding into the seat opposite Chelsea and passing my coffee to me. No apple fritter, I noted with regret.

"She told you?" Chelsea said, her eyes going wide as saucers. "She just told you? Why would she do that?"

"She was worried about Conrad having the DNA test and she thought we could dissuade him," I said.

"Oh my gosh," Chelsea said. "But if nobody else in the family got tested what would it matter? I still don't understand why Yvonne would go to you and just tell you."

"She seemed to be under the mistaken impression that we were required to keep it confidential. We had to disabuse of her that notion and let her know Dinah

Leigh was our client and that our obligation was to her. She didn't take it well."

"And Dinah Leigh still is your client," Chelsea said. "You don't need to tell her about this, you don't need to tell anybody."

"We *do* need to tell her, and we need to tell Conrad, too. We're only missing a few pieces of the puzzle, and I suspect we might learn those inside a blue envelope you told me you didn't remember seeing."

Chelsea tilted her head and gave me a hard look. "Yvonne didn't tell you about that. She couldn't have."

Neither of us said anything. I was debating whether to rat Emma out, but in the end there was no need.

"Emma," Chelsea said, but without malice. "I knew somebody had been snooping around my room. I thought it might be her."

"She swears she didn't, and if it means anything, I believe her, but she did see you put the envelope in Dinah Leigh's jewelry case. So I assume it's in the hotel safe now?"

"Yes," Chelsea said.

"I think you'd better tell us what's in it," I said.

"You mean you don't already know that, too," Chelsea snapped.

"No," I said, my voice calm. "I only know that it was something important enough for you to lie about it. If you want my guess, I'd say it was a letter from Conrad's father. Emma said the handwriting was spidery and I know Herbert Nelson had to retrain himself to write with his left hand after the accident. Did he provide some sort of documentation about the adoption?"

"It was a letter," Chelsea said, nodding. "And it was from their father, but there are no documents about the *adoption*, if that's what you want to call it. He knew he was dying and he wanted Conrad to know the truth. I hope it made him feel better to write it all down but I wish he'd burned it afterward. It's going to cause a lot of misery for a lot of people now."

"There's no help for it, Chelsea," I said. "They have to be told."

"Did Aunt Yvonne tell you everything?" she asked. "Did she admit her part in it?"

"Yes," Esme said. "I think she's worried about that."

"She should be," Chelsea said. "And she'd better get a good lawyer."

"Oh, I doubt they'll take any legal action against her at this point," I said, figuring the forgery of county documents from more than a half century ago probably wouldn't be on any prosecutor's list of priorities.

"Why not? Don't tell me there's a statute of limitations," Chelsea said.

"There probably is," I said. "And anyway, what she did wasn't *that* bad."

"Not that bad?" Chelsea said. "It was horrible."

I couldn't decide if she meant Yvonne forging the birth certificate, or if the letter might support Esme's theory about Yvonne being the mother.

"We've seen far worse," I said with a shrug, hoping she'd be forthcoming.

It didn't work.

"What kind of cesspool do you people work in?" she asked. Before I could answer, she got up from the table and grabbed her bag. "Come by the hotel later this morning and I'll give you the letter," she said. "At least I won't have to be the one to tell them."

She started to walk away, then froze in place. She turned slowly and approached the table almost in slow motion. "You don't think this had anything to do with Lincoln getting killed, do you?" she asked.

Esme and I looked at each other. "I can't see how they'd be related," I said. "It's bad, but it's certainly not worth killing over."

"Are you kidding me?" she said. "I don't think you have any idea what this is going to do to all of them."

We watched her make her way to her car and get inside. She sat there for a full minute and I could see she was sobbing. Finally she collected herself and drove away, and Esme turned to me. "Are we that jaded?" she asked.

"Maybe," I said with a sigh. "Guess we've uncovered too many dark family secrets."

*   *   *

We walked back to my house, showered, dressed, and headed to the hotel. I didn't want to give Chelsea a chance to change her mind. Dinah Leigh was in the spa when we arrived at the family's suite, and Chelsea told us she needed to make a couple of phone calls that were time sensitive. "Then I'll go down and get it for you."

We told her we could wait and she went into her room and closed the door, leaving us with the lovely Aunt Yvonne, who speared us with death stares.

"What's she getting for you?" she demanded.

I figured now was as good a time as any to let Yvonne know the jig was up, and as disagreeable as the woman was, I felt sorry for what she was about to go through with her family.

"Your brother-in-law wanted Conrad to know the truth. He wrote a letter toward the end of his life and told him everything about the circumstances of his birth."

"I seriously doubt that," Yvonne said with a sniff. "Herbert was a coward."

"Maybe facing death made him brave. And he did write the letter," Esme said. "Chelsea's getting it for us. Then we'll all need to sit down and have a serious conversation."

I sat down next to Yvonne and tried to make my voice sympathetic. "Yvonne, are you Conrad's mother?"

Her head snapped up and for the first time I saw shock in her eyes. Her doughy face went through several changes of expression, none of which I could read. She worked her mouth and I could see she was trying to speak but couldn't get words to form. Finally she sighed and her voice came out ragged. "You two are pretty smart, aren't you? Yes, I gave birth to Conrad, and Herbert and Marie raised him. None of us wanted him to know. And since I'm the only one of us three left, I still don't want him to know. Don't I have any rights?"

"Not legal ones," I said, "but we're listening."

"Okay, fine. Marie was carrying a baby when they came to live with me after Herbert lost his job at the graphite plant. She lost that one, too, and she was nearly 'bout crazy. Like I told you, she lost three right in a row. And I was running around with a no-account man I met at a bar when I was sowing my wild oats and I came up pregnant. I didn't want a child. I knew I couldn't raise one by myself and I surely didn't want to tie myself to that side-winding sot. So we worked it out between us, Herbert, Marie, and me. Our business. Family business. Nobody else's. Wasn't then, isn't now. Now I need to be by myself for a while, so leave me alone."

With that she rose and picked up her cane, which I thought for a moment she might use on Esme and me. But she snatched up her cigarettes and lighter and headed for the door. For a woman in need of a cane, she was swift.

Fifteen minutes later, Chelsea came back into the room, pale, but with her jaw set. "I'll be back in a few minutes," she said, pausing at the door. "I hope you two know what you're doing."

Clearly she didn't think we did, but there was no turning back now.

Alone, Esme and I had a talk and decided to stick to the plan. It wasn't like there was urgency. Time wouldn't change anything and it could wait until after the wedding. We could give them that one day of joy unsullied by the new reality of their actual blood relationship.

Dinah Leigh came in, looking refreshed and happy. "Sophreena, Esme, I didn't know you were here. More questions for us?"

"No," I said. "We're all set. We're waiting for Chelsea. She's got something for us that got left out of your memorabilia box."

"Where is she?" Dinah Leigh asked, moving briskly around the room, depositing her gym bag in a closet and helping herself to ice water from the minibar.

"I think she had an errand," I said vaguely. "Don't let us interrupt what you need to do. We'll be on our way as soon as Chelsea gets back."

Patricia came in just then, eager to discuss some

campaign plans with Dinah Leigh, and the two settled at the table by the window. Esme and I twiddled our thumbs for another ten minutes.

Yvonne returned and, still skewering us with her coal-black eyes, settled into the chair opposite the sofa. She picked up a ragged paperback mystery from the table and started to read, or pretended to. I leaned over and said to her sotto voce, "We're going to wait until after the wedding."

"Aren't you generous," she spat back.

Another fifteen minutes passed and I began to fear the worst. Chelsea had decided against giving us the letter and was destroying it as we sat here like saps.

A few minutes later a near hysterical Chelsea opened the door of the suite and practically fell inside. She was breathless and disheveled. "Somebody jumped me in the stairwell," she said. "Dinah Leigh, they got your jewelry. I'm so sorry."

We all rushed to her, all except Yvonne, who showed her concern by casually putting down her book and turning in Chelsea's direction.

Patricia picked up the phone and called the front desk, requesting security.

"No, don't do that," Chelsea said, her eyes wild. But it was too late.

She stammered out the story, which was a little disjointed, but I had no doubt it was true. "I was in the stairwell. I always take the stairs when I can; everybody knows that. Someone came in behind me when I reached the landing on the floor below us and slipped a pillowcase over my head. He told me to get on the floor and tied my hands behind my back. Then I heard footsteps on the stairs. He was going up, not down, which didn't seem right to me. I got my hands free—they'd been tied with only a shoestring, I mean literally a shoestring. I ran up the stairs after him, but there was no one in the hallway."

"You poor dear," Dinah Leigh said, guiding Chelsea to a chair and stroking her hair. "Don't worry, the jewelry is insured. I'm just so grateful you weren't badly hurt."

Almost immediately the room was filled with people. Marc came scurrying in along with three or four hotel staff. No one seemed to be in charge and everyone was asking questions and fussing over Chelsea. Finally Cyrus came into the room and restored order. He made profuse apologies to Chelsea and to Dinah Leigh and turned to his men.

"Search every room," he said. "I don't care how disgruntled the guests are, I want this thief found. Dinah Leigh, would you describe the case for them."

Chelsea, who seemed to slowly be regaining her wits, put up a hand. "You don't need to do that," she said, choking back a sob. "I know who it was. It was him." She turned to glare at Marc.

"I think she's delirious," Marc said, looking totally

taken aback. "Maybe we should call the doctor to sedate her again. She's out of her head."

"I saw your shoes, Marc," Chelsea said through clenched teeth. "They're custom, remember? You like to remind everybody about that. None other like them. I saw your stupid shoes." She looked to Cyrus. "The case is a circular zipper case, tan leather."

Cyrus narrowed his eyes. "Search Mr. Benson's room first, if you would," he told the security guys. "And be thorough."

"Marc?" Patricia said. "What's going on?"

"I don't know," Marc protested. "I'm telling you, she's off her rocker. That happens to some people. I don't know why she's making these wild accusations, but clearly Lincoln's death has messed her up. Dinah Leigh, you know I'd never steal from you."

"I thought I knew that," Dinah Leigh said. "But I also know Chelsea is quite stable and she doesn't lie."

One of the security men came in a few moments later holding a round zip case in his gloved hand. "This it? Found it in the suitcase in his closet," he said, jerking his head in Marc's direction.

Marc set his lips hard. "I was protecting this family," he said. "I was protecting *you*, Patricia. I wasn't after the damned jewelry. I just wanted—"

He was interrupted by the sharp rap of Yvonne's cane on the coffee table. "Shut up, Marc. Close your mouth and use your head. I'm sure we can straighten this all out without having to air our family's dirty laundry in front of outsiders."

"This particular family member will be coming with these outsiders," Cyrus said, motioning for his men to take Marc. "The police are on their way, and he can explain everything to them."

"I want someone to explain all this to *me*," Dinah Leigh said. "*Right now.*"

"To me, too," Patricia said, stepping forward to stand beside her mother.

I looked across to the hotel security man who still held the case. "Would you mind unzipping the case so we can see the contents?" I asked.

"Already did," the man said. "Lots of jewelry, looks expensive."

"Only jewelry?" I asked and looked a question at Chelsea. She took in a deep breath and looked down at the floor.

The man looked to Cyrus, who nodded. "Open it."

The man put the case on the table and zipped it open. Lots of sparkly stuff but no blue envelope, no paper of any kind.

"Please, Cyrus, what's going on here?" Dinah Leigh pleaded. "Sophreena? Esme? Do you know anything about this? Will somebody, for the love of God, tell me what's going on?"

Esme and I exchanged a look. "We need to talk," I said.

"Does it have to do with this thief?" Cyrus asked.

"It relates to his motive, but that's all," I said, nodding toward Marc, who was still protesting being escorted from the room. "You can take him down. We'll come talk to the police," I said, "but give us a few minutes."

Once they'd all cleared out, with Dinah Leigh and Patricia still demanding to know what was going on and Aunt Yvonne sitting silent as a sphinx, Chelsea found her voice. She rose slowly and turned to Esme and me. "I'll go get Conrad. He should be here," she said, her voice robotic. "You'll have to do it. I can't. I can't even be here for this. I won't be able to bear it." She went over and hugged Dinah Leigh, who was totally perplexed. Chelsea bit her lip as the tears started to fall. "I'm sorry. I'm really sorry," she told her, then turned for the door.

We waited, with Dinah Leigh and Patricia growing ever more strident in their demands to know what was going on.

"Keep your britches on," Yvonne said. "These two will drop everything on you soon enough," she said. "And you can blame Conrad for all of it. Didn't I tell you digging around in the past is only asking for trouble?"

"I should go down and be with Marc," Patricia said. "I don't know what's going on here, but Mother, you know he'd never steal anything from you."

"I know, Patricia, but they did find the jewelry in his suitcase—what are we to make of that?"

"They won't let you see Marc right now," I said. "And I think maybe you'll want to stay for this discussion. Just be patient a few minutes longer."

Just then there came a rap at the door and Dinah Leigh opened it on a clearly curious and confused Conrad. Phoebe came in behind him looking equally bewildered.

"Family only," Yvonne barked. "Phoebe, you can go wait in your room."

Conrad's face reddened. "Phoebe is family, Aunt Yvonne, and she'll be staying. Now, what is this about?"

Esme rearranged the seating as if preparing for a therapy session and I had the fleeting thought it might be a good idea to have a therapist on standby. When we were all seated I turned to Yvonne. "I'll do you the courtesy of letting you be the one to tell it if you wish," I said. "But given new developments, it looks like we can't wait any longer."

It didn't take me long to rue that decision. Yvonne told it with all the tenderness a hammer has for an anvil. There were gasps and protests and shocked silences. But Yvonne plodded on as if reciting a grocery list. "And so, all this fuss over a little biology. I was your birth mother, Conrad, but Marie and Herbert raised you and they were your parents. And lucky you were to have them. Lord knows I wasn't cut out to be a mother."

"But I remember the day he was born," Dinah Leigh protested. "My mother was pregnant with him when she left Quinn County."

"You remember the day we *told* you he was born," Yvonne said. "Your mother lost that baby and I was already in trouble when y'all got there. We made the agreement and she stuffed her shirt and kept up the plan. I was a big-boned girl back then and I was able to hide my condition even when I was well along. And then I took leave from work to take care of my sick sister. At least that's what I told people. We had to make a little adjustment in the baby's age, so that's why I kept him at my house for the first few months, so we could keep him out of sight."

Conrad spoke, his voice constricted. "So I wasn't a sickly baby?"

"You were fit as a fiddle," Yvonne said.

"But I saw him," Dinah Leigh said. "I saw him when he was a newborn."

"You saw him through the window at my house," Yvonne agreed. "We told you he was too frail for you to see him close up or hold him. You saw a baby's face. We had him all wrapped in blankets. You were young and anyway, you didn't know anything about babies; you'd never been around any. And everything worked out fine for everybody, so I don't see why everybody's getting so het up over this."

"So," Conrad said, "Dinah Leigh, we're actually cousins, not siblings at all. They lied to us all those years. I feel I've lost something. Something very precious to me."

"Me, too," Dinah Leigh said, wiping at her eyes with an already sodden tissue. "And I'm angry about being deceived. But in the end it doesn't change anything between us, not really. We've been brother and sister all our lives."

"*What*," Patricia said, injecting herself into the conversation with such force some of us jumped, "does any of this have to do with Marc taking my mother's jewelry?"

"I'll tell you what," Yvonne snapped before I could reply. "Herbert went soft in the head in his last days and left a letter to Conrad telling you all this, which Marie and I never wanted another soul to know. I don't know what got into the man. I didn't know the letter existed until these two told me," she said, jerking her head toward Esme and me. "I was hoping they'd honor my wishes and not tell you about any of this, but they showed up here saying Chelsea was going down to get that letter for them. So I called Marc and told him he needed to get to it and burn it. Patricia, this would not be good for your career if it came out to the public. Marc was looking after you like he always does."

"By attacking Chelsea?" Patricia cried.

"He didn't hurt her," Yvonne said. "But I trust he got that letter and did away with it and now nobody outside the family needs to know about any of this."

"Idiot!" Patricia spat. "He didn't think getting arrested for assault would hurt my career?"

"He hasn't been arrested. Chelsea won't press charges—whatever else you can say about her, she's loyal," Yvonne said with a swat. "So there you have it." She spread her gnarled hands as if ending a presentation. "You all know every bit of it and meteors didn't fall, the seas didn't dry up, and the world didn't end. No one else knows other than these two, and I understand they have to keep mum. That only leaves one weak link," she said, turning a hard stare on Phoebe.

Phoebe clutched Conrad's arm. "As long as you don't try to make me call you my mother-in-law, I'm fine with whatever Conrad decides. But let me go on the record as saying I think you're terrible."

"Duly noted," Yvonne said. "Can't say I'm deeply wounded. I've got no apologies to make, so if any of you are waiting for that, you'll be waiting until they're pouring frozen margaritas in hell. If I had to make the same decision over again I wouldn't do a thing different.

Except maybe visit Herbert more often in his dying days and make sure he couldn't get his hands on pen and paper."

"You had no right to destroy that letter," Conrad said. "It was meant for me. What did it say?"

"I don't know," Yvonne said. "God knows what was going through the man's mind. But it doesn't matter. Now you know and you can all just wallow in this, or you can accept it was all for the best and get on with your lives. I don't have much life left, so I'm surely not going to squander it fretting about something that happened way back then."

I looked around the room. Yvonne was right in one respect. It was all out there now and the world hadn't ended. But there was pain traced on every face; even Yvonne's eyes were dark.

I began to feel like an intruder, and judging by the way Esme was shifting in her chair, she felt it, too. I asked to speak with Dinah Leigh privately and we stepped out into the hallway. "I'm really sorry about this. I wasn't going to tell you until after the wedding," I said. "And I'd hoped to break it a little more gently, but I couldn't hand over research I knew to be false. I'm so sorry for the pain this is causing."

"You did your job," Dinah Leigh said, and I noticed her hands were trembling. "Don't apologize for that. This will take some getting used to, but we'll be okay."

She slipped back into the room to be with her family, in whatever form that family had rearranged itself into, and Esme and I headed home.

I felt like I'd been run over by a truck.

Esme and I were so demoralized by the time we got home, we decided to withdraw from the senator's project as well. It was depressing. Two failed jobs at once; that had never happened to us before. Though technically we hadn't failed on Dinah Leigh's job, it had just blown up in our faces.

There are times you just have to take your losses. We'd be okay financially. We had several small jobs waiting and if we started in tomorrow, we'd be able to wedge those in before our next big job, which would take us to Louisiana, Esme's old stomping grounds, in about a month. That would give us some time to lick our wounds over these failures and get our mojo back.

But more important than our business failings, Lincoln Cooper's murder remained unsolved and that was casting a pall over everything. We'd been so busy since his death we hadn't had the time to properly mourn the passing of a friend. It seemed to hit me all at once. He was probably killed by someone he knew. And there was a good chance it was someone we knew, too. That thought made my skin crawl and I found myself in the weird position of rooting for Chad Deese to be a killer. This was wholly unfair, since I'd only met the guy once, but if the choice came down to him or Chelsea, J.D., Damon, Ken, or any of the others we knew from Lincoln's world, the rude reporter got my vote. Now if Denny could just find some way around his pesky alibi.

We started packing up the materials from the workroom. "I wish I could've read that letter," I said as I put the Nelsons' memorabilia into an archival file box to be delivered back to Dinah Leigh. "Now I'll always wonder what it said."

"Me, too," Esme said. "It must've been hard for Herbert Nelson to write. I mean psychologically and physically. And judging by the headache I've come down with, I don't think he's too happy somebody interfered with his message to his son."

"Doesn't seem fair. Yvonne got a chance to confess to her part in the story, if you could call what she had to say a confession," I said. "But Herbert never had a chance to tell his side."

"And now he never will since Marc destroyed the letter. Denny called while I was getting the boxes from the garage. They found burnt paper bits in the wastebasket in Marc and Patricia's bathroom."

"Enough to reconstruct?" I asked, hopeful.

"Tiny bits," Esme said. "And a few in the toilet bowl. He burned it and flushed it. He really didn't want that thing getting out and that's all he had time to do. He had to know shoelaces weren't going to hold Chelsea long."

"No, but that's what was available on the maid's cart," I said, remembering I'd seen it in the hallway when we came to the room. "She had her spray bottles hooked onto the cart by shoelaces. So while he was helping himself to the pillowcase he took shoelaces, too. What I don't understand is his level of desperation. I guess I *am* jaded. It probably would've caused a minor scandal if Patricia's family background had gotten out to the public, but I don't think it would have been an insurmountable one. Politicians have overcome much worse chicanery by their relatives than this."

"You forget the candidate," Esme said. "Benson's already fighting an uphill battle trying to mold Patricia into somebody likable."

"Yeah, well, the incline just got steeper."

fourteen

I FELT FREE AS A BIRD THE NEXT MORNING AS WE left the hotel, having resigned both jobs and submitted zeroed-out billing statements. I knew in the days ahead I'd start to dwell on these defeats, but at that moment I was happy to be rid of the burden.

Lenora and the senator had been very understanding. They'd insisted on payment for the work we'd already done and in turn we'd insisted on a reduced fee.

Dinah Leigh, on the other hand, flatly refused any reduction. "You did your job, and you did it well, maybe too well," she said with a rueful smile. "Just because the result is troubling for us doesn't mean we deserve a refund."

"How are you doing with it all?" I asked.

"We're still in shock," she said, "but we'll be okay. Aunt Yvonne was right, about one thing at least: Chelsea declined to press charges against Marc, though I wouldn't have blamed her one bit if she had, and I told her so. Cyrus was so upset he wanted Marc evicted from the hotel, so he's gone on ahead to where we'll be staying for the wedding in Raleigh. Patricia's not speaking to him right now and has decided to stay on here with me. I'm so angry with him I don't want him in my sight. That was a reckless stunt. He could have hurt Chelsea."

"It wasn't the soundest judgment," Esme said.

"That's a generous assessment," Dinah Leigh said. "Right now, I'm trying to concentrate on the upcoming wedding and Phoebe and Conrad's impending parenthood and on my happiness for the brother I've always loved with all my heart. The rest I'll deal with later."

"Good approach," I said.

She held up our bill. "Chelsea's gone. She left last night. She's taken a few days off with my blessing and encouragement. I think she's more upset than I am. She seems to think I blame her for something. That it came to light at all or that she didn't tell me sooner. I don't know which. I told her I don't hold her responsible but that I'm still absorbing everything and I'm not ready to talk about it yet but we'll straighten it all out when she gets back. She'll take care of this then," she said, waving the invoice. "Or I could see if I can find the checkbook. I'm sure I still remember how to write a check."

"It'll wait," I said. "I hope Chelsea has someone around to look after her. She's been through a lot."

"Oh yes," Dinah Leigh said. "I wouldn't have wanted her to be alone, even if she thought that's what she wanted. She's gone back out to spend a couple of days with Lincoln's father."

"That'll probably be good for both of them," I said, wondering if Lincoln's father lived near a body of water.

Once we were out in the sunshine with the sweeping front steps before us, I suddenly wished I knew how to tap dance. It would've felt so good to do a Ginger Rogers down those steps in a little swirly costume. I had to settle for bunny hopping all the way down.

"I'm glad you're so happy," Esme said. "But you do realize we totally bombed on these jobs."

"But our clients aren't mad, at least not at us. Yes, we took a little financial hit but if it means getting out from under these two cursed projects, I'll happily eat ramen noodles for a month, cut my own hair, and ride my bike to save gas if that's what it takes to make up the loss."

"Preach it, sister," Esme said. "Except for the noo-dle part. That's just disgusting."

Denny came by that evening and he, too, seemed to have more pep in his step. "I can't stay," he said, "I'm on a food run. We've got Chad Deese in custody. The hotel's security records show his car was in the visitor lot the night Cooper died, and the tiny hole in his alibi has turned into a big rip. Security video at the gym shows him leaving the weight room and going out the side door just after midnight. He was AWOL for at least forty-five minutes. Enough time to make it to the hotel and back. We brought him in and while we were questioning him, the ME called. He'd found skin scrapings under Cooper's fingernails. It wasn't much, but enough to get DNA and the results had just come in. It's a match for Chad Deese."

"Why is he on file?" I asked.

"He tried to infiltrate a cult out in the mountains a couple of years back to do an exposé. There was a mishap in one of their more bizarre initiation rituals and somebody died. They took DNA from everybody they could round up during that investigation."

"What's he saying?" Esme asked.

"The usual—he didn't do it, he's wrongly accused. But he hasn't lawyered up yet. We're trying to keep him talking, see if we can't give him enough rope to hang himself."

I couldn't decide what to do with this news. Part of me felt relieved, but another part felt guilty for ill-wishing Deese. When I expressed this out loud I got a huff from Esme.

"Sophreena, much as you'd like to believe in the power of your thoughts, they don't influence anything that's already been done. If Deese killed Lincoln he deserves whatever he gets. If he didn't I trust Denny to get to the truth."

"Appreciate the vote of confidence," Denny said.

"Keep us posted," Esme said, handing over a foil-wrapped package that I suspected contained the left-over pineapple upside-down cake she'd made the day before. I watched wistfully as he thanked her and left with the package.

Another small loss. I love pineapple upside-down cake.

We spent two days in a blessedly normal daily routine. Walks to the coffee shop in the morning, work on several easy-peasy jobs during the day. Esme was cooking. I was spending lots of time with Jack. Denny was feeling better because they seemed to be building a solid case against Chad Deese.

Esme finally got around to getting some moving boxes and we moved more of her things. The plumber, a friend from Esme's church who was giving her a deal by working on her house on the side, finished repairing her upstairs shower. The window people were slated to put in new windows on Monday.

Life was good again. Or should have been, but I'd started stewing. The failures weren't sitting well with me. I'd made myself a promise not to look at anything about the fire for at least a few months and come at it fresh again. I did, however, plan to contact Chelsea and ask her to try to reconstruct from memory as much as she could remember about the letter Marc had destroyed. It was really bothering me that Conrad never had a chance to know what his dying father wished to tell him.

I'd decided to pamper myself the next morning by sleeping in, so I hadn't set the alarm. I was righteously irked when the doorbell rang at seven freakin' thirty. I knew Esme was already up because I smelled coffee, so I snuggled back under the covers and tried to will myself asleep again. But two minutes later Esme came knocking.

"Up and at 'em, Sophreena, we've got company," she said. "Make it snappy."

I groaned and asked who it was, but Esme had no mercy. "Hurry up and come down dressed," she said, giving my door one last pounding.

I found Chelsea, looking rested and more together than I'd seen her since before Lincoln died. She was sitting on the sofa in the family room and Esme had brought her a cup of coffee, which she doctored with cream and sugar with calm precision. She was placid. Serene. Spooky.

"Chelsea would like to discuss something with us," Esme said, "and she'd like Denton to be here." She gave me raised eyebrows. "He had a late night; I woke him up. He'll be here shortly."

"Would you like to give us a clue?" I asked Chelsea.

"I'll wait until Detective Carlson gets here. It's complicated and I want to make sure I tell it clearly. I'm sorry; I'm not trying to be mysterious. I just need to wait."

"No problem," I said. "I'll just grab a cup of that coffee." I jerked my head toward the kitchen and gave Esme the wide eyes.

"I'm gonna get a warm-up. Can I get you anything else, Chelsea?" Esme asked.

"I'm fine," she said, sounding about four ticks below the lowest register of fine.

Esme whispered furtively in the kitchen. "If this turns out to be just a rehash of that whole situation with the Nelson case, Denton is not going to be happy with me. He was exhausted and he's only had three hours of sleep."

"Has Deese admitted anything?"

"Through his lawyer," Esme said. "He says he and Lincoln got into a wrangle earlier that night and Lincoln scratched him when he tried to grab him by the collar. But he's still claiming Lincoln was fine when they parted ways."

"What do you suppose she wants?" I asked, nodding toward the family room. "She was really outraged at the idea that Aunt Yvonne wouldn't pay for her hand in the forgeries and all that, remember? Do you think she's going to push Denny to look into it? The false papers, I mean? That's not even in his jurisdiction."

"I guess we'll find out shortly," Esme said.

Denny arrived a few minutes later, looking exactly like a man who'd gotten only three hours of sleep.

After he'd been supplied with a cup of wake-up, he sat across from Chelsea in the big armchair Esme had bought especially to accommodate his body. It would soon be going down the street to its new abode and I had the thought I might get a Jack-sized chair to replace it.

"Have you changed your mind about pressing charges against Marc Benson?" Denny asked.

"No, that's not why I'm here," Chelsea said. "I've been thinking about nothing but this since I got back and learned from Dinah Leigh what Yvonne told you. And I've thought of what you said, Sophreena and Esme, about how people need to know where they came from. I was wrong before. This is the right thing to do. Lincoln knew it all along. I wish I'd listened to him."

We all waited in silence as Chelsea took a long breath and put her coffee mug on the table. She folded her hands in her lap and began.

"First off, Dinah Leigh doesn't know I'm here. I wanted to give her the gift of the wedding. Let it be a joy to her. It was marred a little by everything Aunt Yvonne told them, but it wasn't ruined. Also, I know if I told her and she asked me to keep quiet, I'd probably do it. And that would ruin me. It would eat at me for the rest of my life. Lincoln was right. The truth is always better."

I looked over at Esme and she pushed out her bottom lip and raised her eyebrows again. She had no idea where this was going either.

"I should have stayed that day, the day you told Dinah Leigh and Conrad, or I should say the day you allowed Aunt Yvonne to make her confession," Chelsea said with a mirthless laugh. "I left that night without talking with Dinah Leigh about it. Though I don't know what I would have said or done right then. Maybe this way is better. I know the whole family is torn up. It's a heartbreak to learn you're not who you thought you were. But they have no idea the kind of real pain they're in for, and I'm in the unfortunate position of being the instrument. I don't think I'd have the strength to do it but for Lincoln. Still, I'm afraid. I'm afraid after what happened to him. I think his death may be tied up in all this."

Denny leaned forward and put his elbows on his knees, clasping his hands together—his intense listening pose. "All this?" he asked.

"That letter was from Conrad's father, or I should say from Herbert Nelson," she corrected. "That much is true. But it wasn't what Yvonne claimed. I wish it had been. Marc destroyed the original but what nobody knows is that I scanned it that night. I read it and I knew what it would mean. I kept the original on me at all times until I put it in the safe. I knew somebody was going through my room. I don't know how they knew about the letter, but I had the idea that's what they were after. I was afraid Lincoln had betrayed me and told someone, but I don't think that anymore. I have a copy of the letter on a password-protected partition on my computer's hard drive, and I also made a backup copy here." She took a chain with a small flash drive on it from around her neck and handed it to Denny.

"I couldn't for the life of me figure out why you two seemed so casual about this," she said, turning toward Esme and me. "Now I realize we were talking about two different stories. Yvonne's and Herbert Nelson's. And I believe Herbert's. I don't think it'll take much to prove who Conrad Nelson really is, not once they realize it all goes back to that fire."

The room started to spin and I had to hold on to the arms of the chair. Finally I breathed the word. "Kidnapped."

Chelsea nodded. "The letter is twenty-two pages

and the man went into great detail. He was trying to wash his soul clean."

"*He* kidnapped John David Sawyer?" Esme asked, sliding forward in her chair.

"That's what he says in the letter," Chelsea said. "You can read it all there, but the gist of it is that Margaret Sawyer and Marie Nelson were casual friends. They belonged to the same ladies' club and one day, shortly after baby Johnny was born, Margaret made what I'm sure was an offhand remark to Marie about how having three children was a challenge. Marie, having lost two babies in the span of that year, was incensed that Margaret would complain and fixated on the thought that the baby would be better off with her. After she lost the next one she became convinced that she needed to *rescue* the baby from the Sawyers. She somehow convinced Yvonne and Herbert, and together the three of them conspired on a plan to take him. I don't think Herbert would have gone along with it if he hadn't been afraid Marie was going to harm herself. In the letter he claims he thought he'd be able to talk them out of it if he just let it play out awhile. But once the plan got under way there was no way to pull it back."

"Who took him? Who actually took the baby?" Denny asked.

"Yvonne," Chelsea said. "She took him out his

bedroom window and went into the woods, cutting across to the Nelsons' house. Marie was already in Norfolk by then and everything was at the ready. Yvonne put the baby in the car and drove. She was probably already over the county line before the fire at the house got going good. Herbert, I imagine you've guessed, is the one who set the house on fire, trying to cover up the kidnapping. But he miscalculated and got a bad burn on his hand and arm. He faked an accident the next day at the graphite plant to cover the injury."

"The hand," Esme said, staring into the mid-distance. "That hand. It's reaching for the lighter. Yvonne is handing it to him as she crawls out the window with the baby."

"Probably," Chelsea said, frowning in puzzlement at Esme. "That's one detail he didn't include, but otherwise, it's all in there," she said, nodding toward the flash drive. "I think he felt worse about setting that fire than he did about taking the baby. He never intended to burn the whole house, just the extension where the baby's room and the kitchen were located, but something went wrong. The grain alcohol he used didn't react the way he'd thought it would and the house was old. It went up quick. He stayed out in the woods, watching to see if Margaret and Lenora got out. In the letter he claims he would've gone back in for them if he hadn't seen them come out. Like that makes him a good guy. I don't understand people. I don't understand how they could have done this and justified it to themselves."

I went to get my laptop and we all gathered around and focused on the screen as I read aloud. It was mostly an apology to Conrad, for stealing his life. But while it was confessional and, as Chelsea had said, very detailed, it was also self-serving, placing most of the blame for the kidnapping on Yvonne and on his mentally ill wife. No reference at all to the wrong he'd done the Sawyers.

"I found the letter in Conrad's baby book that day I inventoried the box of family memorabilia for you," Chelsea said. "Just like Emma said. I glanced over the first couple of paragraphs and realized it was a very personal letter and that it was about something serious. I set it aside because I wasn't sure Dinah Leigh would want to pass anything like that on to you at that point. Later I pulled it out of my desk drawer and read the whole thing. I was sick. I panicked. I didn't know what to do. I called Lincoln and told him I needed to talk with him. He was tied up just then but I was so upset, he excused himself from his meeting for a few minutes so he could come talk to me. I've thought a lot about that conversation and tried to replay it in my head. I wasn't thinking too clearly at that time, but I'm pretty sure I told him I'd found something out, and that it meant Conrad wasn't who everybody thought he was and that Dinah Leigh would be devastated if it ever came out. Then I asked him to meet me so we could talk it over. I had to go to the post office and when I came out my door to tell Dinah Leigh I'd be out for a few minutes, Yvonne was standing right there, right beside the door to my room. I think she overheard."

"This was what time?" Denny asked.

"I'm not sure. I've tried to remember how everything went that day," she said, pulling out a notebook where she'd obviously been making her own notes. "I think it was probably about four in the afternoon, but I could be off by an hour either way. I met Lincoln later in the afternoon when he could get free."

"And you let him read this?" Esme asked.

Chelsea nodded. "I wasn't thinking about the bind that would put him in at that point. His loyalty was to the senator and Lenora, and I was asking him to keep this from them. I was trying to protect Dinah Leigh from finding out. I should never have told Lincoln until I'd had a chance to come to terms with all of it myself. He was adamant. He said we had to tell immediately. Our argument got interrupted when the senator came in, and we arranged to meet later that night where we could be assured of privacy to talk more about it and decide what to do."

"So that's how you ended up out on the exercise trail that night?" Denny said.

Chelsea nodded. "Lincoln had calmed down and so had I and we talked about it. At first we agreed we had to be careful with the information. These people have been friends for their whole lives, but I don't know if even the tightest friendship can overcome something like this. Then the more we talked, the more our divided loyalties came to the surface. Lincoln insisted that we tell J.D. He said he was the most levelheaded person in the family and that someone from the Sawyer side should know and have some input in the decision about how to handle it."

I thought of Damon's eagerness to be rid of Esme and me. "J.D., not Damon?" I asked.

"Lincoln wouldn't have even suggested telling Damon. Lincoln always said he wasn't ready for prime time. But he trusted J.D., especially when it came to ethical calls. Anyhow, by then I was equally convinced that we should wait until at least after Conrad's wedding before we told anyone anything. And really, at that point, I was hoping that no one would have to know, ever. I knew—I know—what it will do to Dinah Leigh."

"And the argument escalated?" Esme asked.

I sucked in a breath.

Chelsea nodded. "It was a terrible, bitter argument. But not a physical one," she said softly, looking over at Denny.

He nodded as if to acknowledge her meaning.

"But after what happened with Marc grabbing me to get the letter, I started rethinking everything that happened. That look on Yvonne's face when I caught her listening at my door was chilling. I'm wondering if she called Marc then, too. What if he confronted Lincoln about what she overheard?"

"His wife claimed he was asleep in bed with her at midnight that night. We checked on everyone's whereabouts," Denny said.

"Patricia takes sleeping pills," Chelsea said. "You could drive a freight train through her room and she wouldn't wake up."

"And you think Yvonne might have convinced Marc to confront Lincoln?" I asked. "He'd have done that to protect her?"

"He may not even know the whole story himself," Chelsea said. "Marc is absolutely paranoid about keeping everything around Patricia contained, controlling the news, controlling her image. Even if he thought the story about Conrad being illegally adopted was the real story, he'd still have wanted it hushed up."

"Yvonne's story 2.0," I said. "The first one involved Conrad being parented by a teenage girl. I overplayed my hand on that one. I think I gave Yvonne the idea to confess to something more innocuous—her being the mother—in hopes of keeping the lid on something worse, the kidnapping and Conrad's true identity."

Chelsea leaned forward, her voice intense. "I don't think she knows what the letter says, or else she's counting on my loyalty to Dinah Leigh to keep me quiet. But what if she decides I can't be trusted to do that? I don't know how much Marc knows or what he's done, but I'm concerned for my own safety."

"A reasonable concern," Denny said. "I'd prefer you not stay at the hotel right now."

"You're welcome to stay here," I said. "We have a guest room."

"That's generous of you," Chelsea said. "I'll let you know. I need to talk with Dinah Leigh face-to-face. I dread it, but I owe her that. After that I may have to find another place to go, permanently."

"My job right now is to get justice, both for the Sawyer family and for Lincoln and his family, including you, Chelsea," Denny said. "I don't have any way to prove the veracity of this letter, especially since I don't have the original. But that doesn't mean I can't use it for leverage. Do you know where Yvonne Bayley and Marc Benson are at this present moment?"

"Not specifically," Chelsea said, "Yvonne is back in Norfolk. Neither Dinah Leigh nor Conrad wanted to be around her right now. And I think Marc may still be in the hotel over in Raleigh where we stayed for the wedding. He and Patricia are estranged still."

"Thank you," Denny said. "I believe we'll see how

loyal those two are to each other. There is no statute of limitations on kidnapping, so I'll have the Norfolk PD pick her up and I'll go over to Raleigh and invite Benson to come have a talk." He rose and looked down at Chelsea. "Thank you for this," he said, holding up the flash drive. "You've done the right thing. Doesn't mean it won't hurt a lot of people, but it's the right thing."

"That's what Lincoln would've said," she said.

Denny called late that night, and Esme put him on speakerphone so Jack and I could hear.

"It's a sing-off," he said. "Each of them is trying to out-cooperate the other to see who can get the best deal. You wouldn't believe what a pitiful little old lady Yvonne has become all of sudden."

"I hope nobody's falling for that act," Esme said.

"Her fate will be decided by a jury," Denny said. "Maybe she'll fool them, but I'm betting she's messed up somewhere along the line, and we'll try to find it. Maybe she'll even do some time, though she's old and I don't know if she's got enough time left for it to really be considered justice."

"How about Marc?" I asked. "Has he confessed to murdering Lincoln?"

"Not murder. He claims self-defense. He says he didn't go out there looking to hurt Cooper. He just wanted to warn him off disclosing anything he'd learned from Chelsea. He swears he didn't know anything about the kidnapping. He thought it was just a matter of an illegal adoption. In any case, he and Cooper got into it, and in the heat of the moment he ran at Cooper and knocked him off his feet and over he went. We'll see what the DA makes of it. But one way or the other, he's done for and he knows it. I'm sure they'll offer him a plea and if he's smart he'll take it, involuntary manslaughter maybe. He'll probably be out in a couple of years."

"Somehow I don't think that will satisfy Chelsea. It doesn't satisfy me," I said.

"Above my pay grade," Denny said. "But the man's ruined. Everything he built his life around is gone. I guess there's some justice in that."

"Precious little," Esme said.

fifteen

MOVING DAY CAME, AT LONG LAST. ALL THE CLUB members were back in town and on deck, and Jennifer came along with Denny to help. Even Chelsea, who'd taken refuge at my house for the past couple of weeks, lent a hand.

Marydale, Chelsea, and I were put to the task of putting Esme's clothes away, which was not a minor mission, since Esme is a thoroughbred clotheshorse. As we worked, Marydale questioned Chelsea about her future in that motherly way she always uses with me. "Will you go back to Dinah Leigh when things calm down?" she asked.

"I don't think so," Chelsea said. "She says she doesn't blame me for anything and I know she means it, but I think she finds it hard to be around me, and frankly, the feeling is mutual. I'll always love her and I appreciate everything she's done for me, but I think it'd be difficult to work together right now."

"Any idea what you'll do?" I asked.

"Cyrus Hamilton offered me a job at the hotel. I think I'm going to take it. I like him and I need a fresh start. Losing Lincoln has helped me realize that however much I love Dinah Leigh and however much I owe her, I owe it to myself to live my own life. And anyway, free massages," she said with a smile that didn't quite reach her eyes.

"Speaking of being your own person, how's Patricia holding up?" I asked.

"You know," Chelsea said, "it's the weirdest thing. I thought she'd come at me like a wildcat after everything that happened. Blame me for everything. But she's been really nice to me."

"Her political aspirations must be in tatters," Marydale said.

"Definitely, but she doesn't seem too disappointed by that," Chelsea said. "She's filed divorce papers and Ken told me she's thinking of trying to adopt a child as a single parent."

"Poor child," I said before I could stop myself.

"No, I think the child will be lucky," Chelsea said. "At one time Patricia and I were good friends. But then she married Marc. I never liked him. I thought he was sleazy. And of course now I think he's far worse. But when I tried to warn Patricia about him, things soured between us. While she was with him she changed, and not for the better. But now that Marc will be out of her life, I believe she'll have a chance to find herself again. I hope so."

"And Senator Stan and Lenora, how are they taking it all? This must have created a terrible strain between them and Dinah Leigh," Marydale said. "Have you talked with them?"

"I have," I said. "They're still reeling. They're feeling joy and sorrow, regret and anger, and probably a hundred other emotions, but they're trying their hardest to come to grips with it. The senator talked a lot about the sins of the fathers not being visited on the sons. He and Lenora were skeptical at first. After all the false claims that have been made over the years, you'd expect them to be, but Yvonne has finally given a full confession and the DNA evidence is in. There's no longer any room for doubt. Conrad is John David Sawyer."

"Dinah Leigh is struggling with shame and a crippling sense of betrayal," Chelsea said. "At first she just did not want to believe her parents were capable of this, but after she read her father's letter she knew it was true. I think she and the Sawyers will eventually work through things. Maybe things will never be exactly the same. After something is broken, even if you fix it you can usually still see the cracks. But I think they'll salvage the friendship in some form. They're all trying. They've even been able to make a little joke about shared custody arrangements for Conrad."

"And how is he feeling about it all?" Marydale asked.

"He's coping better than I could've imagined," Chelsea said. "I think it helped that it came to light at a time when he's so happy. He says this actually explains a lot of things he's always wondered about and he believes it might actually be helpful to him as a father. He's planning to keep the name he's lived under all these years, at least for now. And he's talked with Lenora and the senator and made the legal arrangements to have the foundation plans go ahead. Except now it will be named the Alton and Margaret Sawyer Foundation."

"And there's another change as I understand it," I said. "Damon will no longer be heading the foundation. I gather he hasn't been dealing well with all this. The senator has decided he needs a little more grooming."

"Who'll take over?" Marydale asked.

"Phoebe Nelson," I said. "She's an attorney and has quite a bit of experience with nonprofits."

"I'll bet Damon isn't taking that well," Chelsea said.

"Not well at all," I said. "But the senator says his father is due home in a couple of months and that he'll take him in hand and straighten him out. In any case, despite all their conflicting feelings, the senator and

Lenora did get one thing they wanted out of this—their parents have been vindicated. Sadly way too late, but still."

"Yes," Marydale said. "I've seen several articles this last week and some of them are odes to the parents for their perseverance and their faith."

"And one of them was written by Chad Deese, of all people," I said. "That guy is shameless. He'll go whichever way the wind blows if he can get a story out of it."

"Did you ever find out where he was during that hole in his alibi?" Marydale asked.

"His car wouldn't start—that's why it was in the parking lot at the hotel. He had a service truck jump it early the next morning. He'd gone to the gym with his friends, but he wasn't with them the entire time. He slipped out and walked to a convenience store to get some ice for his eye at some point. He was mortified about getting a shiner from a female and didn't want to tell that part."

Coco came into the room wearing her trademark gauzy skirt, but this time with a carpenter's apron fastened around her waist. She reached in and brought out a shiny chrome cone. "Water-saver showerheads," she said. "Esme tells me you need to get one on the shower at your house, too, *immediately*. I'll come by tomorrow." She disappeared into the bathroom and I could hear the scrape of metal on metal.

"You all have been friends for a long time, haven't you?" Chelsea asked.

"Some of us," Marydale said. "I've known Sophreena all her life. Her mother and I were the closest of friends. But some of us only became true friends about seven or eight years ago. I don't think it's so much the time as the fact that we have *deep* friendships."

"I wonder if I'll ever have that kind of relationship again," Chelsea mused.

"You will," Marydale said with certainty.

"Listen to her," I said. "Marydale always knows what she's talking about."

"Out to the kitchen, y'all," Esme said, putting her hand through the doorway to wave us in.

The kitchen was assembled. Esme had seen to the placement of every pot, pan, whisk, and ladle, and the pantry and fridge were stocked. I had no doubt she could've whipped up a meal on a moment's notice. There were plastic glasses on the table and Esme was pouring sparkling cider. She passed around a glass to each of us and gathered us around her: Denny, Marydale and Winston, River and Coco, Jack and me, Chelsea, and Jennifer Jeffers.

"I'd give you champagne but there's still work to be done and I don't want anybody sleeping on the job," she said. She stretched to her full height. "Now, you all can clearly see I'm Irish, very Irish, and I want to do an Irish blessing on my house. Sophreena, you do not look at me or you'll make me cry." She lifted her glass and we all did the same.

May the roof above us never fall in.
And may the friends gathered below it never
*   fall out.*
May you have warm words on a cold evening,
A full moon on a dark night,
And the road downhill all the way to your door.

"Or in this case," she added, "the road downhill all the way to my door."

Jack put his arm around me and pinched the back of my arm—hard. For which I was profoundly grateful. He's like one of those companion dogs that alerts you when your body is about to betray you in some way. It mortifies me to cry in front of people, and I was close to blubbering.

I thought of Lincoln and of the life he never got to lead. Of the Sawyers, the Dodds, of Chelsea, and Conrad Nelson and his new wife. I hoped they'd be able to come to terms with everything that had been revealed and find peace with it.

I sipped, swallowing hard to get the cider past the lump in my throat. There were big changes ahead for Esme and for me, and for all of us gathered here. But as

I looked around the kitchen I knew we'd be okay if we just stuck together.

There's family by blood and family by choice, and sometimes neither of those work out the way you might hope. But at that moment I felt like the luckiest person in the world to have been chosen by this family of friends.